BLOOD OVER BADGE

WAYNE FARQUHAR

BLOOD
OVER
BADGE

3L Publishing
Sacramento, California

The information contained in this book is intended to be educational and not for diagnosis, prescription, or treatment of any health disorder whatsoever. This book is sold with the understanding that neither the author nor publisher is engaged in rendering any legal, psychological, or accounting advice. The publisher and author disclaim personal liability, directly or indirectly, for advice of information presented within. Although the author and publisher have prepared this manuscript with utmost care and diligence and have made every effort to ensure the accuracy and completeness of the information contained within, we assume no responsibility for errors, inaccuracies, omissions or inconsistencies.

Library of Congress Control Number: 2010923355

ISBN-13: 978-0-615-35911-3

Blood Over Badge soft-cover edition 2010

Printed in the United States of America

For more information about special discounts for bulk purchases, please contact 3L Publishing at 916.300.8012 or log onto our website at www.3LPublishing.com.

Book design by Erin Pace.

For Cari and Christian, the shining stars in my life.

ACKNOWLEDGEMENTS

Thanks go to Peter Heyrman and Michelle Gamble-Risley for their keen vision of creativity. Greg Kihn for inspiration and wonderful support. My family and close circle of friends for believing. And special thanks to the brave men and women in law enforcement that make huge personal sacrifices on a daily basis so we can live safe.

ONE

Kyle Sanders fidgeted and his ankle shackles clinked. One of the jurors peered at him with a look of disgust. He tried to stay still just like his lawyer, Douglas Taylor, had told him, but it was hard while chained up like a dog.

The hotshot lawyer had taken his case only because the court told him to … something owed to someone somewhere Kyle figured. In 18 months of meetings and court dates, Taylor never let his eyes meet Kyle's once. To Kyle, that meant the guy was a fuckin' coward … maybe crooked. He probably had a Mercedes Benz, two houses and belonged to a golf country club. Rich people like Taylor saw him as white swamp trash.

He and Taylor rehearsed everything for the trial. Taylor said it was necessary. Taylor told him how to act remorseful and most of all, keep his mouth shut.

The lawyer first wanted to know everything. He said to tell the truth because it was confidential between just them. He needed to know the whole truth so he could do a better job, and the law protected them and everything they talked about. So he started telling Taylor everything about the murder; but when he started talking about the tingling and the total rush of killing, Taylor stopped him.

"No thanks," Taylor said. "I only need to know the facts. Save the rest for your cellmate or a priest."

"Cellmate or priest? What the fuck? You got me guilty before the court even started," yelled Kyle.

Taylor raised both hands in defiance and shook his head.

Kyle got it. Why bother with the truth? The truth wasn't gonna get him off, no way. His lawyer saw him as a guilty monster, so fuck it, he didn't give a shit.

Taylor swallowed hard. "We'll call it a victory if I can keep you alive. Where there's life, there's hope."

Kyle nearly laughed out loud. Like *his* fate, the fate of a murderer meant anything to Taylor. Kyle heard about Angola. Life there was hardly better than death, but he'd take it. That asshole Taylor was right about one thing: Maybe, in 10 or 15 years, he'd get a parole hearing. Kyle considered breaking out more likely.

Taylor was accustomed to twisting the facts to fit the circumstances. He once said, "Nothing is a lie. The Constitution requires me to defend my client as well as possible." Kyle figured "as well as possible" meant getting creative. This morning, Taylor said he would have to be creative. Today was closing arguments — the last chance to sell the jury on the idea that he was something less than a total fucking monster.

Alicia Clarke was one of the best deputy district attorneys in the Parrish. She could sway any male juror just by looking at him. Even the disgusted expression she gave him was enough to make him jack off in his cell at night. He imagined her big tits and pouty lips. The way she pulled her hair back and wore reading glasses was hot. She was the "bitch-ho" that always got what she wanted. What would she know or care about a guy like him? He knew one thing for sure. She wasn't raised by a crack whore who kept telling her she was nothing but the wrong end of a busted rubber. His momma said the only thing good about him was a few extra bucks in the welfare check. He never saw a dime of that dough and neither did his half-brother. They survived because of one another. Their momma spent all the dough on booze and dope, just giving them enough red beans and rice to keep their mouths shut while she was fucking for more dough. That lawyer couldn't understand even if she wanted. He fucking hated his momma and that lawyer — and that made that bitch-ho even hotter.

She started her closing argument. Every damning word was mixed with underlying sex. Kyle felt it. Taylor whispered in his ear. "She's good. She's a real pro ... just don't react. Don't stare. Don't do a thing." He could see Taylor wanted to fuck her too. No one could miss that. Kyle sat motionless as she laid it all out, step by step to the jurors. She fucked him over real good with her story and he knew it.

"Once she's finished her part it's our turn," said Taylor.

Kyle didn't react.

"She'll get another chance afterwards. They get the last word."

Kyle smelled the sour acidic odor on Taylor's breath when he whispered in his face. It smelled like shit. It was like his lawyer was throwing up in his own mouth cause he had to defend him. *This whole thing wasn't goin' so good,* thought Kyle. Not as good as he thought it would when Taylor was talking to him all them past months.

Kyle remembered Taylor saying, "The Peoples' lawyer always got the last word because they had to prove the case or something like that." All *his* lawyer had to do was make the jurors have some doubt and they had to let him go. It was the law. Now he figured that there wasn't much doubt after she finished talkin'.

"I'm up, our shot," whispered Taylor close to Kyle's ear. As he stood up, Kyle hoped none of the jurors smelled his lawyer's shitty breath.

Taylor's chair creaked as he pushed it back from the table. Now it was time to argue for freedom, or at least something less than death.

A spark lit Kyle's dark eyes. He saw Taylor put his hand on the table to help himself up. His lawyer looked wiped-out. Kyle felt the burning glares of the jurors upon him. *Don't look nervous,* he repeated in his head. His stomach churned with gas pain, and he clenched his ass, fighting the urge to shit.

The hums of air conditioning and cool florescent light were only starting to dent Louisiana's hot summer morning. Even through sealed windows they could hear crickets. Most of the jurors had driven here on muddy roads.

"Ladies and Gentlemen of the Jury, thank you for all your patience and attention through the course of this trial. Each of you has given grueling days, and no doubt, sleepless nights to your judicial tasks, and I know I speak for the whole court when I express my gratitude to each and every one of you."

Taylor's booming voice reverberated through the silence of the courtroom. He tilted his head back and gave a slight smile as he opened his hands and arms to the jurors. He was well-trained in the arts of sincerity.

"Now is time for judgment. Now you must weigh the intentions and actions of every witness. The prosecutor argues that Kyle Sanders is a cold-blooded murderer. And that Kyle Sanders walked into that store planning to kill the man behind the counter." Taylor shuffled his position by several steps causing a pause." Kyle was a scared 17-year-old boy, lacking guidance or any parental love, what-so-ever." Taylor let the message linger a moment in the jurors' minds."

Kyle liked what Taylor was saying.

"And that Kyle Sanders enjoyed shooting and killing his long-time neighbor. I beg to differ."

The truth wasn't that good, thought Kyle. Images of that night flashed through his mind. He felt so fuckin' powerful yelling at that old man. The gun barrel hit the old man's head a couple of times because he held it right up against his skull like he'd seen on TV. He felt a rush of heat in his body and craved the feeling to finally whack someone. He'd killed a thousand times on video games. It was easy and addicting. It was like a dream, and he was outside his own body watching and digging the action. The old man was frail and moved too slow. His hands quivered, and his arched back bent him forward. And then the real excitement happened. Kyle yanked the trigger, and the gun and old man's head exploded at the same time. His nostrils filled with the smell of gun powder and a fog of bloody vapor floated in the air. His face suddenly felt moist and tacky. He licked his lips and his tongue caught the sweet distinctive taste of blood. Old man Whitman lye dead on the floor with his head lookin' like a fuckin' canoe. It felt better than he imagined. Taylor's voice snapped Kyle back to reality.

"Kyle made mistakes in life. As a young boy, he suffered years of abuse from a drunken mother, as well as others who were misguided and desperate. Every adult in his life somehow or another took advantage of him. There was never a father figure in his life. Kyle to this day doesn't know where or even who his father might be. The only men Kyle was exposed to his adolescent life were the sexual clients of his abusive mother. By the time Kyle turned 16, he'd been abandoned by everyone close to him and robbed of the chance to finish school. Kyle was no different than the ones lucky enough to ride the school bus or sit in Sunday school."

Kyle watched Taylor suddenly pause and breathe. *Is he disguising his true emotions — or showing them he feels for me?*

Taylor recovered and began working into his rhythm. The jurors followed, focusing, acting curious, and nodding with each word and move. In the course of a gesture, Taylor glimpsed toward Kyle. The jurors' eyes followed and fell upon him. Kyle sat motionless: Shoulders rounded into a small clump, eyes staring into the hard shine of the wooden table, jagged teeth hidden behind pursed lips.

Taylor walked over and stood uncomfortably next to him. Kyle's skin crawled as he sensed Taylor was going to touch him; but Taylor's fingers hesitated. Instead he strolled around the table. He methodically moved toward the jury. They were hanging on his every word. Their eyes were fixed on his face.

"We cannot forgive Kyle. After all, a life was lost. We all wish we could change that. But let's focus on why. Let's be fair when deciding Kyle's future.

"The prosecutor wants you to believe that my client drafted a crafty plan and intentionally shot Mr. Whitman. I believe we have shown you a different Kyle Sanders. We have introduced the real Kyle Sanders. The young intoxicated country boy who panicked after he accidentally shot Mr. Whitman. Kyle went into that store for one reason. Taylor simultaneously shook his forefinger. "He only wanted to steal beer so he could keep drinking that hot-and-muggy summer night. When Mr. Whitman tried to stop him, he panicked and pulled a gun, only to escape." Taylor paused to let the message sink in deeper. "It was at that tragic moment, the gun accidentally went off and Mr. Whitman was hit. My client was devastated by what he had done. He was a frightened child, he ran away like all kids do when they get into trouble. Certainly, each of you has known children or have children of your own. Sometimes in life, even good kids make terrible and irreversible mistakes."

Kyle felt afraid after it happened. He did run away. That part was true.

"Today, he is before you, wishing he could turn back time, undoing that mistake. Ladies and gentlemen, I ask you to resist compounding one mistake with another. A verdict of murder in the first degree would be a mistake. Please, look at him. Kyle is a young boy who made a terrible error. The law has given you the power to be merciful. I ask you to exercise that absolute power in the case of this very frightened young boy, thank you."

The knot in Kyle's gut loosened. His lawyer did just as he said he would. "His speech was smooth as silk and polished like a new penny." Kyle remembered those were his exact words when he would later describe it to Kyle. He didn't feel like a total monster. After all, his lawyer was a pretty big sack-of-shit liar himself. Still, he couldn't help admire Taylor's speech.

Taylor sat down and folded his hands on top of the table. Kyle looked at him but Taylor didn't dare glance over. He was staring forward and appeared lost in thought.

I hope they really believe him, thought Kyle. He returned his gaze to the polished table and saw his gaunt reflection staring back at him.

Kyle felt a nudge on his arm. "Now it's their turn again. She's going to put on one helluva show. Sit tight," said Taylor.

Alicia got up from her chair. "Ladies and gentlemen of the jury, I will not waste your time in my final argument. However, I do have to address a couple of issues Mr. Taylor brought up." She glanced at Taylor with a slight hint of disgust: In an indication to the jurors, she had a filthy mess to clean. Alicia skirted around the large table littered with opened law books, legal pads and pens strewn about. She strolled with stern confidence past the display table cluttered with items of evidence. She stepped to the podium and tapped the laptop computer. The large courtroom video screen came to life. "Deputy, please dim the lights."

The image of Kyle's twisted face exploded onto the large screen. It showed him smiling, revealing his rotten devilish teeth. His skin was pockmarked and ashen. Dope and beer already gave him dark circles under his eyes. He was unshaven with scrappy growth on his chin and sideburns. His eyes looked beady and bloodshot. His frozen black pupils pierced the screen. The white tiled wall in the background was clean and institutional. The flash of the booking photo camera defined its subject in stark relief.

Kyle studied the image and remembered very little of that night. *I was so fucked up; I hardly remember how they even caught me. Actually, how the fuck did they catch me? I just know I did a shitload of crank. I kinda' remember that picture being takin' ... I think.* Kyle remembered bits and pieces of the night, but it was like something he watched rather than something he'd experienced. Now several jurors glanced at the screen, then at him.

"I have only two exhibits to show you," said Alicia. "I realize you've already seen them along with the many others, but please, ladies and gentlemen, be patient."

Kyle had to strain to hear her because she was talking real low. It was strange because usually her voice was loud. *She had a big fuckin' mouth.* Then, he noticed it. The jurors were leaning forward. They were straining to hear too. She was doing it on purpose! Kyle looked to his lawyer to say something, but Taylor shook his head and waved his hand.

"Please, have one more look at the photograph taken of Mr. Sanders after he was arrested for murdering Mr. Whitman. In searching those eyes, I have great difficulty in finding a troubled little boy. Alicia's eyes flared and her penciled brown eyebrows arched. "I see an evil, twisted man! Not a scared boy!"

Her outburst startled Kyle. Several of the jurors jumped too. Their wooden seats creaked from the sudden weight shift. The bitch-ho turned and pointed directly at him. Her fingers were long and slender and her nails were polished. She glared at him with a pinched angry face.

"A grown man who was completely aware of his actions." She paused a moment. "You may see it the way I do, I believe Mr. Sanders appears to be enjoying himself in this picture!" She allowed the suggestion to sink in while scanning the jurors. Kyle saw several jurors nod in agreement.

"Let's move on. The second picture exploded onto the screen with even greater impact. Jurors rocked back in their seats and Kyle heard a gasp from the courtroom. It was the crime-scene photograph of old man Whitman's body. He was lying all crumpled up on the floor behind the cash register counter. The same way Kyle remembered. Kyle studied the picture seeing blood and brain spattered everywhere. Much of the blood pooled thickly on the floor. *Yeah, I guess I fucked up old man Whitman pretty good,* thought Kyle.

The lawyer took a lighted pen marker and pointed it toward the screen.

"Notice, the empty cash register? Also notice the currency holders all flipped upward," she said. "Ladies and gentlemen, this was no accident. This was an armed robbery resulting in a murder of a gentle, caring man. This was a total disregard for human life: Mr. Whitman's life."

Kyle heard quiet sobs from the courtroom. He remembered that the old man's family and friends were sitting directly behind him. "Don't ever look at any of them," Taylor had said more than once.

Now Alicia raised her arm to the picture. "Please, ladies and gentlemen. Do not allow Mr. Whitman to die in vain!" Her volume was near a scream.

Now the bitch is screamin' and pleadin' with the jurors, thought Kyle. She lowered her voice as quickly and easily as yelling. Kyle realized she was in complete control. She quieted just long enough for everyone to hear several people sobbing. And then long enough to hear the air conditioners' hum.

Alicia's gaze took in the entire jury, and she had their complete attention. Her eyes were wide. "Please take your time and reflect on the statements of the witnesses. Look at the evidence that has been presented before you and don't be fooled by red herrings … stay focused and look at every fact. Trust your heart and have the strength to make the right decision, thank you." Alicia clicked off the computer. The picture of Mr. Whitman was gone, but it burned in an after image like that of a flashbulb.

The people and the defense rested. The judge instructed the jury. They were now the pilots of Kyle's future.

Kyle was escorted and locked up in a six-foot square cell outside the courtroom. Inmates shuffled right past him as they entered and exited the courtroom. He was directly behind the bailiff's desk on the opposite side of the courtroom wall.

Kyle could hear the bailiff's telephone ring and often heard the bailiff's side of the conversation. Every time the phone sounded, Kyle's stomach got tight. Was this it? The verdict?

During the first few days of deliberation, the jury called the bailiff for clarification on various details. The bailiff then called Taylor, who would arrive in court a few minutes later. As this went on Kyle noticed jury deliberation was hard on his lawyer. He looked depressed. One time, he smelled like whisky and peppermint. It was just after lunch and while they were talking, Taylor's head lazily fell to one side. He mumbled something about "time spent reflecting on the should-haves and should-not-haves." Kyle didn't completely understand and really, didn't give a shit.

The ring of the bailiff's phone awakened Kyle. A moment later he heard the bailiff speaking. "Mr. Taylor, the jury has reached a verdict." The deputy's voice was stern and professional. "The judge would like you to return to court, sir."

Kyle couldn't sit still. Both his knees were jittery with tension. He bounced around the tiny cell on the balls of his feet. Every nerve in his body twitched. The door from the courtroom opened and the bailiff's body filled the opening. He held ankle shackles in one hand and the key to the cell in the other. "It's time to hear about the rest of your life." The bailiff opened the cell door and threw the ankle shackles on the floor at Kyle's feet. Kyle mindlessly went through the routine of shackling himself. When finished, he stood awaiting direction. Kyle paused momentarily in the threshold of the doorway leading into the courtroom. The courtroom felt different than before. For the first time, He felt the cool air circulating. The ceiling felt taller and the room seemed larger. The judge's bench was empty. Taylor was already seated at the table. His eyes stared vacantly across the courtroom toward Kyle. He figured Taylor had no clue what they decided. Murmurs ran through the audience, and he felt a sudden chill in his spine and the strong urge to shit came back. He clinched his ass and felt a pit in his stomach. Many in the crowd jotted things down in small notebooks. Once he stepped forward, they all stopped writing and stared at his face. They were looking straight into his eyes — and their stares burned like the hot sun. He shuffled the short distance from the doorway to his seat, ignoring the stares. He sat next to his lawyer for the very last time.

"All rise!" the bailiff's voice thundered over the whispers of the audience.

The courtroom fell silent, with only a few creaking chairs and the swooshing sounds of settling clothes. Taylor nudged Kyle. They both stood.

The door behind the bench swung open and the black-robed judge swiftly took his seat. Kyle hardly noticed the jury filing into the courtroom in a single line from the rear doors. He was thinking that those were the only doors that led to freedom.

The jurors filed into the box. None looked toward his table. "If they avoid looking at you that's bad," Taylor had once told him. Kyle figured it didn't matter much to Taylor now; it was done and out of his hands.

"All be seated. This courtroom is now in session," said the bailiff. He stood and watched as everyone in the courtroom sat down.

The judge slammed his gavel twice on his bench. "Juror foreman, have you reached a verdict?"

"Yes your Honor, we have."

"May I have the verdict." It wasn't a question. The bailiff walked across the floor, took the paper from the foreman and turned toward the judge.

Kyle stared at the paper verdict as it moved across the courtroom toward the judge. His focus so intense he heard the crinkling of the paper as it passed hands. The rest of his whole life was written on that piece of paper. Kyle couldn't stop his legs from shaking. His ankle shackles clanked. The future of his life was now in the hands of this judge.

The judge was expressionless as he silently read the verdict. He didn't look up or toward anyone. Kyle searched for a hint in the judge's face. He watched the judge's eyebrows, eyes, mouth: Anything that might hint what it said. He saw nothing. The judge passed the verdict to the clerk. "Madam Clerk, please read the verdict aloud for the courtroom."

The clerk rose and methodically unfolded and placed reading glasses on her face.

Hurry the fuck up you cunt! My whole fuckin' life is on that paper and you act like you don't give a rat's ass, thought Kyle.

Kyle saw Taylor wring his fingers. His own palms were sweating. His head spun with thoughts and emotions. He could almost hear the faint words floating in the air like the scent of sweet wildflowers. *Did they say not guilty?*

"We, the members of the jury find the defendant, Kyle Earl Sanders, *guilty* of murder in the first degree!" The courtroom exploded into applause and sighs of relief. The words jolted him back to reality. The tension broke and Kyle knew it was over. He'd lost.

Taylor sat motionless. His vacant expression never changed. He showed no emotion. Kyle figured his lawyer could care less about him at this point.

The judge pounded his gavel and screamed. "Order in this court-room! I said, order in this courtroom!" Several minutes passed before the audience settled down.

Kyle slowly stared at each juror, stopping to study every face. Most of the men stared back. All the women turned away. Taylor would have killed him if he did such a thing during the trial. *Why care? It's over.*

He slowly turned to Taylor. How could Kyle respect a lawyer who couldn't even look him in the eye? This was the asshole who had told him they had a chance.

Kyle then stared at Alicia. She replied with a look of disgust. She didn't look away. *That fuckin' Bitch-ho. She wants to laugh at me.*

As the courtroom buzzed, Kyle returned his gaze to the polished ta-bletop. He disengaged reality and got lost in his thoughts. *If I ever get outta here, which one am I gonna kill first?*

TWO

When the new eligibility list went up in the briefing room Inspector Casey Ford couldn't believe his eyes. Officers slapped him on the back. "Congratulations Casey! Good job dude!"

Casey knew from experience that the San Francisco Police Department was a political animal. He doubted that he had the juice to get into Homicide. Obviously, he had a godfather somewhere because his dream had come true; he was officially assigned to that elite branch. His plan was finally coming together.

Casey flushed the urinal and zipped his slacks — his third trip to the toilet in an hour. The coffee was going through him, and his hands jittered from too much caffeine — that just made the butterflies in his stomach jumpier. Casey nervously pulled the knot on his tie; he peered into the mirror. His deep blue eyes were studying and evaluating his own presentation. He realized the importance of the first impression. Four years in the Army and 10 years on the police department had taught him one principle: Look your best and be your best. The rest will fall into place.

Casey took a deep breath and walked into the Homicide Unit. He approached his new partner, who looked up and identified him before Casey said a word.

"Hi Casey, welcome aboard, buddy. I'm Jack Paige. We'll be working together."

Casey noticed Jack's smooth, almost soothing voice. He didn't expect that from this bear of a man. Casey had only seen Jack on the news, walking around chaotic homicide scenes. On screen Jack always looked confident and calm. He directed others, like cops in the movies. Here in real life he seemed bigger than he had on TV.

"Thanks man, I mean, Jack. I'm totally psyched to meet you." Casey beamed his smile. "It's very cool to be here and I'm really looking forward to it." Casey brushed his hand against his slacks to wipe the sweat from his palm and extended his hand. Jack's hands were like mallets. He wrapped his around Casey's as if he was holding a baseball, and his handshake felt like a vice. Thirty-two years on the force hadn't weakened Jack, at least not physically.

"I sit here and you sit right there," Jack pointed.

"Excellent." Casey nodded and pointed. He felt jittery. "Cool, thanks." Casey sat down and discovered his chair was worn. The rollers stuck and the back support bent too far back when he leaned against it. The padding on the arms was torn. It matched perfectly with the World War II surplus desks scattered around the detective floor. The walls were stacked with makeshift shelves holding file folders with case numbers written on the sides. Casey gazed around in his new surroundings.

"Those are all homicide cases," said Jack.

"Yeah? Open or closed?"

"Both. We never close a homicide case until it's solved. Remember ... there's no statute of limitations on murder."

"Oh okay, yeah, that's right. I remember now." Casey realized murderers only escape justice when they hide themselves, their crimes, or they die.

"Some of the older cases have boxes full of cassette tapes. The newer cases have compact discs or thumb drives. They take a helluva' lot less space."

Casey nodded his head without speaking. He thought about the tapes, discs and thumb drives holding the entombed voices of people experiencing sorrow, shock and anger: the recordings of the many people who found themselves in the interrogation room of the homicide unit. Every person was there for his or her own unique reasons. Some were willing, others were not.

The stale stench of cigarette and cigar smoke lingered in the room. Smoking was not permitted in the building, but Casey knew that in the middle of the night, in the heat of a murder investigation, simple rules don't always mean much. Cops do what they have to do.

"Bottom line, Casey, we get the job done and don't screw up! No chief wants his department on CNN for screwing up a murder case. Especially ours. Got it?"

Casey didn't answer because Jack wasn't looking for an answer.

"You drink coffee?" asked Jack.

"Ah yeah, sure," *Shit,* more *coffee,* thought Casey. He didn't protest. He'd smelled burnt coffee since he'd arrived. He saw that he would be following Jack. After all, that was the progression.

They walked to the coffee station in the back of the office. It was centered on a long counter in a makeshift kitchenette.

"Look at all them snacks, man. And Cup-o-Noodles," said Casey.

"There's soda, water, whatever, in there." Jack pointed to a white fridge. Sometimes we eat breakfast, lunch and dinner here."

"I'm cool with that. Hell, I've lived on microwave popcorn and Cup-o-Noodles for days."

Jack poured two mugs of coffee, handing one to Casey. "I hear you're a damn good cop."

"Huh? Uh, yeah, I guess. Thanks." Casey didn't expect Jack would check up on his reputation, but then again, why wouldn't he?

"First thing, check any cockiness at the door. This is just like any other specialized unit around here. You gotta' prove yourself all over again."

"Naaa, I don't carry that shit. I just wanna' do a good job and work hard."

"I know you will. I'm just giving you a friendly reminder."

"Got it, thanks."

Casey relented to the fact he would keep his mouth shut at least until he got a "who-done-it" solved. He realized all investigative units had idiosyncrasies and boundaries. In time, he would figure this one out too.

*　　　*　　　*

Jack made it a habit to have his new partner over for dinner. He had been through a number of different partners during his career, and he found that this gave them a chance to get to know one another; but most of all he wanted Sarah to meet them. Sarah was almost always a supportive wife. There had only been one or two instances over the years when she hadn't agreed with a job Jack accepted. Even at those moments he was lucky to have her. Jack had 12 months until he was eligible to retire, but he knew that in that year he would be spending more time with his new partner than with Sarah. That's why it was best she meet Casey. It doesn't take long for the wife of a homicide detective to understand the relationship between partners.

Sarah sprinkled the steaks with salt and pepper while Jack opened the wine.

"Is he married or what?" asked Sarah.

"I don't know. He didn't say and I didn't ask."

"Was he wearing a ring?"

"I don't know. I didn't look. You'll see soon enough."

"Hmmm ... have you heard anything about him?

"Yeah, I heard he's a great cop. He takes care of business."

"C'mon Jack, you know what I mean."

"I don't."

"Does he have a family? How old is he?"

"I don't know if he's got a family. He's just your typical thirty-something looking cop."

 "Is he gay?"

"Gay? Where'd that come from?"

"Nowhere, really. I'm just trying to get a mental picture before he gets here."

"I don't know what he is. He didn't seem gay. I mean he's not flamin' or outright like most of them around that place."

"You said he could bring whoever, right?"

"Yeah, but he said it was just him and I didn't ask."

"Hmm, interesting."

"I never met the guy until today."

Sarah nodded and gave Jack a smile. "I hope he enjoys a good steak and potato — not one of those young yuppie cops that only eats vegetables and yogurt."

Jack chuckled, realizing his wife was nuts. Then again, she had to be in order to survive 27 years of marriage with him. Not to mention, three kids and two grandkids. He wrapped one arm around her slim waist and lightly slapped her ass with the other hand.

"I know I bug you, but I love you," said Sarah.

"Yeah, you do."

"Now finish pouring my wine," said Sarah.

Jack jokingly pushed her away.

*   *   *

Jack and Sarah lived in a beautiful little San Francisco neighborhood, not far from the oceanfront homes of the celebrities. They bought the house back in the old days when cops could afford to live in the city. The lawn was perfectly manicured, and surrounded with mature junipers and black pines twisting into shapes that reminded Casey of the contour of the cityscape. The fog seeped through the cracks of the jagged hills that separated the city from the sea. It found its way into the rich greenery, as well as the concrete, and wood. It looked like a painting. The Tudor home was cozy. The coping, shutters and trim were painstakingly painted, perfectly accenting the design. It had an incredible hue, reminiscent of old San Francisco. The cobblestone walkway gently curved toward the porch. Orange light spilled through the beveled glass of the front wooden doors.

Casey paused a moment before getting out of the car. He absorbed the environment while trying to free his mind of his negative thoughts. He knew Jack's kids had it made, growing up here with this silver spoon in their mouths. Not every kid has it so good. Casey knew that.

Casey caught the aroma of food cooking before he got to the front door. The sound of soft music drifted out. Shadows passed at a distance on the other side of the beveled glass. Casey rang the bell. As soon as Jack opened the door, the aroma and music came to life, wrapping around Casey's senses.

"Hi Casey. Welcome. Come on in buddy." Jack swung the door wide open. Jack wore a comfortable pair of cotton pants and a button-down casual shirt. Casey had only seen him in a suit. He looked less intimidating in casual clothes.

Casey stepped in. "Hey Jack. This is a smokin' house, man. It's beautiful.

"Thanks. We like it."

Casey saw a thin, pretty blonde woman enter from the kitchen.

"This is my wife, Sarah," said Jack.

"Hey Sarah, I'm Casey." Casey extended his hand.

"Hello, Casey. I'm glad to meet you," said Sarah with a friendly smile and nod.

"Me too." Casey noticed her hand was soft and delicate. Her handshake was gentle. He knew she was definitely not the one who clipped the shrubbery. "Nice house, too. And man, whatever's cookin' smells great. I'm lookin' forward to some good ole' home cookin'," said Casey.

"Good. Jack, how bout' getting something for Casey?" Sarah turned with a smile and headed for the kitchen.

"What can I mix up for you?" asked Jack.

"I don't know? What you got?

"I got everything, name it, cocktail? Beer or wine?

"Bourbon and water would be good if you got it."

"Comin' up," Jack stepped behind the small wet bar.

Casey recognized Jack and Sarah had great taste in design. The front room was furnished with as much attention to detail as the exterior. Rich, dark-colored gumwood-trimmed windows and doorways, and every door had beveled glass and lovely crystal handles. The walls were painted rich colors and the hardwood floors were beautifully polished. It reminded him of those perfect houses you see in magazines.

Family portraits of all ages hung on the walls. The only way Casey could determine generation was by the age of the pictures and the style of the clothes.

"You have a good lookin' family," said Casey while admiring the portraits.

"Thanks," said Jack without looking up from mixing drinks.

Sarah came back into the room at the same time Jack rounded the bar with drinks in hand.

"I was just sayin' to Jack, you guys got a good lookin' family."

"Thank you, how about you, do you have children?" Asked Sarah.

"Naaa ... no kids. I'm single." Casey didn't elaborate. He noticed Sarah accepted the compliment well about her their family. She'd obviously heard it repeated over the years. Jack smiled and nodded, his chin rising slightly. It was body language of a proud father. Casey's ability to read body language had kept him alive more than once growing up, and again later, as a soldier then a cop.

"Jacky Jr. is our oldest. He's 25." Sarah pointed to the portrait farthest left.

"He looks like you, Jack," said Casey.

Jack chuckled.

Casey thought the photo looked like it was taken during Jack Jr.'s college days. He had the same eyes, square chin and strong look of his father.

"He and his wife, Beth, live in San Diego. They have twin boys, one year old. We're always trying to convince them to bring the grandkids up more often." Sarah's voice only partially masked her disappointment.

"Her family's down there and they help out quite a bit with the twins," said Jack. His frown told the rest of the story.

"Got it. Yeah, twins, that's gotta' be a handful, man" said Casey. It was an obvious ripple in this perfect family.

"That's Jenna and that's Jarrod." Sarah pointed.

Casey thought, *Fuckin' weird ... All the kid's names start with "J."* Why do parents do that shit? He sipped his drink, keeping his thoughts to himself.

"Jenna is a senior at UC Santa Cruz. She loves the beach." Sarah's warm smile reappeared.

Casey noticed Jack's smile didn't bounce back. Maybe he wasn't so happy about UC Santa Cruz.

"Jarrod is going to graduate high school this month. He's probably looking at junior college or the military." Sarah didn't sound happy about the military option.

Casey didn't respond.

Jack spoke to fill the void. An awkward silence hung in the air.

"A couple of his buddies think they can see the world by joining up. They got him thinking about it too." Jack frowned and shook his head.

Sarah grabbed Jack's arm and gave it a jerk. "Jarrod's always been a wanderer. It drives Jack crazy. They're too much alike. That's the problem."

"I think the military is great. I joined as soon as I was 18. It was a good gig for me, you know?" said Casey.

"I think it's great, as long as he finishes college, said Jack.

"Yeah, the college thing wasn't really an option for me. The Army gave me a good start on life. No baggage if ya' know what I mean."

Jack and Sarah didn't answer. They just stared at him.

"The Army don't care who you are or where you came from. Just sign up, boy! We'll take care of you from here on out!" Casey chuckled. "Them recruiters jus' smile and kiss your ass. Next thing I knew, I had a DI screamin' two inches from my face. 'You belong to me, boy!'" Casey chuckled and looked toward the floor. He caught himself reflecting on his life. In a softer voice, almost apologetic, he tried to explain: "I'm just sayin', it was good for me, you know? Growing up in the south, we didn't have a lot." He looked up and caught Sarah and Jack staring at him. "If it wasn't for the Army, I wouldn't be a cop."

"Yeah?" asked Jack.

"Yeah," Casey nodded and stopped talking. He smiled and looked back at the portrait of Jerrod.

"Let's sit down. Dinner's ready in a few minutes." Sarah was already moving back into the kitchen. Casey followed Jack through the family room around the bar and into the formal dining room. Three beautiful place settings were on the table. Casey sat across from Jack. Sarah brought out dinner.

"I hope you're a meat-and-potatoes man Casey. It's one of Jack's favorites."

"Oh hell yeah I am. Most my dinners come wrapped in plastic or a paper bag. My idea of a home-cooked meal is ordering Chinese from the family-run Chinese joint downstairs from my apartment." Casey chuckled. "Being single and all, I don't have real home cookin'. Thanks again for tonight. This is really cool." Casey was careful to keep his hands off the table, politely in his lap. Just like the Army taught him. The room fell silent for an awkward moment.

"You know, Jack, I only knew of you from watchin' TV."

"Really, TV?"

"Yeah, you know ... On the news. You don't look nervous. Are you?"

Jack smiled. "Yeah, I get nervous. You get over it. Give it some time." Jack seemed amused that Casey saw him on TV.

"Casey, don't compliment him too much. He's bad enough now." Sarah smiled and placed the dinner on the table.

The dinner smelled great. The aroma immediately reminded him of walking through the front door and being engulfed in warmth and comfort. This was something Casey never had as a boy.

"So, Casey, you mentioned you're originally from the South?" Sarah peeked over the top of her wine glass as she took a sip, awaiting his response.

Jack was serving a piece of meat and glanced up from his plate.

"Yeah. Actually, I was raised all around the South. We moved between Georgia, Louisiana and Alabama." Casey looked into his plate. His voice trailed off to almost a whisper. Noise from the knives and forks almost drowned his words. "Didn't have much really ... growin' up." The pause seemed forever. "Guess that's why the Army was good." Reminiscing about the Army brought a sparkle to his words. It was something good in his life. He rarely spoke about life as a younger man. "I was at Fort Benning for basic training. Man, it was frickin' hot in Georgia. It gets cookin'. I was sweatin' like a dog and learnin' to be a grunt." He noticed Jack and Sarah stopped eating and were smiling at him.

"How'd you end up in California?" asked Sarah.

Casey saw that Sarah was good at interviewing people. You didn't see it happening with her, she was so sweet. He would have to be careful. He was never one to reveal too much about his life.

"I had what they call one-station training at Fort Benning. I was Infantry, assigned to a line platoon. I was a rifleman. Basically, it was because I was young and dumb. I mean young and strong." Casey chuckled. "I carried the heavy guns. After 14 weeks, they assigned me to my primary duty station at Fort Ord in Monterey. Typical Army thinking, they send you as far away from where you came from. It was cool for me, though. It worked out."

Jack wasn't saying much. He watched and listened.

"Yeah ... Once I got here, I loved it. The city grew on me, so I went to night school and here I am." Casey raised his arms and smiled. "What I'm sayin' is, the Army gave me a great background and got me on the PD."

"I have always had a lot of respect for military personnel." It was the first thing Jack had said in several minutes. "I wasn't in the military, but I understand the sacrifice, commitment and drive it takes to be successful there."

"Yeah, thanks man. I appreciate that." Casey raised his cocktail glass. "Here's to the men and women of the Armed Forces, cheers." They clinked glasses.

*   *   *

"Wow man, this dinner is fantastic. Thanks again for havin' me," said Casey while devouring his dinner and washing it down with bourbon and soda.

Sarah smiled while sipping her wine. "You're welcome Casey. You're a good eater, like Jack. I can see you two will make good partners."

Casey nodded in agreement. He smiled with tight lips because his mouth was full of food.

"So Casey, do you get to see your family much? Where did you say they were again?"

Casey had left that open and vague, but Sarah wasn't going to let him get away with it.

"Naw, I'm not a big fan of the weather down south, and I really don't have much a family to speak of. I left for good reason." He didn't volunteer the reason. He wasn't used to talking to people that had a real interest in him. He found that most people like to talk about themselves and usually he could spin the focus of the conversation from him, back to them — most of the time they didn't even notice. It made him a good listener, a good detective. "I've focused on my career. I guess that's why I'm still single. Either that or nobody's willing to put up with me." Casey smiled.

"Well if you hang around with Jack too much, I guarantee you'll stay single." Sarah winked at Jack.

"Now why do you have to be like that? Here we are having a nice time. Where's the love around here?" Jack acted offended.

"Speaking of dating ... I hope Jack mentioned you could bring anyone tonight?"

Casey nodded at Jack. He noticed Jack's eyes flare up at Sarah's last comment.

"Uhh yeah, he did. Thanks." *Jack didn't mention anything about a date. He probably forgot. Casey thought. This would be a good time to cover Jack.* Casey recognized that Sarah and Jack had their own intimate way of teasing and joking. It had been refined over years of sharing lives and raising a family. They also hid their frustration with one another as well

Sarah let the relationship issue go. Casey decided it was a good time to change the subject. "So Jack, how's it work? You know, when we pick up a case?" He was anxious to start learning.

"I'll get a call from the detectives at the scene. If it's a solid homicide or looks at all like a suspicious death, we'll send crime scene guys out and we'll roll out too. I'll get the ball rolling from the phone, give you a call, and we'll decide where to meet." Jack fell into a calm demeanor during his explanation. Obviously, he had done this a hundred times before. He was careful and methodical.

"I hate to say it, but I can't wait to get a case. Not that I want someone murdered, but I want to work a homicide."

"We'll pick one up soon, buddy, society guarantees it. Just remember, homicide is just like any other assault, except the victim dies." Jack winked at him.

"Yeah, I guess so." Casey smiled politely. *I know much better than you could ever imagine, buddy.*

Dinner was over and it was getting late. They said their goodbyes on the porch. Casey wanted to be fresh for work. Who knew? Maybe they would get a customer tonight.

*   *   *

Jack and Sarah washed dishes. "You're not saying much, Jack."

"About what?"

"You know, about Casey, and how the dinner went."

"It went good. I like him."

"He seems kinda' quiet, private. Or like one step back." Sarah tilted her head.

"Don't you think you were prying a little too much?"

"Jack, I was just trying to figure the guy out!" Sarah put down a plate, faced Jack and dried her hands.

"Okay, okay. You asked." Jack kept rinsing dishes and didn't return Sarah's look.

"I get a sense about him." She was pensive for a moment.

"Sarah, I know you are very perceptive. But give the guy a chance. That's all I'm asking, okay?" Jack wasn't in the mood to argue. He wanted to dismiss the whole conversation.

"It's not so easy for me Jack. I'm home wondering if you're okay, while you're out chasing murderers. I know you may have to depend on Casey with your life. I have to feel good about him for my own peace of mind."

Jack felt selfish. He knew that he kept himself from thinking about that from his wife's perspective. He stopped rinsing plates and faced her. "I'm sorry babe, you're right."

Sarah breathed a sigh of relief.

"Let's go to bed," Jack took her hand and they went upstairs.

THREE

The swearing-in ceremony for the new correctional officers was more recruiting effort than anything else — fanfare. Officers marched around in dress uniforms. Hundreds of family members with cameras sat in folding chairs, waiting for a reason to clap.

Justin Pierce took it all in. It was a happy day. Finally, he was getting his badge. Justin looked forward to starting his career as a Louisiana State Correctional Officer. *The best thing about being a prison guard is that you run your own piece of the world. After all, who the hell is gonna listen to complaints from a bunch of convicts?* Justin grinned, showing teeth stained from years of chewing, twisted dried tobacco. Every man in his family chewed Cotton Bowl — at least, every generation he could remember. People watched Justin receive his badge. They even applauded.

When Justin arrived at the prison he found it was better than he'd expected. There was a shortage of guards, so he could work all the overtime he wanted, but first he had to attend the orientation for new guards.

Justin was bored and antsy from sitting in the classroom for the two-week in-house training program. He didn't completely understand what the instructor was saying when he explained prison issues on a state-wide scale, but Justin doubted that was important. He paid attention to day-to-day operations, figuring that was all he needed to know.

Justin had never realized that prisons are like little cities, with their own society, with layers between staff and inmates. He learned to separate inmates mostly by color. Blacks stayed in one area; Mexicans in another; and Whites had their spot. If an inmate was in a gang, he couldn't stay too close to a member of a rival gang. If he did they'd kill each other. Lifers and death-row inmates stayed in a designated area. Homosexuals, child molesters and cops were completely isolated; everyone wanted to kill them.

During training Justin walked the yard, decks and catwalks. He felt uncomfortable around inmates that weren't locked up. In the main yard area, inmates hung out in groups. The blazing Louisiana sun baked their shirtless, tattooed bodies. Justin felt the tension in the air as he walked past them. They watched him and the other guards constantly. They watched other inmates even more. Justin quickly learned that inmates were like caged wild animals. They become very dangerous. Always prepared to attack or be attacked. Justin found that no matter where an inmate was housed, he would do push-ups and pull-ups constantly. The bigger and stronger an inmate was, the better his odds for survival — exactly like being in the wild.

Justin sat in the classroom waiting for the final class to begin. The guard who was teaching was 6'3" and weighed about 275, about the same size as Justin. The guard carried a large box into the room, and heaved it onto the front table. It clanked then Justin heard sounds of metal settling. The guard wiped his rolled-up sleeve across his brow and then grunted his name. Justin didn't catch it, but he really didn't care.

"Gentlemen," the guard boomed. "The difference between peace and riot is a delicate balance. The venting of frustration must be controlled so it doesn't become explosive. If you don't understand this concept, lives will be lost. That life may be your own."

It sounded scripted but it still gave Justin a chill. He would never let that happen.

The guard reached into the box and started pulling out crudely made, edged weapons. He handed different ones to the guards seated up front. "Keep passing them back," he said. "There's plenty to go around."

Weapons of different designs, shapes and sizes passed hands. Once everyone had one or two weapons to examine, the guard stopped, and looked at the class. A hush fell over them. "Every weapon you see here was manufactured and confiscated in this prison," said the guard.

Justin looked down at his weapon: a handle with a sharp, crude blade. It could be an effective killer.

The class of recruits was completely silent and focused on the guard.

"There's a helluva lot more where those came from. That's just the ones I could carry." The recruits further examined and fondled the various weapons.

"There is no greater issue in prison than respect. Plenty of people get killed in prisons for lack of respect."

The guard had Justin's attention.

"My point is ... inmates have access to anything they want — cigarettes, sex, drugs, and, as ya'll see, deadly weapons. It's amazing so much can be secreted into cement walls. But, just like on the outside, nothing's free. And these men can give a fucking rat's ass about your life — or their own."

Justin decided he would try to work on the decks. Less likelihood of getting hurt.

"My class is short, but effective, I hope." The guard paused until the entire class was looking at his tired, lined face. "Remember, when you lock a man in a cell 23 hours a day, he has a lot of time to think.

They all think about the same thing; how to beat the system. This is just a small example of what these guys come up with. Class over."

*　　　*　　　*

Justin's first assignment was the midnight watch on the Double Red Wing Deck. Here every inmate was a lifer. They wore red pants and red tops whenever they were moved. Most were a select group of murderers and serial rapists. They were generally cooperative, resigned to the fact that they would never get out.

In his first few days, Justin tried to get a feeling for the place — guards and inmates. The cells were somewhat private, no bars, just cement walls and solid metal doors. Justin learned how to pass food and medications to inmates through the small openings in the doors. Guards had little contact with inmates. Each 8' x 15' cell had a single bunk bed attached to one long wall. Each had a freestanding stainless steel sink and toilet. Most cells were cluttered with letters, books, magazines and court documents. The walls were papered with photographs and hand-drawn pornography.

The midnight shift worked well for Justin. It was lights-out for almost his entire shift, and few other guards were on duty. Justin liked going solo, even if it was more work. Justin had always liked working alone.

The prison was never quiet. One night Justin was startled by an inmate's screaming. He noticed that the training officer next to him didn't move a muscle. The man had eased back in his chair, feet parked on his desk, and when the scream came he didn't raise an eyelid. "What the hell is that?" asked Justin.

"Don't worry about it. Some inmates scream during the night. They get frustrated in the dark. Their eyes got nothing to focus on so their minds concentrate on being caged up. I guess it drives some guys' nuts. You'll get used to it."

"That sucks if they want sleep."

"Yeah, I guess."

Justin realized the training guard didn't give a damn about anything. He made a mental note of it for later.

After several hours Justin tired of sitting. He tapped the training guard's arm. "Hey, I'm bored. I'm gonna make the rounds."

"Whatever ... I'll be right here ... sleeping."

Justin walked the deck. His sinuses burned from the re-circulated stench air combined with the pungent bite of ammonia that made up the universal aroma in the prison. Justin cut a corner too short and his shoulder rubbed against the wall. Even the walls stunk. The odor rubbed onto his skin and clothes.

Justin stopped here and there to listen. Beds squeaked. Muffled whimpering was suppressed with pillows. Those noises disguised the sounds of men pleasing themselves. Listening made Justin's loins tingle. He got hard.

The crackle of the walkie-talkie startled him. "All guards return to the main control center," said the lead training guard. Justin returned quickly and discovered they were assembling teams to conduct routine cell searches. Justin arrived as the briefing began.

"We'll break up into three-man teams. Each team will hit a specific cell. We hit them at the same time so nothing gets flushed down the pot, any questions?"

The supervisor gave each team leader a cell number and a set of shackles. Justin followed his team leader to the section that housed the lifers.

They stood quietly outside the cell door, waiting for the electronic lock to click open and the lights to turn on. Justin heard the click. The team leader yanked the heavy metal door open.

Kyle Sanders lay on top of his sheets. He wore only prison-issue underwear. Justin could tell from the shocked look on Kyle's face that the inmate had been asleep.

Justin noticed Kyle's skin, pale and fragile. It hadn't seen much sunshine in 16 years. The inmate's cell and body both had the stale day-to-day stench brought by years of poor hygiene. There were no colognes or deodorants on the shelf above Kyle's sink. Justin figured this guy didn't give a damn.

Justin dropped the shackles on the floor of the cell. "Get up and take off those shorts."

Kyle complied. He rubbed his face with his hands, yawned and shook his head as if to rattle his mind awake. He removed his shorts and stood naked in front of Justin. As Justin directed Kyle moved robotically through the search sequence. Justin paid special attention to Kyle's mouth and rectum, his *prison purse*: The ports of concealed contraband. Kyle's were clear.

"Put the shackles on your ankles."

Kyle complied, never saying a word.

Justin shackled Kyle's wrists and escorted him from the cell. They moved slowly because Kyle had the "lifer walk," a 12-inch shuffle ingrained from the exact length of chain that connects the shackles.

Justin returned to the cell and searched through Kyle's paperwork, clothes and toiletry items. It was dirty work. In the air vent Justin found a wick. Kyle had stacked a length of toilet paper and twisted it tighter and tighter until it became a worm-like twine. He took his one contraband match and lit the end of the wick. It had a burning cherry like the tip of incense. The air circulation in the vent kept the wick alive, burning slowly.

Justin carried the wick out and showed it to Kyle. He smiled, and held the wick in front of Kyle's face.

Kyle stood, expressionless.

"What's this doin' in your vent, Sanders?"

"Burnin'"

"I know its burnin' asshole! What do you need it for?"

"Smokin'"

Justin found no other contraband. "What do you have to smoke?"

"Sometimes a cigarette, sometimes crank."

"You're getting rolled up for this, Sanders. It'll cost you thirty days in the hole."

Kyle's steely eyes bore through Justin's glare. Justin realized Kyle Sanders couldn't give a fuck about anything in life. Justin stared back until the icy words broke the silence.

"Oh yeah." Kyle flashed his dirty jagged teeth. "There is one other reason ... I keep it there in case I need to light some asshole on fire." Then he smiled.

*   *   *

After a month of watching and talking to the same inmates, night after night, Justin began to learn the things that made them tick. He saw a side of inmates that most never see. He learned their strengths and probed for their weaknesses. Justin wasn't naïve. He knew they had to pay for their sins. He was going to make sure of it.

*   *   *

The cell door opened, and painful bright light streaked in. Kyle had to squint. The blinding light felt like shards of glass slicing through his eyes. He hadn't walked more than five steps in a straight line for 30 days. Five steps covered the distance of the tiny square cell. He didn't care. Thirty days in the hole was nothing. It built character. A good portion of his 16 years had been spent in the hole. Kyle had learned the new guard's name: Pierce. He decided he wasn't going to let Pierce mess up his world. As soon as he got back to the deck and his regular cell, he would turn the tables on the guy, and gain some respect. It would cost him another trip to the hole, but it was worth the price.

Kyle shuffled along the deck to his cell. He walked slowly and looked around. There was no need to be in a hurry, especially with 12-inch steps. He smiled; it felt good to be home.

"Hey Kyle, welcome home." The voice came from behind a cell door next to Kyle's. A couple of inmates cackled as they peered through the holes in their doors.

"Good to be home, Lester!" said Kyle. He chuckled, acting unaffected by 30 days in the hole. "We'll get caught up soon as I get my shit situated." Kyle swayed his shoulders back and held his chin high as he shuffled. Those who caught a glimpse saw he hadn't been broken.

"Lookin' good, Sanders!" The voices carried a tone of respect.

Kyle's feet were still cold from standing naked on the cement floor. The guard slammed the cell door shut behind him. He looked around his cell. A hurricane had blown through it. Everything was still in the same ransacked condition it had been in when he'd left a month ago. Kyle dressed himself and put on a pair of white socks. He slipped his feet into orange rubber shower thongs. They pushed the socks up between his big toe and second toe. He folded his extra clothes and stacked them in the corner. He replaced the thin plastic foam-wrapped mattress onto the gray metal bunk frame attached to the wall. He pulled a thin, white sheet over the pad and threw his blanket and pillow on top. Then he started on the strewn papers. He separated his personal letters from the other stuff and began the putting pictures and drawings back onto the walls.

He put the letters back into chronological order, newest on top. Many were from other inmates in other institutions. Most were from women, but some were from men. The content was similar to all prison mail: Polite salutation as opener — *My soul mate, Kyle. I hope this letter finds you in good health* — followed by the inevitable update — *My attorney has assured me we are moving forward with my appeal. Cocoa sends her love too. She will be leaving us sometime in December, the parole board agreed to let her out this time around —* then on to longings, and sexual fantasy — *what I'll do to you when I finally see you in the flesh.* Prison mail is fantasy sprinkled lightly with truth and reality.

Kyle had few letters from family. Now and then they would write and give him an update and maybe put money on his books. He needed money to buy things in the joint.

In the following days, Kyle got caught up on what had been going on in the world, both inside and outside. He spent his hour of exercise time talking to guys from other areas of the prison. He got caught up with the happenings on his own deck by way of kites. Kyle was an expert at folding the small scraps of paper with miniature writing on them and using strings to pass them under cell doors. He could communicate privately with anyone with a kite. That way, he didn't have to talk aloud for all the guards to hear.

Television was Kyle's window to life outside. He could read letters and connect them to what he saw on television, in an attempt to figure what people were talking about and seeing in everyday life. He saw what freedom was like; he just never experienced it.

"Yo Kyle, how ya'll been, man?" Lester had a strong southern accent. He'd spent most of his life in Mississippi, until he got arrested for killing a man.

"You know, Lester, it ain't easy but it ain't no thing either."

"Man, we been havin' new ass blood coming thro' here lately. Shit, I can't keep up with all the new people. You know, guards, inmates. It's getting' crazy man."

"I got some business with that new guard. You heard anything?" Now, Kyle was talking as low as possible. He knew other inmates could hear their conversation.

"Shit, he ain't no different from them other mutha' fuckers. He's calming his ass down after they rolled ya'll up that last time. Ain't much going on since then." Lester raised his voice a little knowing the guard down the hall might hear. "You know, them assholes come on in here like the new dog and got to piss in our bowl. They got to let us know they on the block. It's all a fuckin' game!"

"Yeah, like that ain't never happened around here before," said Kyle.

Both men started laughing. So did a couple of other inmates listening in on the chatter.

Kyle drifted off to sleep.

The cell lock clicking open startled Kyle awake. He wasn't used to hearing the door unlock in the middle of the night. The door didn't swing open like usual. He was waiting for the rush of guards to do another surprise search. He froze, with his senses on high alert. No guards burst in. Kyle heard his heart pounding. He inhaled, trying to calm himself and figure out what was going on. The door opened slowly. Light spilled into the cell. Kyle saw the silhouette of a large man wearing a jumpsuit and leather duty belt. The guard slipped in and was immediately on top of him, one hand over his mouth. The weight and size of the large man on top of him felt suffocating. Kyle realized it was Justin Pierce and felt terror. Suddenly Justin grabbed his dick and balls. Kyle struggled, but Justin squeezed his balls harder, sending sharp pains into his stomach.

"You and me got a long time to get along boy." Justin held his face close. Kyle inhaled air that Justin had just exhaled. It tasted bitter from chewing tobacco and stale coffee.

"Guess you and me gonna' learn to get along, real good." Justin twisted Kyle's balls harder. "Now you just keep your mouth shut, or I'll stick my dick in it. Don't say a fuckin' word, just nod your head, got it!"

Kyle sweated from the pain and the weight on top of him.

"Got it boy!" He repeated with a tight voice as spit formed on his mouth.

Kyle frantically nodded his head. The fingers on his mouth and balls relaxed.

"I'm glad we agree boy. Like I said, you and me are gonna get along real good, and you ain't got shit to say about it. I run your world, asshole."

Kyle nodded his head again.

"Good, I'll see you soon." Justin climbed off Kyle, giving his balls one last painful twist and then softly stroked his dick several times. "Goodnight sweetheart," said Justin with an evil grin.

Kyle remained still, frozen.

Justin slipped out just as quickly as he slipped in.

Kyle lay there, his head spinning, as he tried to catch his breath. He still tasted spit and smelled rank breath. The pain was still raw. Kyle had been molested. For the first time in his life, he was the victim. *The rules have changed.*

FOUR

The telephone ring ripped the silence of the dark room. Casey fumbled for the receiver. "Hello," he tried to focus on the numbers of the clock. The red blur sharpened into: "1:45." *Is it work, or something personal? Someone might be dead.* Casey's heart began to race.

Jack's voice came, tired but business-like. "Hey Casey, we got a customer. Get up, take a leak, turn on the light, and grab your notepad. I'll hang on a minute." Jack knew the things men have to take care of when woken suddenly.

Casey followed Jack's directions, adding a splash of cold water to his face. He grabbed his notepad and sat back down on the bed. He shook his head to clear it. It was chilly, sitting in his underwear. He grabbed the phone. "Hey Jack, what's up?"

"Got a call about 10 minutes ago. Uniform guys got a call of a suspicious vehicle at a closed gas station in the Marina District. They got there and found a brand new Mercedes Benz, engine warm, but no keys in the ignition. They snooped around and found some blood on the rear bumper. They opened the trunk and found a young woman, Jane Doe. Her hands and feet were bound, and she had a gunshot wound. Execution-style."

"Holy shit," whispered Casey.

"Casey, we got a bigger issue going on here." Jack sounded more serious.

"Bigger? What's up? What could make this bigger?" Casey was almost afraid to hear the answer.

"The Benz might be registered to the Mayor. Same name but different address. We already got brass all over the place. This is gonna be ugly."

"The Mayor of San Francisco! Our fuckin' Mayor?" said Casey, not believing the words coming from his own mouth.

"Yeah, our fucking Mayor. Welcome to homicide. Now let me bring you up to speed. The car is registered to an address in Santa Barbara, not the Mayor's home. We got a captain and a tactical team heading out to check on the Mayor at his house, make sure they're secure."

Casey had already written the date, time of his call-out, and location of the murder. His pen raced as he noted every detail. He scribbled a few of his own thoughts as well. The notebook would eventually contain all the details of the investigation in chronological order. It would become evidence and be dissected by attorneys and judges. All of this had been drilled into Casey, but right now he was just writing.

"The body is still there and the scene is buttoned up. We can meet there," said Jack.

Casey figured Jack already called the on-scene commander to make sure a large perimeter had been cordoned off securing the crime scene. That should keep the brass and media at bay.

"I'll hop in the shower and suit up. It'll take me about an hour to get there," said Casey.

"Okay, I'll see you there. I'm about the same time out as you." Jack hung up without saying goodbye — this was the Jack that Casey had seen on television.

Water streamed across Casey's back and neck. He wondered about the woman in the trunk. Just hours ago he'd been getting ready for bed. Maybe about that time the victim was out having a good time. Then, something bad happened — sheer terror. A moment came when she knew she was going to die. She'd woken up and gone through the day, never imagining that she would be murdered. Somewhere out in the city people slept, not knowing that the girl they knew and loved was dead. Their lives would be changed forever. Casey felt odd knowing this before they did. Here, he had this awareness, yet he didn't know her name.

As Casey dressed a million thoughts ran through his mind. Where is the murderer right now? What's he doing? What's he thinking? What's his plan? Where's he going? Why? He shouldn't assume it was a man, but what woman would stuff another woman in a car trunk? Casey felt nervous at the thought of having to answer all those questions. He used the toilet again.

The chatter on the police radio gave Casey a good idea of what was going on at the scene. He heard references being made to a staging area and units were switching to backup radio channels to talk more privately. The media listened to police scanners and often beat the police to crime scenes. If the media had known there was a body in the trunk of a car that might be owned by the Mayor, they definitely would have beaten the marked units to this scene.

The flashing police lights could be seen 10 blocks away. Casey slowed as he approached and took in the sight. He tried to focus on everything: landmarks, geography and businesses. Wondering which one might hold a clue or a witness. He reached the outer perimeter. A uniformed patrol officer sat in her car, amber flashers on. Yellow crime scene tape stretched from a tree on one side of the street to the roof of her car. It wrapped around the radio antenna, and then continued to the other side of the street where it was tied to a newspaper stand. This would later be referred to in a police report as the "western outer perimeter."

Casey killed his headlights as he approached. His parking lights were on. Cops learn to do this from day one. Never blind other officers at a scene by driving in with your headlights on. The officer calmly climbed out of her car and raised the tape high enough so the unmarked detective car could drive under. Casey stopped the car midway beneath the tape. He had his badge clipped to the outer breast pocket of his suit.

"Good evening, detective." The female officer smiled.

"Good evening, officer."

They exchanged a few words of pleasantries. This was customary, giving an air of calm.

"Looks like you might be busy for awhile," she said, glancing toward the scene and raising her eyebrows.

"I think you might be right, officer." Casey tilted his wrist so the flashing lights of the officer's patrol car could help him read his watch. "Inspector Casey Ford, badge 12454, Homicide. I got about zero-two-fifty-one hours."

"Thank you, sir. Have a good evening." The officer wrote down Casey's name, badge number and time of entry on a notepad. She would incorporate it onto the log she was keeping for her report and turn it into the homicide unit at the end of her shift.

Casey pulled into the outer perimeter and drove toward the next line of tape, about four blocks ahead.

The officer got back in her car to wait for the next arrivals. Those authorized would pass, but her tape was the last stop for the media. They would use zoom lenses to close the six-block distance to the actual scene to gain shots for the news. Or they'd bring in a chopper and zoom right into the scene for aerial shots.

Casey saw several unmarked police vehicles parked outside the next line of tape. He recognized Jack's car, and then saw Jack standing near the tape, writing in his notebook. Casey parked his car and wrote in his notebook: "Arrived at scene 0251 hours."

"Hey, Jack. Been here long?"

"Nah, just pulled up." Jack was drawing a diagram of the street and the gas station. He also drew the position of the victim's car.

"I write down everything I see when I first get here." Jack didn't look up from his notebook as he spoke. "Weather, lighting, number and make of the cars on the street, and where they're parked. You know, just about anything I can think of. Everything I see. You never know what's gonna be critical later. The crime scene guys do it all to scale, but we may need it before that gets done."

Casey followed Jack's lead and did the same thing.

Two crime-scene detectives approached from the inner perimeter. Their photographers' vests covered casual clothes. Both carried note-pads and flashlights. The field lieutenant broke away from a group of sergeants and walked over. Casey heard another car approach from behind. He looked back and saw an unmarked car with its headlights off. It was Richards, the homicide lieutenant. Two night detectives came from nearby. Everyone gathered in a circle.

Jack got things started: "What do we got here, folks?"

Phil Foster, the senior night detective spoke quickly, fidgeting. "We got a dandy one, Jack." His skinny fingers rustled through scraps of paper and pages of his notebook. Phil looked nervous and jittery, but he wasn't flustered. His suit had always hung off his shoulders. When Jack rolled up to a scene, he always felt relief at the sight of Phil, despite the thinness and jitters. He knew Phil would have matters in hand. "The reporting party is on her way to the third floor. She's like, twenty-five-ish. She stopped to get some gas, saw the place was closed, but noticed the victim's car. It looked out of place so she called in on her cell, then drove home. It was low priority so it pended about

25 minutes. Once they figured out what they had, uniforms picked her up at her place." Phil paused until everyone stopped writing.

"The beat guys said the engine was still warm. No keys. They spotted blood on the rear bumper and figured they might have a live victim in the trunk. So they popped the trunk and found the not-so-live victim." Phil paused again, waiting for his cue to start. Up to this point, he had led the investigation. This field briefing was the formal process of passing the case to the homicide detectives. "Looks like the Benz is registered to Mayor Russell. Same name but it's out of Santa Barbara. Maybe his daughter? Maybe his girlfriend? Who knows? Anyhow, we got the troops and a captain heading over there to see what the story is, making sure they're not all dead in the house." Nobody was shocked by that thought. Phil went on. "I got two patrol teams doing the canvas on both sides of the street, two blocks in both directions, door-to-door. The district sergeant is supervising them. Also got communications working on locating those responsible for the station to see if they got video rolling or any late night employees." Phil pointed in different directions as he spoke.

"The victim's in bad shape. Looks early twenties, white girl, dressed like she's been out at the clubs. Hands bound behind her back and legs bound. All with duct tape. Looks like a headshot, her head's blown up. Execution-style. She looks shitty."

"Did anyone find a purse?" Jack asked.

"I can fill you in on that, boss," said Andrew Mills, the lead evidence technician. Andrew knew his way around a homicide. He would have been a great homicide detective except for one drawback: He hated interviewing people.

"Thanks Andrew. So, how do you see it?" Asked Jack with a smile that gleaned a respect earned over many years and cases.

"The inside of the car looks pretty clean. No purse that I could see, but we haven't gotten into it yet. She was probably done outside the car or maybe even in the trunk itself. We won't know until we get her out." Andrew shined his flashlight beam along the street toward the car. "We got a path cleared if you two are ready for a closer look?"

"Thanks, Andrew." Jack folded his notebook shut and slipped it into his inside coat pocket. "So we don't know if we got a robbery, rape, domestic thing or what?"

"We probably have another crime scene somewhere other than here." Casey chimed in.

Jack was glad to see Casey was thinking and not overwhelmed by his first call-out.

Jack, Casey and Phil followed Andrew in a straight line toward the car. They were all careful to not step on or kick any pieces of evidence. As Jack took up the rear the four men looked like a conga line with flashlights. They stopped several feet from the car trunk.

Coagulated blood had matted the girl's hair. The bright red color seemed to jump to life when the beam from Casey's flashlight struck her upper torso. The duct tape spun around her wrist in a frantic pattern. *She must have fought,* thought Casey. To him, human bodies looked odd when they were dead. Like plastic objects. He was far from the first to notice that a body takes on an incredible stillness once life leaves it.

"We'll have to make sure we get fingernail scrapings from her," said Casey, falling into the homicide detectives' role like a natural. "If we're lucky, she scratched the fucker. I don't see any bullet casings around."

"Maybe they're in the trunk," said Phil.

"Maybe he used a revolver," said Jack.

Casey started getting the feeling all homicide detectives get when they're starved for information, when there are more questions than answers. "Hey Jack, think we should check out the tire treads and the boot soles of all the firefighters and medics that were out here? Just make sure they didn't pick up a bullet casing in a tire or shoe."

"I'll get one of my guys on that right away." Andrew flipped open his cell phone and hit a number in the memory.

Jack's phone rang. "Hello, this is Jack." He paused listening. "Okay, boss. Can you have the family meet us at the station? Also, have them bring a current photo if you can. That'll give us a jump on a flyer." Jack flipped the phone shut and exhaled deeply. Casey suddenly recognized the bags under Jack's eyes. Jack seemed to age years in seconds. "That was the captain. Looks like our gal here is Lisa Russell, the Mayor's daughter, visiting from Santa Barbara. College break."

The cool moist night air suddenly seemed as if it were biting Casey's neck. He felt the chill down his spine and pulled his coat tighter. The group fell silent. They all knew the pressure on solving this one had just cranked way up.

"The first 48 hours." Jack had said at dinner earlier in the night. "Those are the most critical. If the case goes cold in the first two days we're often sunk." Not an option on this one.

"Hey Andrew, what time will the autopsy be?" asked Jack.

"Probably around 10. I'll give you a heads up so you guys can get over in time." Andrew knew Jack attended autopsies whenever essential information might be involved.

"Keep me posted on what you got here. Casey and I are heading over to the station. We'll get the reporting party statement banged out, then see if we can positively identify this as Lisa or not." Jack knew they still couldn't assume this was Mayor Russell's daughter. First step in a homicide investigation: make sure you know who the victim is. Jack and Casey left the crime scene the same way they'd entered it: slowly. Both made notations of time and information.

"I'll follow you in, Jack." Casey glanced down the street and saw the bright lights of camera setups. *Ignore them,* he thought. *There are more important things to worry about.* This was exactly how he was supposed to think.

FIVE

Casey followed Jack from the police department parking lot into the building. When they entered Casey noticed some uniformed officers near the doorway to the homicide unit. The young officers had a deer-in-the-headlights look, eager to help, but not sure what to do. The officers nodded and cleared the way for the detectives.

Casey smelled coffee brewing for the long night ahead. Lieutenant Richards was already open for business, with the reporting party (the girl who'd called in about the suspicious car) sitting in an interview room.

"Casey, need a cup?" Jack was already pouring from the pot.

"Java? Absolutely, thanks."

The men entered Richards' office for the first of several briefings. Richards sat in a blue adjustable chair behind a desk pushed back from the door. Jack and Casey took the two '70s-style chairs in front. A map of the United States covered one wall, with an American flag hanging opposite that. Other walls had plaques and a collage of police memorabilia. Framed pictures of Richards' family sat on his desk next to a stack of papers. It was the stuff of a career.

The blinds were rolled closed and the fluorescent light bathed everyone in a pale hue. Several video monitors sat on a shelf beneath the flag. Three computer video recorders were lined in the corner behind Jack's chair. The interview rooms were all wired for video and sound, and Richards could monitor them from here.

"Hey Casey, got a hot one right out of the chute," said Richards, raising his bushy eyebrows and grinning.

"Hey, whatever, boss. I'm good with it."

"Good, that's what I expect. That's why you're here." Richards looked at Jack. "What do we got here?"

Jack took his notebook from his pocket. "Looks like it's the Mayor's daughter. We got a closer look after you left. She was tied up with tape and shot in the head, at minimum. We're waiting for an update from Andrew. Is the family here yet?"

"No, they're on the way." Richards glanced at his wristwatch. "Should be about 15 minutes. The Chief's coming in too. He's going to notify City Council members as soon as we get positive identification."

"We got the canvas in the neighborhood going. So far, nothing. I also got a call into radio, trying to find the owner or manager for the gas station." Jack checked his notes.

Richards read from a note on his desk. "Radio already called with the information. The owner of the station said he shut down about 11:00 last night, got out of there about 11:45. He didn't see anyone in the lot. No video either. Here's his horsepower." Richards handed the note to Jack.

Jack saw the owner's name and contact information written on the note. He slipped it into his notebook.

"I talked to him on the phone. I'll email you the digital recording." Richards linked the digital recorder on his desk to his computer, clicked the mouse and said, "Done. It's in your email." Every conversation with a potential witness or suspect had to be recorded, though the station owner hadn't been aware of it.

"We'll contact this guy and see if the victim was a regular customer. Maybe she had friends in the area."

Casey chimed in. "You want me to call Andrew and get the phone number of the pay phone at the station?"

"Yeah. Have him process the phone for blood or prints. We'll get working on a search warrant for any calls from the phone before or after," said Jack.

Casey made a note of it.

"Boss, we'll start a full work-up on the victim. We'll get a credit history and start tracking her credit cards to see if anyone is using them. Maybe we can get one of the night detectives rolling on that." Jack knew they would have extra resources on this one, so why not start using them.

"I'll get that going," said Richards. "Once we get positive identification, I'll have Andrew take the photo and make a flyer for your canvas."

"Can you get someone started on finding out if there was a bus running out there?" Casey asked. "Also hit up the cab companies and see if they had a pickup? Maybe they can track that down while we start interviewing."

"Sure. Meanwhile, get the reporting party done and out of here. I don't want that girl to see the Mayor or his wife. Keep them apart. I don't want the general public to know the Russells are involved yet."

"We'll get on it right away." Jack reached behind his chair, grabbed a fresh disc and popped it into the recorder monitoring the interview room. "Let's get going buddy."

Casey followed Jack out of the lieutenant's office. Richards reached for the phone.

Between calls Richards watched the monitor where Jack was interviewing the reporting party. Casey sat, taking notes.

"How did you end up at the gas station?"

"I was ... out with friends earlier. I pulled in to get gas and realized it was closed." She paused to blow her nose into the crumpled tissue she was holding.

Richards noticed her hands trembling.

"I'm sorry. It's horrible. Is a woman really dead?"

"Unfortunately, yes." Jack nodded solemnly. "Take your time."

"Something felt wrong. Her car was out of place. Not parked or anything. I drove out and called 911 on my cell phone."

"Did you see anyone around the pay phone?"

"No."

"Did any cabs or buses pull up? Any cars in the area?"

"No. I'm sorry. I'm not much help, am I?"

Jack patted her hand, and then gave it a slight reassuring squeeze. "You're doing great. You're brave and very helpful. Thank you for being here."

It was exactly what she needed. She smiled with a new sense of strength. "I drove home and went to bed. A half-hour later, the police called and told me what happened. Now I'm here."

Richards saw she didn't have much to offer and wasn't surprised when Jack wrapped it up. Richards popped the disc from the recorder, wrote her name on it, and added the date and time. He met Jack and Casey outside the interview room and handed them the disc.

"The Chief is talking with the Mayor and his wife. We got the photo of Lisa. I had one of the boys scan it so they could both text it and run a hard copy out to Andrew for confirmation. They also described the clothes she was wearing when she left the house. It looks like it's going to be her, but I want Andrew to see the photo to confirm."

"You got the photo with you?" asked Jack.

Richards fished the small photo from his shirt pocket and handed it to Jack.

Jack looked at the photo of the beautiful young woman. Smiling, she was all life and future. He thought of all the pictures of his own children. Moments preserved forever, but what did such images mean when the last one was a bloody death in the trunk of the car?

"Yeah, it's her," said Jack, handing the photo back to Richards.

Richards took the photo. Lisa Russell: murder victim number 49 this year in the city of San Francisco — and absolutely, the daughter of the Mayor.

All three men were silent for a moment.

"How do they look? How they taking it so far?" Jack asked.

"It ain't good. They look like shit as you can imagine. I hope you guys can get a decent interview out of them."

Richards knew the fallout would start with the morning news. "I'll run interference so you guys can concentrate on the case. Freshen up your coffee. It's gonna be a long one. I'll let the chief know about the ID so he can make the notification." Richards knew protocol. "Let's give them time to gather themselves before you do the interview."

He was gone before Jack or Casey spoke.

*　　　*　　　*

Fifteen minutes later Richards watched the monitor. The Mayor and his wife sat in the interview room. There wasn't the slightest hint of the political powerhouse couple who had won the last election, but merely two crushed parents trying to survive a nightmare.

Jack suggested that they make an exception and interview these two together. Richards agreed. A box of tissues sat on the table. Richards saw that both had taken tissues and both held tight to each other's shaking hands. Their nerves were shredded.

Jack and Casey entered the room. "I'm terribly sorry for your loss Mr. Mayor, Ma'am."

Jack looked at the floor, his hands folded in front of him. At the sound of his voice the woman broke into tears. She leaned over holding her arms around her abdomen, a mother holding the womb that once held her baby. She wept.

The Mayor put his arm around her and held her close. In a weak and broken voice he rasped, "We're just trying to understand this, Detective. We'll do our best for you."

Jack nodded. "Thank you, sir. I don't know how to make this any easier for you and your family, I'm very sorry."

"Please, call me William and my wife is Susan."

Susan Russell raised her head and looked at Jack. Her red eyes were swollen with tears. She nodded her head to her husband's words.

"Thank you, sir." Jack avoided the issue of first names by not using names at all. "Can we get either of you something to drink? Coffee or water?"

"Water, please. Susan and I can share."

Casey left the room. He returned a moment later with water.

"This is my partner, Casey Ford."

Russell and his wife nodded.

"Hello sir. I'm very sorry for your loss." Casey put the water on the table, took out his notebook, and sat next to Jack.

"First of all sir, I want you to know we will be recording our conversation. There's a hidden microphone and camera in the wall. We use the tape to preserve the interview. I thought you should know that."

In the office, Richards nodded. Jack knew that you don't tape record the Mayor without his knowledge.

"Sir, would you tell us about Lisa, her living conditions?" Jack opened his notebook.

Russell began, "Lisa's 21-years-old. She's a junior at UC Santa Barbara." His face seemed to squeeze, his eyes closing up to stop tears.

Susan Russell wept and cried out, "My god, she's my baby! Please God, help us!"

Richards saw Jack pause and inhale deeply. Richards was single but Jack had once shared with him his greatest fear: losing a child. He watched as Jack maintained — a professional sitting in a room full of pain.

Pushed over the edge by his wife's outburst, the Mayor's breath escaped, sounding as if he'd just been punched in the stomach. Tears rolled from his eyes. He wrapped his arms around her and buried his face in her hair.

Jack sat, head down, barely holding it together.

Russell composed himself first. "I'm sorry, Detective. It's so difficult."

"I can only imagine, sir. Please don't apologize. I'm sorry we're here tonight."

Richards noticed Jack did not say he understood what they felt. He was sure Jack prayed he would never know what the Russells were feeling.

"She lived in a dorm with some other students."

Richards made a note to have her dorm room secured. They would have to search it.

"Lisa wasn't the perfect student, mostly A's and B's. Although, she was very popular. She talked about going to a lot of parties with friends."

Richards noticed the Mayor had started talking about his daughter in past tense. Jack did the same. "Did she speak of boyfriends or dates?"

Russell looked confused and glanced at his wife. Obviously, Lisa didn't talk to her dad about such things.

Now Lisa's mother finally spoke, her voice little more than a whisper, "No boyfriends. Dates yes, but nothing serious. She never brought anyone home to meet us. She'd been home for two days and she went out a couple of times. We thought she was getting caught up with old high school friends." Her voice stopped.

Jack looked back at the Mayor. "Sir, her car?"

"She drove home in her own car. Well, our car. We gave it to her when she first went to school. We wanted her to have a safe, dependable car for the long drive back and forth from school."

"We didn't want to see her stranded on the highway," said Susan.

"I understand. How about her activities while she's been home?"

"Lisa's been staying in her old room. She likes sleeping in her old bed. She went out tonight, but I didn't ask where."

Susan Russell spoke of her daughter in the present tense. Richards scribbled another note: "Secure and search her room at her parent's house too. Check phone calls, voice mails, pagers, emails and social websites."

In the Lieutenant's office Jack's voice broke into Richards' thoughts, and he looked back at the monitor. "Sir, I would like to talk to both of you about some issues of the investigation, logistical things that will help us; especially while your family is making preparations. Also, I'll discuss the first steps we will be taking to catch this person." Jack was establishing secure avenues of contact with the parents. No leaks. He knew they needed to get Lisa's rooms secure, both, here and in Santa Barbara.

"Sure detective, what can we do?"

"First, sir, Casey and I would like to have some crime scene investigators examine your home. We're especially interested in Lisa's room, but we would like to examine the entire home. Maybe Lisa wrote a note. Maybe dropped it into a garbage can or something. We would also like to check your answering machine, email and voice mails. Maybe someone left Lisa a message." Jack was making notes in his notebook as he spoke. We'll also need Lisa's cell phone number as soon as possible.

"Her cell number is 805-893-0897." His voice was a whisper. "Anything you need, detective, anything at all." The Mayor looked at the floor.

"We would also like to do the same with Lisa's place in Santa Barbara. Hopefully, we can get the address from you as soon as possible?" It was a polite request. Jack looked toward the floor too. He knew to mirror people as he spoke to them. People subconsciously react to mirrored demeanors by becoming more forthcoming or cooperative.

"Yes, yes of course. Good idea." The Mayor was doing all the talking now. His wife was lost in thought.

"Sir, it would be a good idea that in the future, Casey and I speak with you or your wife directly," said Jack, laying the ground rules. "Can we exchange phone numbers? I would prefer it to ensure we have no miscommunication. If you have questions, you can ask us directly. This maintains security and integrity during the investigation. As you can imagine sir, there will be great interest in your family."

Susan looked up, flinching at the thought of the media's interest.

Mayor Russell answered, "All right, we appreciate that too."

"Sir, Casey and I will see if provisions have been made for your family for tonight. We can talk later, after you take care of your daughter and family needs." Jack and Casey got up and left the interview room.

Moments later, they were back in Lieutenant Richards' office with the door closed. The video of the interview played, but the sound was down, leaving a ghostly image of the Mayor and his wife holding one another.

Richards consulted his notebook. "We have our press officer and the Mayor's press officer working on the press release. We also have the Mayor's security detail standing by. Russell and his wife will be staying with relatives until the crime scene investigators get the house processed. I've got the information on where we can find them. I also got Special Operations to provide security at the funeral. As soon as the family decides the plans for the funeral services, they'll develop the security plan. The chief's office already made notifications to the city manager, council members and the governor's office," said Richards. Richards closed his notebook, leaned forward, and looked at Jack directly. "You guys got to put this case down. And fast. No mistakes and zero exceptions." Lieutenant Richards was a master at coordinating resources and making notifications. He wanted his investigators to focus on solving the case.

Jack looked at Casey and nodded his head. "You're right boss, we will." Both men got up and left.

At his desk Jack banged out a quick search warrant for Lisa's cell phone records: all calls and all text messages to and from Lisa's phone for the past three months. Jack had done hundreds of these papers; most of the necessary detail was boilerplate.

Jack's phone rang, and when he picked up he recognized Phil Foster's voice. "We wrapped up the neighborhood canvas. Not much from it. No new witnesses."

"Thanks, Phil. Can you bring your guys in? I'm working on the search warrant for the cell phone and we need a flyer for a larger canvas."

"Got it, Jack. We're on our way."

They needed the larger canvas to find out where she had been, whom she was with, and what they were doing. Jack thought about the basics of any murder investigation. *All victims have three lives: A public life, a private life, and a secret life.* Everyone has secrets. He and Casey would have to discover Lisa's.

                    *   *   *

Killing her wasn't his plan and fucking him wasn't hers: even though she acted like it was. The killer played out the whole night, over and over in his head. *Sweet.*

SIX

The County Coroner's Office is in a single-story building bordered by trees and flowers about a short drive from the police station. The brick building has a prominently posted street number, but no sign stating its business. Its windows are tinted, and most of the neighbors have no idea what actually happens within. The building's parking lot is secured by a slatted cyclone fence, keeping all ingoing and outgoing cargo private. There's a call box with a keypad at the lot's entrance, and a closed-circuit television camera monitors everything.

This is *the Morgue.*

Casey followed Jack into the coroner's lobby. With its table, black vinyl chairs, magazines and box of tissue, it looked like any medical office. Casey noted that there was even a small counter with a sliding glass window. The glass was obscured. A small bell sat on the counter, along with pamphlets with advice on bereavement.

"I have to warn you about Jenean," said Jack.

"Jenean? Who's she?"

"She's the receptionist here. She's nuts and always spun up."

"I thought you had to be somber in this business."

"Not her. She's a crazy red head."

The window slid and Jenean beamed a big smile. "Hey Jack, where the hell you been? I haven't seen you in ages." Her boisterous voice was out of place for the environment.

"Been busy, I've ..." Jack didn't even finish his answer when Jenean turned to Casey.

"I see Jack is keeping better looking company these days." She reached out her hand. "Hi, I'm Jenean."

"So I've heard." Casey shook her hand. It was soft and warm. "I'm Casey, I'm his new partner."

"Nice to meet you. I've never seen you before. First time?"

"Ahh, Yeah it is."

"Let me guess, the Russell case?"

"Yeah, lucky us," said Jack. He reached into his pocket and handed Jenean his business card.

"Hey Casey, do you have a business card?" Jenean asked.

"Yeah, sure." Casey fumbled into his pocket and handed his card to her. He leaned in toward the window and watched her put the cards in a folder attached to a logbook — part of the documenting system for visitors' names, dates and times, he figured.

"Come on in, I'll buzz the door."

There was a buzz. Jack pushed open a door to the office area behind the window. Jenean sprung to her feet and gave Jack a hug and then hit him on the arm. "You'd better visit me. None of this showing up just for work." She winked at Casey.

"Okay, okay ... I promise," said Jack.

"Go on, they're waiting for you guys back there." Jenean waved them off with her hand.

They passed through a maze of partitions and cubicles, then through a swinging door into a locker room, and then into another hallway. A sticky mat pulled all the debris from the soles of their shoes. They entered the staging area. Casey sat down on one of the two chairs while

Jack got what they needed.

"Here, put these on." Jack handed Casey two shoe covers and a smock.

Once they were suited up they entered the laboratory. Casey felt the cold bite of chilled air. Rows of overhead fluorescent bulbs cast white light on everything.

The coolness couldn't mask the rank smells of rotten flesh, human innards and formaldehyde. Those permeated nasal passages and taste buds. Seven stainless steel tables sat on the left. Naked bodies lay flat on their backs on three of them. The bodies were different ages, and each had suffered a different manner of death.

The tables could be tilted toward a sink that ran the length of the wall. Each table had a large overhead gooseneck spring-neck faucet with a hose attached. It reminded Casey of the busboy's faucet in the kitchen of the Chinese restaurant below his apartment. Next to each faucet sat a scale. A portable X-Ray machine was pushed into the corner. Lighted panels lined the wall so X-Rays could be viewed.

Casey saw the large green body bag lying on top of a table. The body inside wasn't cooperating, and the bag had contorted.

"Is she in that bag?" Casey asked.

"Yeah, that's the one. By the looks of the bag, she must be in rigor mortis," said Jack.

Casey looked around in disgust and horror. "This is one creepy fuckin' place, Jack. I've uhhh, seen a lot of shit, but never been to one of these."

"Yeah, I figured as much when you were fumbling with your card for Jenean. To be honest, Casey, I'd never been to one either until I worked homicide."

Someone called their attention. "Hey guys, Doc Irwin and Larko are getting started in a few minutes, come on down." Casey saw that Andrew, the crime scene technician, was already there. Casey kept staring at the bodies. He'd seen hundreds of dead people on the streets — and it was no big deal. Seeing dead people lying around this place felt weird. It was morbid. Andrew's equipment was scattered on a table near the body bag. He was fitting a zoom lens on a 35 mm camera. A smaller digital camera, also with a zoom lens, sat on the table. Andrew was dressed like Jack and Casey with the addition of a pair of latex gloves.

Casey walked to the steel table where he studied a whiteboard on an easel. The left side was a laundry list of internal body parts. Next to each was a space to write the weight and any other comment describing the part. A small portable cart contained several crude surgical tools. The large, worn butcher knife didn't look sterilized, nor did the other instruments. A sharpening steel hung on a hook from the cart. An electric bone saw sat next to the butcher knife. A coroner's assistant could butcher and disassemble any human body with those two basic tools. Casey also noticed a large stitching needle with a roll of twine-like suture string. He shivered at the thought of what he was about to see.

Suddenly, the room came to life. Two men walked in. Casey could immediately tell from their demeanors which was Dr. Irwin, the coroner; and which was his assistant, Larko. There were no introductions. People just started doing their jobs.

Dr. Irwin wore a headband with a small light attached, reminding Casey of a miner's helmet. The doctor took out a small tape recorder and tested it.

Why in the fuck would someone go through all the work to become a doctor and then become a coroner? Casey stared at Dr. Irwin and wondered. Larko approached wearing a large rubber smock and fishing galoshes. His forehead and hair were wrapped in a tie-dyed bandana. He had three earrings in his left ear and two in his right. He wore a band around his head with a Plexiglas facemask attached. The Plexiglas was flipped up like a welder's visor. Larko grabbed the wooden-handled butcher knife and the steel, and started sharpening. He looked as if he might be about to filet a fish.

Casey had pictured scalpels, not butcher knives, but now he realized there was no reason to be sterile. Dead people don't get infections.

Larko pulled a pair of metal mesh gloves and two pairs of rubber gloves from under the cart. He put on the metal mesh gloves then pulled the two pairs of rubber gloves over the mesh pair. "I wear this stuff so bone fragments won't cut me to shit when I'm up to my elbows in a body," he told Casey.

"I bet." Casey couldn't think of anything else to say. The squeak of casters grated on Casey's ears. Andrew was pushing a metal rolling stairway toward the table. It was the kind you would find at Home Depot.

Jack took Casey by the arm. "Stand right here, buddy." Jack walked Casey to a spot about eight feet from the metal table, next to the portable X-Ray machine.

Jack nodded upward. "Vent," he said. The air vent directly above their heads made this the coolest, cleanest-smelling spot in the room. Casey loosened his necktie and the top collar button of his shirt. Jack took his notebook from his jacket pocket and began writing.

"Let's get started, gentlemen." Dr. Irwin cued Larko, who undid the wire twist on the body bag. "The Coroner's seal was broken and removed by my assistant," Dr. Irwin said into the recorder.

Larko unzipped the full length of the bag exposing the body. Casey could clearly see every awkward twist and bend. Lisa Russell was positioned on her left side, bound in the fetal position. Blood was caked in her hair, on her face and clothing. Casey could smell her blood. Her eyelids were partially open and her eyes had a glazed dead fish look.

Her mouth was slightly open and her body was frozen in position from the rigor mortis that had set in.

"It looks like she was rolling around in the outdoors," said Jack, nodding at leaves, twigs and dirt stuck in the dried blood in her hair and on her clothes.

A camera flash startled Casey. Andrew stood on the top platform of the rolling stairway taking photos. The doctor climbed the same stairway with his own camera and took a photograph. Both men climbed down. Andrew grabbed a small brown paper bag and held it open for Dr. Irwin.

"Thank you, Andrew." The doctor used a pair of tweezers to remove plant and dirt debris from the body and drop them into the bag.

"No problem, doc." The process took a moment and required more bags. Andrew numbered each bag.

"Let's get her out," said Dr. Irwin.

Larko unzipped the full length of the bag.

"Grab her feet and calves. Don't touch the tape."

Larko grabbed her feet.

"Here we go. Up and..." Dr. Irwin pulled the bag out from under Lisa, while Larko held her on the table. Her body was still in the same position as had been in the car trunk. Casey blinked at the flashes as the others photographed every detail.

One shoe was missing.

"She is totally fucked up," whispered Casey.

"You got that right," said Jack.

"Andrew, do you remember seeing her other shoe in the car?" asked Casey.

"Not off the top of my head. But we haven't done the car yet. We just did the preliminary search. We'll get into it later on."

"Where do you think she was, Jack?" Casey whispered, not wanting to be picked up on the doctor's recorder.

"Could have been Golden Gate Park. I don't know. Maybe even outside the city limits." Jack changed the subject. "Notice she's missing her right ring fingernail?"

"Oh yeah ... you're right. You think she put up a fight?"

"It looks like it. No stamps on her hand either. You know how some nightclubs put stamps on hands when they go through the door. Her clothes are in pretty good shape but, her pants are buttoned and the zipper is down. The shoe being gone is weird, maybe she lost it after she was dead."

"So, you think it was a sexual assault?" Casey asked.

"Hard to tell if it got that far. We'll be sure to get a SART exam done, just to cover all the bases." SART was the Sexual Assault Response Team. There was a countywide protocol on sexual assault cases to make sure survivors had proper support and advocates. The other side of the protocol was a system for collecting physical evidence in sexual-assault investigations. The systems were designed so nothing would be overlooked.

"Hey doc, we'll need a SART exam and scan for sexually transmitted disease too," said Jack.

"I figured as much," said Dr. Irwin, stepping back from the table. "Let's get her undressed and see what the hell happened here."

Andrew began opening the paper bags he would use to individually package each clothing item.

Larko grabbed Lisa's legs. It took all of his strength and body weight to straighten her so she would lay flat on her back. There were grotesque snapping sounds as he broke her rigor mortis. He flipped her onto her side so photographs could be taken of the tape job on her wrists and ankles.

"Do you want to remove the tape or you want me to do it? I don't want to screw up any fingerprints or anything." Dr. Irwin said to Andrew.

"I'll get that doc, thanks." Andrew carefully cut away the tape, putting each piece in a separate bag.

Larko undressed Lisa, bagging one item at a time, until she was stripped to her bra and panties.

"The bra and panties go in the SART kit," said Jack.

"Okay, it's the same as for live victims," said Casey.

"Do you know if she had sex last night?" Dr. Irwin asked.

"We don't know. We haven't traced her evening yet," said Jack.

Larko left and then returned with a shoebox-sized container. He opened the top of the box and removed two envelopes. He took the panties and bra from Lisa and placed each one into an envelope. He put it on the foot of the metal examination table. Now Dr. Irwin, Andrew and Larko got busy, taking more photographs from every angle. "Hold that ruler next to her hand," said Dr. Irwin to Larko and he snapped the shot. "Now, take the ruler away." Click, another shot.

"This was the hand with nail torn off the finger." He said into the recorder. They placed a plastic ID tag with date and case number with every photo.

When the first photo session was done, Dr. Irwin reached into the SART Kit, retrieved a comb, and went to work on Lisa's pubic hair. He placed the combings into an envelope and placed it back into the kit. He took plucks from the pubic hair, scraped material from under her remaining fingernails, and then took prints of all her fingers and both thumbs. *They would need these as elimination prints when processing Lisa's car,* Casey figured.

With three large Q-tips he swabbed inside her mouth, vagina and rectum. All would be analyzed for semen presence. Casey watched as Dr. Irwin quickly and methodically dabbed various bloody areas on Lisa's body with Q-tips soaked with saline solution. Then he would drop each one into a separate bag being held and marked by Andrew.

Every location was documented.

"They'll enter all that into the DNA database," said Jack.

"Let's get her ready for X-Rays," said Dr. Irwin, stepping back from the table.

Larko grabbed a hose that hung above and turned the spray on the body. With a broom-like brush he scrubbed caked blood from her head, face and upper body. He tilted the table so the bloody runoff drained into the sink that ran the length of the wall. *He might've been washing a car,* thought Casey.

I could never understand how the hell he can do that," whispered Jack.

"I thought I'd seen it all, man. That dude's got absolutely no fuckin' emotions," said Casey.

"Yeah, but thank God guys like him exist. Every single thing he does is critical."

"I hear ya', but he's still a freak," whispered Casey.

Larko grabbed a couple of cotton towels and dried Lisa. He and Dr. Irwin visually examined every inch of her body, looking for cuts, bites — any clues. Larko got a gurney from an adjacent room, and he and Dr. Irwin slid Lisa onto it. They wheeled her into the room the gurney had come from, and then closed the heavy door behind them.

Casey saw a warning light above the door. It read X-Rays.

"How long does this take?"

"About 15 minutes. They're fast," said Jack.

Casey gazed around the room and wondered how these guys could do this shit every day.

The warning light blinked off, and they wheeled Lisa back in and returned her to the table. Larko placed a large, black rubber block under her neck and shoulder blades. Her shoulders and head fell backwards, and her collarbones were thrust upward.

"That looks weird, man," commented Casey.

Dr. Irwin snapped the large X-Ray film onto the box on the wall and squinted as he studied the film. "I see a bullet, maybe two."

Casey tried to discern bullet fragments from skull fragments. It wasn't easy.

"There's a good-looking fragment here." Dr. Irwin pointed to a lighted area, and then snapped more frames of film onto the box. "Everything else looks pretty good. Nothing remarkable." Dr. Irwin said into his recorder as he flicked off the light.

Larko shaved hair from around the entry wound. He glanced up at Casey. "We need a good photo."

"The first cuts are always the worst," Jack warned Casey.

Larko placed the butcher knife under Lisa's collarbone, pushing down on the top, pulling with his other hand, and steering around the top of her breast, stopping midway in her chest. He quickly repeated the motion on the other side of her chest. The third cut started at the meeting point of the first two cuts and extended lengthwise, down her stomach, stopping at the top of her pubic hairline. There was no blood. In a corpse the blood pools at the lowest points. Blood anywhere else would indicate she was moved after death.

Larko peeled the side flaps open like wings, exposing her entire rib cage. The wings were bright reds and yellows: muscle tissue and subcutaneous fat. The aroma of human innards filled the room.

"Holy shit dude. Thanks for getting me under this fuckin' air vent, man."

Larko set down the butcher knife and grabbed the bone saw. The saw whined as he cut from under Lisa's armpits to the bottom of her ribcage. He grabbed the underside of her ribs and ripped upwards. A sick crack split the air as he tore out ribcage and laid it next to her body.

Casey began to feel lightheaded. *Pretend it's a science project. It's not real.* Then, Casey noticed a sweet smell.

"Yep, she was doing some drinking. You guys smell it?" said Dr. Irwin.

"That sweet smell is booze?" Asked Casey.

"Yep. They have to have a pretty high level to smell like this." Dr. Irwin took several blood samples with a syringe.

"You think he gave her some of that date rape shit?" Casey asked Jack.

"Rohypnol or like, Ecstasy?"

"Yeah, I heard that shit knocks them on their ass. Maybe he dumped some of that crap in her drink."

"I wouldn't be surprised," said Jack. "Hey doc, how long for 'tox' results?"

"Six weeks. We'll screen for anything in her system, including stomach contents. Maybe you guys can figure out where she ate."

Larko grabbed a small waste paper can, lined it with a heavy black plastic bag, and put it at the foot of the table below the butcher's scale. He grabbed a metal cook's ladle and began scooping blood from her chest cavity. It reminded Casey of getting served soup in the chow lines in the Army. As Larko finished, Dr. Irwin stepped in with a scalpel, removed her heart and dropped it onto the butcher's scale. As he read off a number, Larko wrote down the weight. The two followed the same process with her liver, kidneys, lungs and spleen. The organs wound up on a cutting board.

Casey watched with fascination. "What are they doing now?" Casey asked Jack, not wanting to bother the doc with questions.

"They're taking tissue samples of all the organs. They have to show she didn't die naturally."

"Naturally? Are you fuckin' kidding me?"

"We have to check everything, even if it's obvious."

"That's crazy."

"The cause and means of death is our whole case."

Dr. Irwin sliced flat strips and closely studied each piece.

"What are you looking for, doc?" asked Casey.

"Abnormalities or foreign objects. Really, I'm checking to see that everything looks normal." Dr. Irwin plopped what was left into the plastic-lined pail.

Dr. Irwin fished through Lisa's innards until he found an organ Casey didn't recognize. What's that?" he asked.

"Her uterus." Dr. Irwin cut it free and then sliced it open.

"What are you looking for?"

"Tissue growth. I'm checking to see if she was pregnant."

This is fucking disgusting, thought Casey.

"I'll get a urine sample from her bladder but I don't see anything. It can be hard to tell, especially if she was in the very early stages." Dr. Irwin cleaned his hands and grabbed his camera. He focused his attention on the top of Lisa's head. He tilted her head sideways to get a better view of the gunshot.

Casey peeked around Andrew and Dr. Irwin as they were taking the usual photographs. "It was a large caliber gun," said Casey.

Jack nodded without looking away from the procedure.

Casey noticed tattooing. He'd seen a lot of this while working the streets. Mostly on suicide cases where the gunshot is point blank. Burning gunpowder spits out of the gun barrel, sticks to the skin, and finishes burning, causing a tattoo of black and red speckles.

Dr. Irwin put down his camera and grabbed a three-foot long metal rod and inserted it into the entrance wound. "There's the trajectory."

Casey could see it in his mind. *Lisa was on all fours and the fucker was behind her, like doggie-style. And then he put the gun barrel close to the back of her head and blew her fucking brains out:* More photos.

"Let's take a closer look." Dr. Irwin stepped away pulling out the rod.

Larko stepped in with his butcher knife. He straightened Lisa's head on the table, and then began above her right ear. He sliced her scalp around the rear of her ear and followed the nape of her neck to the bottom of her hairline. He turned the knife and sliced across the back of her hairline to the opposite side of her neck. He turned upward and cut behind, then over the top of her left ear. He stopped at her left temple, exactly opposite of where he began. Her skin was still connected across her forehead.

"This is the worst part. I hate this sound," said Jack.

It was an ugly tearing noise, like something glued being peeled from a melon. Larko worked his fingers between the scalp and skull and pulled. By the time he was finished, her scalp was inverted and resting on her face. There was damaged skin and her hair was bundled into the inside of the peeled cap. Her shattered skull was completely exposed. Andrew and Dr. Irwin clicked away with their cameras.

Casey heard the bone saw whining again. This time, Larko cut a circle around the top of Lisa's skull about the size of a soup bowl saucer. The distinctive smell of burning flesh and hair filled the room. "That stink is making me fuckin' sick, man," whispered Casey.

"Breathe through your mouth."

"Fuck no, then I'll taste it."

"Hang in there. They're almost done."

Larko grabbed what looked like an opener for paint cans. He inserted it into the skull and gave it a twist. A loud tearing sound filled their ears as the cap separated from the tough fibrous membrane between the brain and the skull bone. He lifted the cap enough to get his fingers under it and tear it away from the skull.

"Look at that, the brain's totally blown up. It looks like fucking Jell-O," said Andrew.

Death was instantaneous.

Once the brain was out, Larko took what appeared to be pliers and went to work near the brain stem.

"What's he doing now?" asked Casey.

"He's gonna' pull out the pituitary gland."

With a twist of his wrist, Larko tore out the dime-sized gland.

"Remember years ago, that marine went nuts on that college campus is Texas?" said Jack.

"Yeah, the dude went into the tower and sniped a bunch of people. It was a like, a little before my time, but I saw some old video of it.

"Well, they found his pituitary gland was messed up. That's what made him go nuts."

"That's a trip. That little fuckin' gland controls everything?"

"Yeah, they'll test that too."

Dr. Irwin sliced the brain into several sections, recovered one large bullet fragment and another smaller bullet jacket. Andrew placed those into plastic containers. "Looks like a 45 caliber or a 44 magnum. Hopefully they're in good enough shape to get striations," said Andrew while holding the fragments up toward the light.

Dr. Irwin plopped the brain into the plastic-lined can. "Looks like we're done here gentlemen. Thanks for your company." He smiled, peeled his gloves off and dropped them into the garbage can.

Jack stepped forward. "Hey doc, can you not release the report when you're done. We need to keep this one under wraps for a bit."

"Yeah, no problem Jack. My office will give the usual 'Confidential for police investigation' line to the media."

"We gotta' Ask them not to release the report? I thought it *was* confidential?" said Casey.

"Autopsy reports are public information. We gotta' make the formal request to hold them back."

Casey was due one more shock. Larko pulled the plastic bag from the can, gave it a spin and tied the top into a knot. He dropped the bag into Lisa's chest cavity, mashed it around until it was level, then put the ribcage back. He flipped the skin flaps back, unwound some heavy twine and threaded a large needle. With that he stitched her chest back together. Next, he replaced the skullcap and pulled the scalp back into place. Lisa's hair flowed back to life. He sutured the scalp just as he had done with her chest.

"Dude, those are some huge sutures," said Casey.

"Nobody will ever see them. They'll hide them with her hair and a dress with a high neckline," said Jack.

"Man, that's some twisted shit."

As they left the building bright sunlight pierced Casey's eyes, and even outdoors the smell of human innards seemed to linger.

"Hey Casey, wanna' grab some breakfast?"

"Breakfast? Are you fuckin' kidding me? I'll be lucky to not blow chunks in this parking lot. That was nasty shit man."

"Casey, that 'nasty shit' is part of what we do. We get paid to deal with it. Those guys in that office and us gotta' step up. We owe it to the victims and their families."

Casey nodded and looked down with a bit of shame for complaining. "I got it. I hear ya'."

Jack looked at his watch. "We got about six hours until Andrew processes the car. And we got about 24 hours before the media gets wind of Lisa's name. Then all hell breaks loose and I wanna be fresh for that."

"Yeah, me too," said Casey.

"The car's a lot easier. It'll go pretty fast."

"Tell you what, grab some sleep and I'll meet you at the office in six hours."

"Cool, six hours. See you then." Casey was figuring out that this would be the pace of the investigation until they got a handle on the pre-liminaries: work for two days; sleep a few hours, then back to work.

They climbed into their cars and drove home. Casey's head spun. His first homicide case was well under way.

*　　　　*　　　　*

He thought about raping her when he first spotted her parking her car. She moved fast and headed straight into a nearby bar. He didn't notice it wasn't his kind of bar until he was inside. He'd never seen her before, but then again, what difference did that make? She drank alone, never once looking toward the door, like she was waiting for a friend. She didn't seem to know anyone either. She just sat there sucking down wine. Hot bitches never drink alone unless they're look-ing for it. She was real nice when he first sat next to her. She giggled and touched him: Totally leading him on. Everything she did, said let's fuck. He saw it. And then, the look on her face when he said they should go. Her mouth open and laughing at him. He played it cool even though he wanted to smash in her laughing face. All his life, fucked-up women laughed at him — and that bitch paid for them all. He cranked up the tunes and kept driving.

SEVEN

Casey's alarm clock startled him awake. It took him a moment to realize it was 6:30 in the evening, not morning. Time for dinner, not breakfast. He needed to shower, and then get back on the case. It would be another all-nighter. The steamy water cleared his head, breathing life back into him. His adrenaline started up again.

Casey got in the door of the homicide unit just as Jack hung up the phone. Jack looked fresh as ever.

"Get some sleep?"

"Hell yeah. I crashed, it felt good. What about you?"

"Yeah, I did." Jack motioned toward the phone. "That was Andrew; he got some sleep too, but now he's on his way to the warehouse to do the car. Let's meet him."

"Cool." Casey noticed the door was closed to Lieutenant Richards' office. He nodded toward it. "Do we gotta update the boss?"

"He's not in there. I think he's at the chief's office, dealing with their stupid questions. Let's go. I don't want to get stuck here." Jack stood up and put on his jacket. "I got consent on the car and the house before we kicked them loose last night. We won't need warrants."

Casey nodded as they headed for Jack's car.

"You been to the warehouse before?" Jack asked.

"Yeah, a few times when I was in uniform. I had to shoot pictures of a car in a fatal, and I seized some crazy fuckin' exotic cars from this shithead crack dealer. We put them over there on Front Street. Is it still there?"

"Yeah, same hot, dusty place."

"The big fuckin' barn, right?"

"Yep."

They cruised through the industrial area of town and parked in front of the oversized swinging doors of the warehouse. They went inside.

"Why is it always fuckin' hot in this place? And it smells like a fuckin' barn."

"Because it *is* a barn."

"I've been in enough barns in my life. There ain't supposed to be barns in San Francisco."

"San Francisco if full of crap that doesn't belong," said Jack.

Smashed, beat-up, dust-covered cars were littered across the vast floor. A couple of well-kept-up cars had "Narcotics Unit" placards on the windshields. Most likely these were waiting for asset forfeiture proceedings.

Casey saw Andrew walking around the victim's car. He had bright lights on tripods and was snapping photographs. He'd set up his equipment on a portable table. The scene was similar to the Coroner's Office but this time the car was the evidence, rather than Lisa's body. It would get the same care and attention, but Casey knew this job would be easier on the nerves.

Jack handed Andrew a key. "This ought to help. I got it from her folks last night."

"Thanks."

The car rested above the ground on four jack stands. Andrew grabbed a mechanic's creeper and slid under the car.

"Don't see too much here. It doesn't look like it's been off road or anything," He pushed himself around the car examining every tire tread, inch-by-inch with his flashlight. "There's gotta be something here that will tell us where this car has been."

You find anything yet?" Jack asked.

"Nadda!" Andrew pushed himself up from the creeper and slid it away from the car. "Let's see if we can lift a print." Andrew took a fingerprint kit from his bag and opened the bottle of black graphite powder. He began to dust the car.

Sunlight from the high warehouse windows streaked through the dust in the air. It reminded Casey of clouds floating.

Andrew circled the car, stopping occasionally to lift a print. "We got some good prints here guys. Hopefully our guy touched the car and hopefully he's in the computer."

"You got high hopes, Andrew," said Jack.

"Only the asshole crooks have the good luck," chimed Casey.

"I'll be a little more hopeful with the tape off Lisa," said Jack.

"Don't get your hopes up. I didn't see much on it when I was cutting it off."

"You're nothing but good news," said Jack.

Every time Andrew lifted a print, he made notes on the card, and then dropped it into his shirt pocket.

"Done with the prints, let's have a closer look inside." Andrew lay across the door jamb examining the foot pedals with a flashlight. "I think we got a little dried blood on the gas and brake pedals."

"He drove the car after shoving her in the trunk?" said Jack.

"Yeah, I'll get a swab of it." Andrew swabbed the blood, and then measured the distance from the gas pedal to the lumbar area of the seat. He went on to measure how far it was from the base of the seat to the level of the rear-view mirror.

"Why you measuring?" Casey asked Andrew.

"Seeing how tall the dude might be. Add a couple of inches for forehead and hair and I'll have a height estimate."

"No shit? That's cool. I've never seen that before."

"It's an old evidence tech trick. Sometimes it works, sometimes it don't. Crooks are pumped up. Sometimes they overlook the little bullshit." Andrew made calculations on his notepad. "I think the dude was 6'2" to 6'5." Pretty tall if this seat position thing is right."

"Lisa looked small. What would you say Casey, like 5'4"?

"Yeah, definitely. There's no fuckin' way she drove this car with the seat like that. She couldn't reach the fuckin' pedals."

Andrew wrapped sticky tape around a hand-held plastic block, and dabbed the interior of the car. He focused on carpet, seats and door panels. "This will pick up microscopic stuff. A fiber or hair strand could break this thing wide open." When Andrew finished with the blocks he dropped them into a paper bag. "I always fingerprint the places crooks touch without thinking." Andrew fingerprinted the rear-view mirror, shift lever, seat-belt buckle, door handles, turn signal arm, steering wheel and horn button. He lifted several latent prints. "Don't forget to call the Coroner's Office, Jack. I'll need those elimination prints from them."

"I got that." Casey took out his cell and called, leaving a message saying they would pick up the prints in the morning.

"Thanks Casey."

"Sure dude."

Andrew took the key from his pocket and slid it into the ignition. A bell dinged because the doors were open. With a quick turn of his wrist, the engine started and the car was running. "There's a full tank of gas, Jack. He wasn't thinking about gas when he pulled in there."

"The dude had to be hella' nervous driving with her in the trunk." Casey spoke loud so they could hear him over the engine noise.

"What station is the radio set on?" Jack asked.

Andrew hit a button, and they heard an old George Jones tune ending. "Something country-western. You know what she listened to?" Andrew turned the car off.

"No, we'll find out. We didn't spend a lot of time with her folks ... Just got the basics out of them. We'll get a good interview in the next day or so, maybe when you guys are doing the house?" said Jack.

"When you want us to do the house?"

"Yesterday ... is that too soon?"

"Nope ... I hear ya."

Andrew itemized the contents of the glove box and center console. "The garage door opener and registration are still here."

"A burglar would have taken the opener and used the registration to get the address," Jack observed.

Andrew buried his head into the trunk and began snapping photos and swabbing blood. Casey saw only shadows and the flashlight beam moving around.

Andrew's voice came up from inside the trunk, seeming strangely disembodied. "We know these things for sure: There's no purse, no keys, no bullet casing, no fingernail and no shoe."

"So, this fucker is a cowboy and carries a revolver," said Casey.

"I think you're right about the revolver, that explains why there's no bullet casing," said Jack.

"By the looks of the blood spatter, I think she was shot somewhere else, then stuffed in the trunk," said Andrew.

"She had to be. Who would shoot her in the parking lot of the gas station?" Jack's question was rhetorical. Nobody answered.

"There's no high-velocity spatter here. Its big drops and drainage-type patterns," said Andrew.

"Maybe it was a semi-auto and the casing was ejected at the murder scene?" Casey was still talking about the gun.

"Where'd the duct tape come from? He has to be a sexual preda-
tor. Why the hell else would someone carry duct tape?" Jack added.
Jack pictured the scene in his head:

*Lisa was drunk ... probably drugged. She's stumbling and being
helped by the tall cowboy. He gets her in the car and drives to a secluded area. It's pitch dark. He's too tall to screw her in the car so he
drags her into the bushes. She has enough awareness to realize she's
in big trouble and she fights, tearing off her fingernail. He's trying to
screw her from behind and for whatever reason, he kills her. Lisa
lost her shoe somewhere between getting out of the car and getting
stuffed in the trunk. No doubt, she was already dead when he stuffed
her. He didn't dress her after he screwed her, no way, it didn't make
sense. He was trying to get her pants off when he killed her. It had to
be. But, why didn't he leave her in the bushes? Why even bother to
stuff her in the trunk and leave the car at a frickin' gas station?*

"What if she was a target?" said Casey.

The question snapped Jack from his thoughts. "What do you mean,
target?"

"You know, like the dude really wanted to fuck with the Mayor, so
he kidnaps Lisa. Maybe his politics pissed someone off."

Jack nodded, keeping his mental image to himself. "We'll check if
the Mayor got any threats. The 'Intel' guys will have a handle on the
politics. They track extremist and stuff happening on the college cam-
puses. Who knows? Maybe there's a link between one here with one
down in Santa Barbara."

"We need to get our asses to Santa Barbara, right?" asked Casey.

"Yeah, that and a million other things, like figuring out where they
met and finding where all those leaves and shit came from." Urgency
hung in the air on Jack's words.

Jack's cell phone rang. "This is Jack." He listened a moment. "Thanks, I appreciate the call." Jack flipped the phone closed. "Damn it!"

"What's up?" asked Casey.

"We just can't catch a break. No GPS on Lisa's phone ... nada."

Casey nodded. "That sucks."

"Andrew, we'll see you back at the station. We need to get a flyer out to the patrol officers on the streets quick."

"All right guys. I'll call Santa Barbara and get her dorm secured."

"Thanks, brother, time's a-wastin'." Jack and Casey got back in the car and headed to Homicide.

"You know what we really need?"

"What?" Casey asked.

"We need a snitch."

"Yeah, man. We do."

"We'll get a ton of calls once we do the press release, right?"

"Oh yeah, they'll start climbing out of the woodwork. Unfortunately, so will the crackpots and kooks."

EIGHT

"Well I'll be damned," Kyle Sanders whispered as he watched the news anchor report the breaking story out of San Francisco. *The daughter of that city's Mayor had been murdered.* Kyle stared as figures walked around the crime scene. Police lights flashed, and yellow tape shook in the night breeze. It was footage from a couple of nights earlier, when the girl's identity hadn't yet been released.

Kyle squinted, trying to get a better look at the faces there on the scene. TV lights played on the reporter, and the police tape, but beyond that, he couldn't see shit. The cameraman focused on the girl's car instead of the cops. With its nine-inch screen, the cheap prison TV wasn't much help either.

Kyle studied the picture as a TV reporter interviewed neighbors. *They didn't see shit. They never do,* he thought.

A woman in a bathrobe said, "Normally, it's very quiet here." Yeah, Kyle thought. *I've heard it a million times. It's always quiet till somebody like me shows up.*

The reporter stretched it as far as it would go, but information was thin. The Mayor's daughter had been murdered and the police had no suspects in custody. The detectives hadn't said how she was killed. Nor was there any hint of a motive.

They're no closer to solving it than I am to getting out of this dump, Kyle thought. He flipped through the channels hoping to get another report. Maybe he would see a better camera angle, or maybe some reporter would shake out a comment. He found nothing except the same clip. He turned the television off.

*   *   *

As expected, the time had come: All hell broke loose. Jack and Casey sat in Richards' office. The media wanted a live interview with Casey or Jack. The chief of police was clueless on how to handle it and the whole bag of shit landed in Richards' lap.

A story came to life when the investigators talked for the record. Maybe they couldn't say much, but at least it put a real person into the mix. Reporters seemed to love unsolved murders as much as cops hated them. Ongoing mysteries involving famous people kept viewers watching and readers reading. It gave a producer a hook to throw out before the commercial. "New clue in homicide — details right after this break." The Mayor's daughter killed — it was a story that could go on for weeks.

"You're it Casey. I'm putting you on for the live press release," said Richards.

"I'll be honest boss, I fuckin' hate reporters and maybe ... I mean, I'm like, not the best pick for this one. This is big shit."

Jack interrupted. "We talked about this, remember? I hate those assholes too; but in our line of work, we need them."

"Yeah but, this is my first case, man," pleaded Casey. The reality was; he wasn't keen on having his face front and center on national television.

"I personally know every single reporter. And, you know what? We work together. Well, most of the time, they learn stuff about our cases way before we're ready to release it."

"How's that?" Casey asked.

"This fucking place has more leaks than the Titanic for Christ's sake," said Jack.

Casey looked betrayed.

"If you plan on being successful in Homicide, you'd better build a great relationship with the media. If you don't, they'll fuck you every time."

"He's right," said Richards.

"Okay, okay. But I'm gonna' need some help, man. I'm tellin' you right now; I'm not so good in front of a camera."

"I've got that covered. You'll be meeting with the PIO beforehand," said Richards.

Casey thought about meeting the PIO: *The face of the police department on every news station. The thought turned his stomach. The guy oozed bullshit sincerity from every pore and he had a fuckin' million dollar smile: Just like the asshole chief. The problem was; the PIO never did a single fuckin' day of police work in his life: Just like the chief. And, Casey had zero respect for either of them. They were nothing but a couple of pretty boys with nice smiles not real cops.*

The meeting was more brutal than Casey imagined. The tension was obviously high, and it had nowhere to go except down.

"The most important tip I can give you is: Don't say anything you don't want repeated," said the PIO.

"What?"

"They'll repeat everything you say."

"That's fuckin' brilliant, dude." He chuckled at his own sarcasm.

"I'm just trying to embark some experience so you don't screw up this press conference and embarrass the chief. That's my job!"

"Are you fuckin' kiddin' me? Is that what's important here? Dude, I'm a cop not a fuckin' PIO. I have to solve this murder. Do you think the chief might be embarrassed if this goes unsolved?"

"That's not my business, detective. Remember? I'm a cop too! I just got assigned here, just like you got assigned to Homicide. And now I've been tasked to brief you, and I'm just trying doing my damn job!"

You're not a cop; you're a fuckin' pussy, thought Casey. He calmed himself down. "Okay dude, sorry ... I'm used to catching asshole crooks; not looking pretty in front of a camera. This isn't my gig that's all." He looked away, feeling uncomfortable.

"That's why I'm here." The PIO took a moment to gather his composure. "Don't forget. This is common sense, but it plays out a little differently in an interview."

"Okay, okay ..." Casey became impatient and fidgeted in the chair.

"Remember, they'll have their questions, and what they want is simple: everything. But there's only so much you can tell them. So the key is: only think about what you're supposed to tell them — the information you want to release. It doesn't matter what they ask you. Just say what you have to say. That's all."

"What? That's bullshit. You're telling me to say whatever, even if it makes no fuckin' sense?"

"Exactly! When they show the clip on the air, the question is never shown. It takes too much time. The viewer sees the TV reporter outside the building, giving the background, then they cut right to a clip of you. In reality, the reporter will tailor his report to whatever you've said in front of the camera, so it will all make sense to the viewer."

"So, no matter how fucked' up it feels, say exactly what I want? Even if it makes no fuckin' sense?" said Casey.

"You got it."

"Okay then."

Casey left the meeting with the PIO and returned to the Homicide Unit to meet with Jack and Richards. They discussed the press conference.

"You want me to say she was shot?" Casey asked.

"No," answered Jack.

"We got to give them something, Jack," Richards interjected.

"Why's that?"

"They'll be starving for something. We can't totally hold out."

"That's bullshit. We don't have to say a thing. It's early in the case."

"Not this case. We're talking about the Mayor. So, what do we give them?"

Jack acquiesced. "Okay boss. We say she was shot. We don't say where or how many times. We don't even release the caliber of the gun. That, we hold back. The only people that know that are us and the fucker that killed her."

Richards pondered Jack's idea a moment. "Okay Jack, that's what we'll do."

Jack smiled, knowing Richards was tough to sway. He'd won this battle. Jack scooted up in his chair. "My feeling is this, we stress we need the help of the public. This is a terrible case, and we absolutely need the help of witnesses to backtrack Lisa's evening. We give them the flyer with her picture and the car and ask if anybody saw her or her car. Hopefully, they'll run the flyer long enough for us to flush out a witness or snitch."

"I'm good with it," said Casey.

"Hey Casey," said Richards.

"Yes sir."

"Don't fucking swear on live TV, okay?"

"Yes sir, I won't"

*   *   *

The camera lights blinded Casey. He'd never understood why they needed such bright lights in the daytime. Traci Townsend was closest to the podium. She was the field reporter with the top local TV station. She was absolutely stunning and glamorous, her shimmering blond hair accenting her bronze, tanning-salon skin. Her bleached white teeth and red lips added up to a sexy smile. Though she was petite, her expert plastic surgeon had sculpted just the right exaggerations into her breasts and butt. She might as well have made love to the camera. Traci could charm or turn vicious at will.

To Casey she seemed too shallow for either emotion to be real. Like all reporters, she could twist words in an interesting fashion. She liked to call victims by their names. Of course, this did humanize the victim, but in this particular case, it also reminded viewers that the victim was the Mayor's daughter.

"Detective, how was Lisa Russell murdered?"

"She was shot."

"Shot? Can you tell us where? Or how many times??"

"I'm sorry. I can't release that information without jeopardizing the investigation. We'll release that as soon as possible." Casey said with a firm tone.

"Can you tell us if you have any suspects?" a voice asked from the crowd.

"We have not focused the investigation on any single person or group at this time. We are asking for the public's help. If anyone saw Lisa or had contact with her during the past week, please give us a call."

"Was Lisa sexually assaulted?"

Casey looked at Traci. She smiled, her nose squinted, and she tipped her head sideways as if to say, 'it's my job.' She knew she wouldn't be shown asking the question.

"It's very early in the investigation." Casey wanted to smirk at Traci, but didn't dare. Her lips formed a pout. *Was this girl flirting with him?* ·

Casey reached into his folder and took out a copy of the flyer they had put together. He held it up so the cameramen would get a good shot. "Here is a picture of Lisa and her car. Please call us if you believe you saw her in the days before she died." Casey was ready to finish.

"Detective, do you think this killer might strike again? Have you considered this might be some type of crazed serial killer on the loose?" Traci loved to turn up the meter on speculation. It pushed up ratings.

"We have no indication this is a serial case." Casey knew he had better address this or her theory would take on a life of its own. "We have been in contact with neighboring jurisdictions and there are no similar cases. We are in the early stages of this investigation and it is critical we not begin to speculate."

Traci saw she was not getting any more information about the homicide, so she shifted the focus. "How are Mayor Russell and his family handling this tragedy?"

"As you can imagine, this is a difficult time for them. It would be for any of us. It's important we show our support and respect. Mayor Russell and his family express their thanks for honoring their privacy and your thoughts and prayers."

Jack was impressed by Casey's performance on that last one. "That was smooth," he said to Richards.

Casey ended the conference with a plea. "Please look at the flyer and give us a call if you feel you can help us with any information. I'm sorry I can't answer all your questions, but we need to get back to work. Thank you." The conference was over. The media had their tape just in time to edit and cut for the evening news.

Traci approached Casey while her camera crew folded up their gear. Her stride was sexy and her fragrance was fresh and sweet smelling.

"Detective, can we have lunch? Off the record of course." She raised her perfectly painted eyebrows and her green eyes looked directly at him.

The question caught him off guard and she knew it.

"Lunch? I'm, like, uhhh ... super busy now."

"Not now, later ... anytime." She smiled and held out her card. "Here. This has my personal cell number. Don't wait too long to call, sweetie."

Casey knew few men denied attention from Traci. He also knew that everything he'd heard about her from his colleagues was bad news. Despite that, he took the card.

*   *   *

Kyle flipped off the television, lay back on his bunk and lit a contraband cigarette. He inhaled deep into his lungs, held it, and then relaxed his chest as the smoke rolled from his mouth. He closed his eyes and thought back to childhood when things had seemed so much less complicated. *How did this happen in my life?* He thought about times when he and his brother ran barefoot in the yard. There'd been other kids in the neighborhood — friends even. Kyle had memories of laughing and playing tag. The coarse green crabgrass would make his feet itch.

The weather in those memories was always hot and humid, but an occasional rain shower would cool things down. Late in the day, at sunset, the fireflies would zip around and the armadillos would make their way out of hiding to start rooting in the crabgrass. He could almost smell the pig cooking on the barbecue. He and his brother could hardly wait to check the catfish lines in the creek next to the house. *Who would have known it would end up this way? Kyle missed his childhood. Nobody could have ever known.*

Lost in thought, Kyle was finishing the last of his cigarette. He didn't hear the lock on his cell door click. Suddenly, the door swung open and there in the doorway stood his favorite guard silhouetted against lighter shadows.

"Hey asshole, enjoying that smoke?" Justin Pierce gave a twisted smile.

"Since when does anyone give a shit about a smoke?" Kyle asked.

"Whaddya mean? It's a violation. Get the fuck up."

"But nobody ..."

"Quiet!" Justin snapped.

Kyle stood up. He kept his mouth shut. The cigarette between his fingers smoldered.

Justin closed the distance and stood face to face. His smile turned evil. "I told you!" He paused to take a deep breath, and then spoke in a whisper so he couldn't be overheard. "My job is to enforce the rules. This is my world, asshole."

Kyle felt spit on his face. He couldn't believe this Okie scum was haunting him. All he wanted was to be left alone. Like 16 years in the joint wasn't already enough. Now he had to deal with this jack-off for the rest of his life.

"Well sir, I'm real sorry." Kyle bent over and snuffed the cigarette out on the floor. As he rose, he smashed Pierce right in the fucking balls as hard as he could. Pierce cried out and his legs buckled but he didn't go down. *This fucker is strong*, Kyle thought. The thought didn't last long because Kyle felt a smashing blow to his left temple. His vision in his left eye narrowed and he felt pain radiating across his forehead. With Justin's quick response, Kyle lost track of what was happening. He could feel blows all over his body but he went numb. Pierce beat the shit out of him with a small wooden billy club. Long before it was over, Kyle had lost consciousness.

When he woke up, he was stripped naked on the floor of the hole. He could taste blood on his swollen lips. He smelled piss and shit and wondered if he was lying in it. He tried to feel his body but when he moved he hurt. His whole body hurt. He had never been beaten this badly. He began to recall Pierce standing over him and beating him. There was the cigarette and the fight. He winced, exhaled deeply and fell fast asleep. That was his only escape.

In Pierce's report Inmate Sanders had attacked him while he was enforcing a rule. Pierce fought for his life as Inmate Sanders savagely battered him. Pierce overcame Inmate Sanders' resistance and took him into custody. The Warden reviewed the report and was thankful Pierce had not been severely injured. Pierce might even get an award. The Warden liked justice to be served in-house. Inmate Sanders would not be criminally charged.

One week in the hole would be his punishment. That would give the beating additional value. The other cons would see the consequences before Kyle had a chance to heal.

Down in the hole, Kyle woke again. Three trays of food sat on the floor next to the door. This was the only indication of how long he had been asleep. His head was pounding and fuzzy. He rolled onto his right side to sit up. A sharp pain in his ribs robbed him of breath. He grunted and pushed himself into a seated position. Once he was seated he checked himself. He had shit himself. His eyes and lips were swollen. Kyle struggled to his feet and steadied himself with the steel washbasin. He turned on a trickle of water and began cleaning himself. The cold water helped clear his head. Based on the food trays, he figured he had been in the hole about 24 hours.

The door swung open and Pierce was standing in the doorway with another tray of food. He had that same twisted grin. "Only six more days asshole, then you're close to me again in our private room. I told you, it's my world, not yours." Pierce dropped the tray on the floor and slammed the door shut. Kyle heard a chuckle as footsteps became faint.

There was no television in the hole. Kyle would miss the news for a week. He bent over the sink, splashed cool water on his face, and realized something. *Either I gotta' get out of this prison, or I'm gonna' have to kill that asshole."*

NINE

The media was going crazy. The story broke and, as usual city officials began to panic. Jack made 200 copies of the flyer showing pictures of Lisa and her Mercedes. He and Casey attended as many patrol briefings as possible and distributed the flyers to the street cops. They needed a snitch.

"Jack!" Lieutenant Richards called from the chair in his office. "Grab your partner, come in here a minute."

Jack and Casey went in and sat down. Richards' eyes were more bloodshot, and the bags underneath them had grown darker. The pressure from above was obvious. Jack knew that Richards was absorbing all of it so he and Casey could concentrate on the case. The Lieutenant had always been good at shielding his detectives from political fallout. Jack had a keen appreciation of this. He'd worked for lousy lieutenants, ones who'd only created more pressure. Richards wasn't one of those. He knew how to stay on top of a case without weighing down his men.

"Where you guys with the case?"

"We got flyers out to patrol," said Jack. "We need to do the house and another interview with the Russells."

"When you getting it done?"

"As soon as we get outta here. Andrew buttoned up the dorm. It should be secure. We need to get down there too."

"What do you need from me?"

"Same thing as usual, boss, keep the heat off."

"Not easy on this one, guys."

"We get it. Oh yeah, one more thing that Casey came up with."

"Yeah, what's that?" Richards leaned forward and crossed his hands on his desk.

Jack leaned back, looking toward Casey.

"I don't know ... I'm just throwin' out ideas here, but what if it wasn't random? What if Lisa got killed because someone wanted to fuck over the mayor real bad?"

"I guess it's possible. Will it change what you need to be doing next?"

Jack chimed in. "No, but it is another angle. I think we gotta look into it."

"Jesus Christ. We don't need that complication. This thing is big enough." Richards paused giving the notion a thought. "I'm beefing up the security on the Mayor for a while?"

"That sounds like a good call," said Jack.

Richards picked up the phone and punched four numbers. "This is Lieutenant Richards. I want another security team on the Mayor and his wife until further notice."

Jack heard a voice on the other end of the phone but couldn't make out what they were saying.

"I don't give a shit about the overtime for Christ's sake! Just do it! We're talking about the fucking Mayor here!"

The other end fell silent.

"And you will personally call me when it's done! Am I clear?" Richards slammed the phone down. "Jesus Christ! These guys want everything done but they don't want to spend the money to do it right!" He pointed toward the phone. "They just bust my balls day in and day out!"

The bags under Richards' eyes were darkening by the minute. Jack took that as a cue to leave. He got up and nodded to Casey.

The two detectives headed for the Intel Unit, always a strange place. The detectives there monitored different groups and organizations. They never wrote police reports because those were discoverable under the Freedom of Information Act. Intel detectives monitored terrorist and extremist groups, outlaw motorcycle gangs, prison gangs and any other radical group that might pose a threat to the public or the police. The well-organized groups that pride themselves on civil disobedience plan their tactics well in advance. Intel detectives track such information. A cop or two on the force might have once belonged to an extremist group or even the Communist Party. Intel detectives would be keeping track of them too.

Jack briefed the Intel Unit on the homicide. Casey explained his theory. The Intel guys bit on Casey's theory. Conspiracy linked with politics — it made perfect sense to them. It was in their blood.

*   *   *

Jack called the Mayor's security to tell them they were heading to the Mayor's house. Mayor Russell deserved advanced notice and Jack didn't want to surprise the security officers. They were bound to be jumpy.

Jack and Casey climbed into Jack's car to head over to the house.

"Hey Jack, Is Andrew gonna' process the house?"

"No. I don't want a bunch of cops trampling their house. We'll do it ourselves. If there's something we can't handle, we'll call Andrew."

The street was off the beaten path. It was very quiet with little traffic. The three unmarked police sedans parked with views of the

Mayor's house stood out like sore thumbs. The long cobblestone driveway to the house was crescent-shaped and lined with lanterns up on black poles. Years ago, the city had torn up a number of streets and found old cobblestones under the pavement. The cobblestones were sold at auction to contractors. With the huge demand, most walked away empty-handed, but, as luck would have it, the Mayor happened to get enough for his driveway.

The front yard was well-covered with mature birch trees. The beautiful white bark of the trees contrasted with the shade. A slight breeze wafted through. Branches swayed and leaves gently fluttered to the ground. Jack felt a great sense of loneliness. The doors of the three-car garage were closed, as were the shutters on the windows of the house.

Though the house looked empty, Jack knew the Russells were home. Still, he could sense that this was a house that was not open for visitors. He felt sorrow when he saw the house. It looked dark and sad. He thought about his own children and was thankful he never had to deal with that kind of loss. Jack swallowed hard on the lump in his throat. He began to go through what he would say to these people when he was face-to-face with them.

The front doors were beautiful, arched to a point at least 10-feet high. The hardwood was polished and aged. They reminded him of a grand entrance into a winery he had once visited. When he pushed the doorbell there came the deep ringing of chimes. A moment later, Mayor Russell opened the door. The Mayor didn't make eye contact but Jack could see his eyes were bloodshot and completely encircled in dark rings. The skin on his face hung as if it was unnaturally being pulled to the ground by gravity. His shoulders hunched forward and his head hung low. His hair was stringy and messy and he hadn't seemed to have showered. He'd aged 20 years in two days.

"Good morning sir. We met the other night at the police station. I'm Jack Paige and this is Casey Ford.

"I remember, please come in." His voice was low and raspy. His throat was raw from weeping. The Mayor took a step backward and opened the door wide. The entryway floor had spectacular tile work in a semicircular design. Each piece was cut by hand and fitted into a mosaic. The color combinations were brilliant. Jack had an appreciation for tiles. He'd seen some of the best in European churches many years earlier, and their beauty had never left his memory.

"Can I get you guys something? Coffee, water?" The Mayor motioned toward the kitchen.

"No ... no, we're good. Can we sit and talk?"

"Sure, let's go in here." The Mayor walked toward the kitchen while Jack and Casey followed.

It reminded Jack of the perfect kitchens in cooking shows on television. Stainless steel appliances sat on marble countertops. Yet the room suddenly felt cold as Jack heard the slight echo of his own footsteps. They sat at a slightly distressed, stained-wood table. It didn't seem very old. Jack set his ideas on décor aside and took out a notebook. "Sir, have any of you received any threats?"

The Mayor looked puzzled. "Threats, like death threats?"

"Any threats at all."

"No, none. I mean, my staff would tell me if that happened."

"It's just something we have to look at."

Casey sat quietly, nodding his head.

"You think someone did this to Lisa to hurt me?" The Mayor looked up from the ground and looked Jack in the eyes for the first time.

"Again, sir, we have to look at every angle. I'm not trying to alarm you, but we have to be thorough."

"I understand."

"Did Lisa have her own bank accounts?"

"Yeah, well sort of. We put money into an account for her to live off of. She didn't work."

"So she had a credit card? ATM?"

The Mayor nodded yes.

"And her cell phone bill?"

"We paid that too." His voice was barely audible above a whisper.

"Can we get copies of those bills? We need the account numbers."

"Now?"

"If you could."

"They're in a file in my office." The Mayor pulled himself to his feet and left the kitchen. Jack and Casey stared at one another without speaking. It was deathly silent in the house, as if all the life, love and joy had been sucked out. The Mayor returned and handed the folder to Jack.

"Thank you." Jack passed the folder to Casey.

"We'll need your consent for your phone bill for the time Lisa's been here."

"Sure, please get whatever you need from my staff. They know to cooperate."

Jack saw Casey had the folder open and was busy texting on his cell phone. The Mayor was looking at Casey too, but his mind was obviously a million miles away.

"We need to take a look in Lisa's room."

"Now?"

"Please."

"Sure, it's this way." The Mayor led them up the stairs. He stopped short of the closed door and motioned them to go inside. The Mayor squeezed his eyes shut and tears began to race through the lines and crevices of his weary face. "I'll be ... downstairs." The Mayor was barely able to choke out the words.

Jack nodded his head. His compassion was genuine. He'd heard that failing voice many times on other cases — it was the sound of losing a child. Right now, the Mayor regretted ever denying his daughter anything during her short life. As the Mayor left, Jack wondered what it must feel like to leave men behind so they could examine your daughter's most private possessions. He felt a shiver, and then went to work.

Lisa's room was full of pictures from high school. It was obvious she had decorated it on her own, and her parents had kept it that way since she left for college. A small table with a mirror sat near a twin bed with a pastel-colored comforter. Matching pillows were neatly placed at the head of the bed. A small stuffed bunny rabbit leaned against the pillows. There were a few boxes full of magazines, yearbooks and other knickknacks in the closet. Prom dresses and cheerleader uniforms hung, wrapped in plastic, obviously dry-cleaned then stored.

"What were you texting?"

"I shot the account numbers to Phil: And told him to run her out and see if she had her own credit cards. He's gonna' get the tracking started on all the accounts."

"Good."

Jack noticed a suitcase against the wall and pointed. Casey nodded, walked over to the bag and began to search. Jack searched through various areas around the room.

"This is just clothes, some overnight stuff, and ..." Casey didn't finish the sentence so Jack looked over. Casey was waiting for him to look. He tossed a small container to Jack. It was a pill container. Jack opened it and saw the wrapping: birth control pills. He looked back and saw Casey shrug. Jack nodded and tossed the container back to Casey. He was glad Casey didn't advertise his find out loud. The

Mayor didn't need to learn from them his daughter was having sex.

"Did you find a computer," asked Casey.

"No."

"I wonder where it is?"

"My guess is Santa Barbara."

The job didn't take long, and to a layman's eyes they didn't find much, but in truth they found plenty. Both men were well on their way to intimately familiarizing themselves with a young lady they had never met.

They walked back down to the kitchen. The Mayor had composed himself, but didn't get up from the table.

"Sir, we're finished here. Do you have any questions?"

"No, just find the son-of-bitch that did this." His anger came from deep within. He clenched his fists and his hands trembled.

"We won't stop looking until it's completely resolved."

"I don't understand. Why? How could someone do this?"

Jack knew the Mayor needed a reason. Any reason would be better than never knowing at all. Someone had to be responsible. He needed someone to blame. Someone to hate.

"We're going to Santa Barbara next. There's a lot of people working on this up here. It's not just us."

"Thank you." The Mayor seemed to have calmed.

Jack knew the Mayor was being whipped around on a giant emotional roller-coaster.

"I don't remember if I told you, but, Lisa had a roommate."

"No sir, we didn't get that."

"Julie Anderson. She's already called a couple of times. They were real close."

Jack made a note in his book. Julie Anderson would be the first person they met in Santa Barbara.

As they headed back to the station, Jack thought about the stuffed bunny rabbit on Lisa's pillow. *Time to start learning what she did as an adult, he thought. We've left her childhood behind.*

TEN

Jack and Casey spent most of the night going over the game plan with Richards. They decided to get a few hours rest then head out at the crack of dawn. The drive south was a breeze. As they got further into southern California Jack was shocked. It had been some time since he'd gone that route, and he couldn't believe the number of new vineyards. They consumed miles upon miles of rolling hills from the southern end of the Monterey Peninsula to the base of the coastal mountains northeast of Santa Barbara. "I remember when these hills were full of steers and vegetable crops," Jack said.

"Steers? No way, dude. That must have been awhile ago. I've never seen it any other way. It's always been wine country."

"It was a long while ago. Now, the Golden Crop for the Golden State is grapes."

Jack enjoyed the gradual climb into the coastal mountains. He'd done the drive many times during his college years at Cal-Poly in San Luis Obispo. The highway lulled him into slumber as it wound up to the summit, then suddenly the great Pacific appeared. It spread below them, its blue waters stretching as far as the eye could see.

"Look at this view Casey. I'd forgotten how beautiful it is." Jack paused. "This always makes me think of Charlton Heston playing

Moses, standing at the Red Sea just before he parts the water." Jack raised his hands, gazing through the windshield at the view.

"I don't think I caught that flick," said Casey, his eyes on the road.

"Ahh, forget it. You were just a kid."

They fell silent and the road dove down the steep ocean side of the mountain into Santa Barbara. Unlike San Francisco, Santa Barbara is squeezed onto the beach between the ocean and steep mountains. The mountains protect the valley from the sea. The Pacific there is vastly different from the Pacific that wraps under the Golden Gate. It's a deep clear blue. Oilrig platforms with flames burning like torches lye out in the distance. Even the waves are different. They don't crash onto rocks like they do up north. They roll in and wash across long sandy beaches.

Santa Barbara had grown since Jack's last visit, but the college town beach atmosphere still lingered like ocean mist. Parking was plentiful at the admissions building. The Dean looked younger than Jack imagined, prettier too. His college dean had been an elderly, stuffy bureaucrat.

"Hello gentlemen, I'm Victoria Hall. We spoke on the phone." She extended her hand. She wore her jet-black hair straight, setting off her soft white skin. Her glasses with their stylish tortoise-shell frames gave her a sexy intellectual look. A mid-thigh skirt and medium heels displayed her athletic calves.

Jack shook her hand and smiled. "Hi Victoria, I'm Jack. This is my partner, Casey. I think you talked to Andrew from our office?"

Victoria's handshake was firm, but her long fingers felt bony and cold. She moved with efficiency and wasn't shy — the manner of a CEO. Jack wasn't sure why, but he couldn't help feeling he was tardy for something.

"Yes, I did. Please, have a seat." She pointed to wooden chairs in front of her desk. Jack sat on the uncomfortable chair. It wouldn't be long before his back would start to complain. The chair back was completely upright forcing him to sit perfectly straight. Victoria sat, perfect posture, on the edge of her large leather swivel chair.

She rolled the chair forward and picked up a folder off her desktop. "Here are Lisa's records."

Jack thought it interesting that she didn't offer it to either him or Casey. She wanted to see which one would take it. Jack reached across. Victoria smiled, gave it to him and turned her chair slightly his way. She'd identified her audience.

"There's not much there," she said. "Just her application, standard emergency contact information, parking permit, transcripts and her dorm records."

As Jack went through the papers, Casey asked, "Ma'am, has Lisa's room been secured?"

"Yes." Victoria turned to him, slightly surprised, suddenly uncertain of the hierarchy she'd thought she had detected here. "I secured it the night I was notified of Lisa's death. I made a note on the file. Also, I had the janitorial staff change the lock on her door, just in case."

Jack looked up from the folder. "Great, thank you. How about Julie Anderson?"

"She seems to be coping fairly well, considering the circumstances. I moved her into another room."

"Can we see her?"

"I can have her brought here or would you rather talk in her dorm?" Victoria spoke with the efficient compassion of a bureaucrat.

Jack wondered if Victoria was at all troubled by Lisa's murder. She hadn't asked a single question about what had happened. It seemed as if it might be just another opportunity for her to showcase her organizational prowess to a new audience.

"In here works. It seems private enough." Jack smiled, but the firmness in his tone made clear that this was not a suggestion. Victoria's eyes flared, but she quickly regained her composure. Still, Jack observed that her sexiness had drained away. Jack stood. "If you don't mind, we'll take a look at Lisa's room now."

Casey stood too.

"Of course," Victoria said, pushing her chair back, as she opened the top drawer of her desk and grabbed a single key. She rounded her desk and took the lead toward her office door.

"Follow me gentlemen, I'll show you the way."

They followed through the main area of the administration building. Victoria breezed past the secretary at the desk, snapping: "Please locate Julie Anderson. I'll let you know when we would like to have her brought into the office." Victoria didn't even miss a step.

"Yes ma'am."

Jack noticed the woman at the desk didn't bother to take her eyes off her work. He felt sorry for her, and he glanced ahead at Victoria, thinking: *What a bitch.*

They walked silently across the campus. Some students noticed them, but none seemed interested. The dorm was two stories tall and generic. Lisa lived on the second floor. Victoria unlocked the door and swung it open without stepping into the room. She left the key in the lock.

"Thank you Victoria, we'll meet you back at your office as soon as we finish. It shouldn't be too long, there's not a lot here." Jack smiled. It was his way of politely dismissing her.

"Are you sure you wouldn't prefer I stay?" she asked, practically tapping her foot.

Casey slipped inside before Jack could answer.

Jack kept the smile, but took a firm hold of the door, with her on the outside. "Oh, no thank you. We'll take it from here. You've been a great help." Jack turned away, cutting eye contact, and gently closed the door. They heard Victoria's curt footsteps grow distant then disappear.

"Holy shit, what a bitch." Casey said. "She reminds me of this chick I used to date, for about an hour."

Jack laughed.

Casey looked out the window into the open quad area. Victoria was skirting across. "She'll be back to her building in a minute. Then, I'll go grab the shit from the car."

"Okay." Jack started searching the room containing Lisa's adult life.

A few minutes later, Casey arrived with the evidence kit.

"This room is so damn small; it's hard to get a shot." Jack struggled with the camera.

Casey set the box of packaging materials in the center, put on a pair of latex gloves and searched through the dresser drawer next to Lisa's bed. Jack did the work on Lisa's desk and files. This wasn't a hunt for a particular item, just anything that might tell them about her life. Who was this girl? Where she might go, with whom? What kind of guy did she prefer? Or gal for that matter? They looked for notes, letters, phonebooks or a planner.

"Take a look at these," said Jack, while holding up photos.

"What is it?"

"Friends, I'd guess, from the way they're hanging all over each other."

Casey looked. Most of the settings were bars and beaches — people laughing and being silly. *Girls like her have a pretty nice life*, he thought.

"Here are some with her parents." Jack passed on more photos. "You know what stands out most to me?"

"What?"

"She had a beautiful smile. It's sad."

Casey nodded.

Jack put the items into paper bags — and these went into a box. Andrew would examine them later. Lisa's laptop screensaver was sailboats in San Francisco Bay. "The High Tech Unit will mirror the hard drive and copy everything on here." Jack switched off the computer, unplugged it, and boxed it along with its attachments.

"What about her password?"

"They somehow get past it."

"Huh, nice to know."

Casey found a small CD player with a built-in radio. He turned on the radio and heard rock 'n' roll. Thumbing through a stack of CDs he noticed something. "All the music is rock, blues or hip-hop. This chick didn't listen to country western."

"Was that country station pre-set? Do you remember? Jack asked.

"Naa, it wasn't. It makes sense, the cowboy theory."

Jack rifled the drawers of her desk. "Not much here. A few scraps of paper about classes, knick-knacks ..."

"She didn't collect a bunch of shit." Casey observed.

"How could she? Living in here?"

Casey finished searching the closet and her clothes. "I don't see anything that links the case to here."

"Naa, me neither. Maybe we'll get something out of the photos or her computer, but I've got a feeling everything happened up in our city." They peeled off their gloves and tossed them into the box. They took another glance around, nodded to one another and left the room. Casey carried the box to the car.

Jack pulled the photos from the box before closing the trunk. "We'll ask Julie about these." He slipped them into his jacket pocket.

Victoria was at her desk, typing at her computer when they walked in. She stopped typing, but didn't bother to stand. She seemed to be expecting a progress report.

"We're all set with the room, thanks." Jack looked at the wooden chair with dread. It had stiffened his back. He hesitated. "Is there someplace more comfortable we can use to talk to Julie?"

"Absolutely," Victoria picked up her phone, and pressed a button. "Please bring Julie to the senior staff conference room. We'll meet her there." Victoria hung up the phone without waiting for a response. "Follow me gentlemen." The two men had to trot to keep up. They followed her down a corridor lined with framed photos — staff dating back decades. The senior staff conference room looked like a corporate war room. A large dark, highly polished table was surrounded with comfortable leather chairs. Aromas of leather and finished wood mingled. A refreshment table stood in one corner. Victoria turned up the lighting. She was a quick study, and this time she didn't embarrass herself by assuming she would be present.

"Julie will be in shortly. Let me know if there is anything else I can do for you. I'll be in my office."

"Thank you. And thanks for all your help," said Jack.

Jack pulled out a leather chair. This was a lot better. Casey sat next to him, took his notebook from his pocket, and placed it on the table.

A young woman knocked at the door even though it was standing open. Her cheeks were red as were her swollen wet eyes. She sniffled and then wiped her runny nose with a crumpled used up tissue. "I, uhmm, I'm ... Julie." She barely got the words out: Huffing between syllables and fighting to keep from crying.

Jack got up first. "Hi Julie, I'm Jack, this is Casey." Jack gently touched her wrist and shoulder to guide her. As soon as Jack touched her, she burst out crying. She couldn't hold back a moment longer. He held her arm and stood for just a moment while Julie worked at calming down. When the time was right, he guided her to the chair.

She looked like a child with the large leather chair engulfing her petite stature.

"I'm very sorry we have to talk about this. I know it's very painful."

"I can't believe it ... I mean, I just can't believe this happened," she said while still crying.

Jack sat quietly while she settled down. Casey got up, went to a water cooler across the room, and filled a plastic cup. He returned, setting the cup of water on the table in front of Julie. "Here you are."

She picked up the cup; her hands trembled as she drew it closer to her mouth. She took a small sip and placed the cup back down on the table. "Thank you." Her voice was a little more composed.

Jack took his tape recorder from his pocket, clicked it on, and placed it on the table." Julie stared at the recorder a moment, and then gazed back to the cup.

Jack sensed she was calm enough to begin. "Julie, can you tell us what kinds of things Lisa liked to do?"

"I guess ... you mean like, what kinda stuff we did?"

"Yes, the stuff you guys did besides school."

"I don't know ... I guess, we just liked to hang out with friends, you know?

"School friends or other people?"

"Mostly just like, school friends."

"Did Lisa belong to any clubs or special groups?"

Julie paused to think. "Groups or clubs? No, I don't think so."

"How long have you known Lisa?"

"Umm, Since school started. Just last year and this year." She tucked a lock of auburn hair behind her left ear and shuddered, as if she had a chill. She'd calmed down considerably.

Jack realized that he'd already seen Julie, mostly in blue jeans, a sweatshirt and scuffed brown work boots. That's what she'd been wearing in the photos they'd found in the dorm room. She'd been in a lot of them.

Casey took notes while Jack talked.

"Are you from this area?"

"Me?"

"Yeah, do you have family nearby?"

She nodded her head. "My mom and dad are in Paso."

Jack knew she was referring to the small town they passed through, Paso Robles.

"That's a nice town. What do they do?"

"You mean my mom and dad?"

"Yeah."

"They own a winery ... it's the whole family, really. My grandpa started it." For the first time, Jack noticed a tiny sparkle in her eye.

"Which winery is it?"

"Johannis Estate Vineyards."

Jack suddenly realized this pretty farm girl came from a very wealthy family. "I'm a customer," Jack said with a polite smile. He wasn't exaggerating. He knew the label from stores, restaurants and the modest wine rack in his own home. The small talk was doing its job of easing the tension.

Julie replied with a faint smile.

"So, I take it you'll be working in the winery?"

"Uhh-huh, I'm taking Ag."

Jack figured she would be next in line to run the winery after graduation. *Nice life*, he thought. For the first time, Jack noticed she had unusually deep blue eyes. They were beautiful.

"I take it, you and Lisa got along?"

"We really did ... a lot. She even came home with me a couple of times."

"She liked the winery?"

"Yeah ... she liked the beach a lot, too."

"Really?" Jack acted surprised so he could keep her talking.

"Her dad is the Mayor of San Francisco, right?"

"Yes."

"She told me she liked that nobody down here really knew who she was. She never bragged or anything ..."

Jack took the photos from his pocket and placed them in front of Julie. "Can you tell us who these people are?"

"You took these?"

"I'm sorry, we had to."

Julie nodded and the sadness took over again.

Julie began pointing to different ones. Over the next few moments, she described the event in each photo as well as the people involved. None seemed too significant to the murder. "I can't believe this is happening. Who would do this?" Julie began to cry.

Jack took tissues from his pocket and handed them to Julie. They sat quietly for a moment, letting a little time pass so she could gain some strength.

"I'm sorry," she said.

"No need to be sorry," Jack set his pen down and waited.

Julie inhaled deeply then exhaled.

"Does Lisa have a boyfriend?"

"No, not really ... not like, anyone steady or anything."

"Did she date any of these guys in the pictures here?" Jack pointed at one picture.

"I don't think so. We're all just friends, you know ..."

"Did she say what she was going to do in San Francisco? Maybe she talked about meeting someone?"

"No, I don't know. I mean, she said her friends hung out in the Marina or something."

"Did she mention any bars?"

"I don't know ... I mean, I can't remember any. She just hung out with old friends, I guess. She had a lot of friends."

Jack knew the lifestyle and knew it resisted verbal definition. "I know you may not want to say it, but Julie, this is really important."

She looked at him, anticipating the question.

"Did Lisa ever talk about drugs?"

Her eyes looked to the floor.

"This isn't something we share. It's really important, please."

"Maybe a little, but ... like, she was from the city." Julie said, seeming to equate drugs with San Francisco. "I never saw her do anything like that. Never around me, ever."

Jack persisted. "Did she ever say her friends used drugs?"

"Her friends? Yeah, I guess some do."

"Do you know if she tried them?"

"No ... I mean, I don't know."

"I'm sorry I have to ask you this. A lot of people experiment with drugs, especially in the city. It doesn't mean they're bad people." Jack was sincere.

She nodded her head.

"Did Lisa drink a lot?"

"A lot? Umm, I don't know. I guess not. What do you mean by a lot?"

"Well, did she get drunk? Or would she go to a bar alone, just to have a drink"

"I don't know. I mean she might, I guess if she wanted to." She paused. "There was one thing."

"What's that?"

"Like I said, about the winery ..."

"Yes."

"Well, one time she came with me to this yearly thing at the winery. I mean, everyone was drinking, it's a winery, right?"

"Sure."

"I'm not sure how much she drank, but it seemed like a lot. I mean, I was buzzed and I had less than her. But, it's not like we were driving or going anywhere ..."

"Right, right. Just having a good time." Jack nodded in approval.

"Yeah, exactly. Well, I kinda expected her to be really wasted, but she wasn't. Even the next morning, she wasn't hung over or anything."

"Huh, I understand. Thanks for being open."

She nodded, almost ashamed she mentioned it.

"Julie, I have to ask you a tough question." An awkward silence fell over the room. He continued.

"Again, this isn't stuff we're sharing. It's stuff we need to know to catch the guy who did this."

"Okay."

"Was Lisa sexually active with anyone you know of?"

"No ... not really."

"Would she have sex with someone she just met and liked?"

"No way ... she was not way like that." Julie naturally became defensive.

"Do you know if Lisa was close to her parents?"

"Close? Oh yeah, I think they were real close. She really loved them. She went home because she missed them."

"I see," Jack slipped the recorder into his pocket. "Oh, one more thing."

"Yes?"

"Did Lisa like country music?"

"Country music? No. That's one thing we didn't have in common. I love it, but she hated it." Julie seemed confused by the question.

Jack didn't clarify.

Everybody stood up at the same time. Jack lightly put his hand on her shoulder. "We'll talk again, later," he said. "Meanwhile, if you think of anything, please call us. Okay?"

"Sure."

"Thank you," They handed Julie their business cards.

Julie clutched the cards, and stared straight into both men's eyes. "Catch the person that did this, please."

"We will." Jack couldn't help but stare into those perfect blue eyes.

They found their way back to Victoria's office.

She sat at her desk, busy. "Did you gentlemen get everything you needed?"

"Yes, thank you. We're finished here and we're heading back." Jack somehow became the spokesman for the team. "I believe you'll hear from Lisa's family about her belongings."

"No problem. I'll take care of everything. I'll personally handle it with her family." Victoria jumped up extending her hand to conclude the visit.

Jack was first to shake her cold bony hand again.

Casey went second. "Ahhh, thanks. Thanks for the help." Casey struggled to smile.

As they were leaving the office, Jack paused in the doorway and looked back at Victoria.

She stopped working, peered through the top of her glasses and returned Jack's stare. "Yes, was there something else?"

"Yeah, I'm just curious."

"Yes?" She set down her pen and tilted her head.

"You never asked about the case."

"I assumed you wouldn't say anything, so I didn't ask." Her cold expression didn't change.

"Oh, right." Jack smiled, turned and left.

The drive back to San Francisco seemed shorter than the drive down. Both men digested what they learned. They gazed at the scenery. The radio was off and the tires hummed on the roadway.

"This things got nothing to do with Santa Barbara," Casey said.

"Yeah, I agree," Jack paused. "Man, were her eyes unreal or what?"

Casey agreed. "Hell yeah. Crazy blue."

"And what about that cold bitch?"

"Whew!" said Casey.

ELEVEN

During the drive back, Casey called Richards and asked for someone to coordinate a roundup of Lisa's friends. They wanted to interview as many as possible. Richards said he'd volunteer Phil Foster. When they got back north they found the mood in the Homicide Unit was electrified and hyper-speed, like the last quarter in a close Super Bowl. Everyone wanted the latest update. Jack saw captains and chief officers he hadn't seen in years. Richards was earning his paycheck, doing all he could to shield Jack and Casey from the turmoil. He deflected the meaningless requests, while steering what little was worthwhile their way. That gave them room to work.

"I've got a flow chart of Lisa's friends here," Casey held it up.

"Nice, who did that?"

"Phil."

"Good. Is the list long?"

"Yeah, it is. A few of them are on their way down. Phil organized some of the guys from other units. They're already lined up to help with the interviews."

Jack nodded at Casey is if to say, "Hey, you handling all this okay?" And then looked down at an endless pile of messages on Casey's desk.

"What? You mean this little stack here? Casey chuckled. "Hey man, what the hell do I know, it's my first case."

"So what's going on with these interviews?"

"I've asked the guys to focus on getting background — like boyfriends, girlfriends, dates, you know? Maybe her favorite bars whatever."

"Good." Jack approved.

"Cool, is there anything else we should be thinking?"

"Not now. Just remember, the key might be right under our noses. We just haven't figured out what it looks like."

"Wouldn't that be crazy?"

"That's exactly how it works … every time."

The two components of the Homicide Unit are connected by a doorway. One side has the detective's desks. The other has the crime-scene investigators and their equipment. Andrew came through the doorway from his side.

"Hey Jack." He plopped into the chair next to Jack's desk.

Jack looked over. "How come you always look relaxed?"

"I don't know. I don't slow down enough to get tired."

"That makes no sense."

Andrew shrugged. "Bad news: No hits on the prints from the car. Maybe down the road something will come up."

"How about the tape? Anything?"

"It's a mess, nothing usable. We've got a better shot at making a comparison with the lifts from the car." Andrew shook his head. "The blood on the pedals is hers, a perfect type match. I'm having the lab run the DNA to confirm."

"Thanks Andrew." Jack glanced down, dejected. "We don't have shit."

Casey sat, listened and took notes on Andrew's update. He said nothing to add to the gloom.

Andrew was the one to give a glimmer of hope: "We got one thing.

You were right on that bullet. It's a semi-jacketed hollow point, .44 Magnum. I got the imagery set up to show the likely scenario for bullet path. You guys wanna take a look now?"

Jack and Casey followed Andrew to his cubicle. Casey studied the poster-sized pictures of dead people decorating Andrew's walls.

"Interesting, huh, Casey?" Andrew said.

"It's a lot of violent shit in these photos. I remember some of these cases."

"They're some of the more unusual cases I've worked. I like the bazaar stuff, like the ones over there with knives still sticking out." Andrew pointed to several photos of dead bodies with discolored skin, twisted into awkward positions.

"Crazy."

"In that one over there," Andrew pointed, "the woman is chopped into pieces. It's unsolved. How 'bout you and Jack solve that one."

"Yeah, sure," joked Casey.

They stood behind Andrew, looking over his shoulder as he clicked the mouse on his computer. On his monitor the image of an asexual droid shifted through different positions. It finished in a kneeling posture. With a click Andrew shot a line through the head.

"Just like we thought," said Andrew.

"Yeah, pretty obvious," Jack answered. He couldn't shake the image from his head: The one where Lisa was on all fours with the guy behind her. He could see it clearly and almost hear the attack happening. *The guy's climbing on her back.* That was it, thought Jack: *The guy was fighting to control Lisa and her struggling made it even better. Rape is all about control not sex! He's holding the gun and already has his pants down or at least unbuckled and his dick is hard. He's trying to reach around and undue her pants at the same time which means he's rubbing his dick all over her ass. He's in his glory holding a gun and feeling her fight while ripping at her clothes to strip her naked. He finishes off without even making penetration and then he kills her. He's done.*

"Hey Andrew, are her panties still in the SART kit? Jack asked.

"No, I've already checked them. No semen."

I'm glad he didn't rape her after she was dead, thought Jack. "Do you have her pants here?"

"Yeah."

"Would you check the back of them now?"

"Yeah, Sure. Give me a sec ... I'll grab the stuff." Andrew returned with a brown paper bag and the Woods Lamp. He snapped on a pair of latex gloves and tore off a large sheet of white butcher paper from a roll. He covered the examination table with the paper and then laid out the pants.

"Hey Casey, get the light."

"Sure." Casey flipped the switch and the room went dark.

Andrew clicked on the lamp and the fluorescent stain glowed under the blue hue of the light.

"And there it is. He blew his wad on the back of her pants."

"Our first break," said Jack.

"I'll get a sample to the lab," said Andrew.

Andrew turned on the lights and popped the CD with the shooting angle from his computer. "I'll get to work on that sample." He handed Jack the CD and left.

"Right under our noses," said Jack.

"Lucky we checked."

"Oh, no doubt Andrew would have found it eventually, but time's not on our side. A murder case is like a fumble: You gotta' go after it balls out."

"Okay, yeah, I hear ya'."

Jack and Casey walked back to their side. Several of Lisa's friends had arrived and were going into separate rooms for interviews. These kids all looked shocked. A couple of them were crying. Though they'd known she was dead, the procedures of death were now right there in front of them: the police station, questions, all of it. The common denominator among them was good looks — just like Lisa. The difference was that these kids had long full lives ahead of them.

Jack and Casey went through their side without even stopping at their desks. It was time to update Lieutenant Richards. As usual, he was on the phone. They stopped short in the doorway but Richards waved them in. Jack and Casey sat down, took out their notebooks, and listened to the tail end of Richards' conversation.

"I realize that Chief ... we'll tell the media what we want, when we want ... just like any other case, sir ... yes, a little more time ... thank you, sir."

He hung up, and stared at them.

"Thanks, boss," Jack said.

"Sure, Jack. I keep trying, but they're pushing real hard. Oh yeah, we also got all of Special Operations canvassing the bars with the flyer you put together."

"It's nice to see Patrol Division coughed up some teams to help us out. We'll take all the help we can get."

Richards opened his notebook. "Are we getting anywhere yet?"

"She was home about a day-and-a-half. We haven't gone through all her friends yet, but it looks like she didn't really hook up with anyone. We got her cell phone records coming." Jack laid out the key events of the case: the drinking, sexual assault, interviews and search results. Richards took notes.

"Anything on a suspect yet?"

"Not from a witness."

"Damn."

"Based on the seat position in the victim vehicle, our guy is probably 6'2" to 6'5" tall. He also likes country music."

"Country music, what the hell does that mean?"

"The radio station in the car was on a country station. It wasn't a
pre-set station and Lisa didn't like country music."

"That's interesting. I didn't think country music was popular in San
Francisco."

"You're right boss, it isn't." Jack closed his notebook. "I'd like to
get some uniforms out checking the park. Maybe we can find the
crime scene or dig up a witness. We're a little thin on those."

"You got it." Richards stopped writing. "What can we give the media
now?"

"Nothing!"

"Jack, we have to give them something. If we don't, they'll make
it up." Richards sat up straight, his arms extending out from his sides.
"Work with me a little on this, for Christ's sake."

"Okay, boss. How about we release the flyer, tell them we need
help finding out where she was before the murder ..."

"That's all?"

"That'll be enough," Jack said. "We get the media and public on a
mission. Give them just enough to distract them. They'll feel challenged
to find answers on their own. That lets us off the hook, at least for a little
while. We need as much time as we can get — it won't be much."

"I like it, Jack."

"Also this way, the media can deal with all the psychics and clair-
voyants that come crawling out of the woodwork."

"All right, let's do it." Richards closed his notebook. That was the
cue for the detectives to get back to work.

Most of the interviews with friends were finished up within the next hour. Detectives piled interview sheets, photos and CDs on Jack's desk.

"Did you guys get anything?" Jack asked them.

Phil spoke for the group. "Not really. The stories were pretty much the same. They hadn't seen her yet. One or two spoke to her on the phone. They made plans to meet up with her later, but nothing concrete. She didn't say anything specific about going out that night." The other detectives nodded in agreement.

"Ok, thanks for the help, guys. At least we identified phone numbers that should show up on her bill."

Once the detectives dispersed Jack and Casey organized the case file.

"We have to keep all this organized from the beginning. It's a pain in the ass, but if we don't, it's impossible to sort everything out in the end."

"Sure, I'm super organized too. I like my shit in its place."

Casey stopped filing for a second, "You know what really sucks about this, Jack?"

"What?"

"The asshole that did this has been running from the second he bailed out of that car — and we don't know which way to start chasing him."

"But, we are chasing him. In everything we do. And maybe he ain't running. Maybe he's just hiding?"

"Yeah, yeah. Maybe," said Casey with a nod. Casey glanced down at his desk. Someone had put a written message there from Traci Townsend. She'd called looking for him. Casey pulled her business card from his wallet and stared at it a moment. *Okay,* he thought, recalling the sexy reporter, *it's not that big a risk. I can try something on my own.* A few minutes later he walked toward the bathroom and dialed her private number on his cell phone.

TWELVE

He couldn't believe this. A Nevada State Trooper was pulling him over. Fuck! He screamed out loud and banged the wheel. Red light filled his rear-view mirror, and the blinding spotlight waved across the back of the stolen car. He glanced at his speedometer: 83 mph. He was speeding. *Should I stop or fuckin' punch it? I'm gonna' have to kill this cop. One thing for sure, no way in hell am I going back to Angola ... or any goddamn prison.*

He had cut his hair, shaved, changed and dumped his bloody clothes before he'd left California. *If this asshole tries to arrest me, he'll die.* It looked like only one red light but it was impossible to be sure. He figured running would only draw in more cops. If he was going to kill this cop, his odds would be better with a surprise attack. He flipped his turn signal and slowed his speed. He moved into the right lane, peering into his mirror to see how many cops were in the car. He couldn't see shit. The bright lights blinded him. He slipped his hand between the seat and the console and felt the cold grip of the stolen .44 Magnum revolver. The original owner had kept a box of ammunition with it: 25 hollow point rounds. So far he'd only used one.

He stopped on the shoulder, rolled down both front windows so he could hear better, then shut off the engine. The driver's side spotlight on the cop car moved. Suddenly, the passenger side spotlight turned on, catching him by surprise. *Shit! There must be two of them. The rush of adrenaline and the thought of being caught caused him to flash on the night.*

*   *   *

She was a hot, tasty bitch and her flirtin' got him hard. And then she got that fucked-up look and turned him away. Yeah right, you ain't turnin' me away. I'm gonna' fuck you harder than any punk-ass college boy you ever had. And then she took that next sip and realized something didn't taste right. The frightened, confused look on her face only lasted a second but it was fuckin' great. He grinned and watched the magic happen. Her eyes drooped and her head got heavy. It was time to drag her sorry ass out of that fuckin' yuppie bar. When he got her on her feet, she looked drunk. Nobody paid much attention. He only gave her half a dose for that very reason. He had to bend way over, cause' she was a little tight, hot bitch. He buried his face into her hair so people couldn't see his face. It looked the like two lovers stumbling out of a bar. He could still smell her hair. He tasted the mixture of her salty skin and make-up when he licked and kissed the side of her face.

*   *   *

He could barely see the cop's shadow advancing toward his car. He couldn't see a second cop — or if there was another car behind the first.

The cop called out. "I'll make contact, partner, and you cover."

Fuck! He could hear the cop, but couldn't see or hear any partner. If he couldn't locate the other cop he was done. His best chance might be to shoot the asshole through his window. Sweat poured down his face. His heart pounded in his ears. He tried to control his breathing. *Shit, this is happening too fast!* He closed his eyes and concentrated on what he could hear.

*   *   *

He heard whimpers from the bitch as she tried to fight him off. It was so fucking dark he couldn't really see too good. He pointed his gun right in her face, but she was too fucked up to realize it. Or she did and could only roll and flail. Oh yeah, keep fightin' bitch. I'm just gonna' fuck you all the more harder. He bitch slapped her, then squeezed her face tight and licked it all over. It was good ... it was better than he imagined it would be. Oh yeah, uh huh, I'm gonna' tape you up and fuck you all night. Uh-huh. He turned her over and it happened. Just like it always did. He fuckin' lost his load. He couldn't hold it. Shit! It was too fast. You fuckin' bitch! You made me cum too Goddamn fast! It was over. The rush was gone. Fuck! His chest heaved as he tried to catch his breath. Sweat poured down his face. He could barely make out the sorry ass bitch under him. He stuck the gun against the back of her head.

*   *   *

He squeezed his hand into the crease of the seat tightening his grip on the gun. *Think man, think. What are my fuckin' options here. Okay, I can definitely take the first cop, then I gotta' get the fuck out and find the other cop and kill him too. This is bullshit,* he thought.

He would probably have to reload. That would be impossible in the darkness. And on top of that, he would have to find the second cop before he started blasting away. He could get out of the car without the gun, locate both cops, dive back in, grab the gun and start shooting. His odds of winning that one were slim to none.

Sweat dripped from his face. There was so much crank in his system he couldn't think straight. Then he thought of a third option: *I can get out with the gun and dive into the darkness. Then I can kill both these mother fuckers before they find me. But what if there was another cop car behind that one?* He couldn't decide, and he was out of time. One thing was sure: It wouldn't make sense to pass up the chance to kill the first cop.

The cop was almost to the passenger side window. He heard him say, "I'll make contact, you cover."

He saw the cop in his peripheral vision. He adjusted his grip on the gun and slipped his finger onto the trigger. He could yank it out in a flash and blow the cop's face off. He still couldn't see the other cop. *Where the fuck is he?*

"Sir, I stopped you for speeding. Please put both hands on the wheel so I can see them."

He stared straight ahead. He didn't move a muscle. Sweat burned his eyes. He would have trouble focusing on the gun site.

The cop said, "Hey, partner, this guy is a little hinky." His voice was nervous.

He was sure there were two. *Shit! I can't even hear the other cop talking back.* As the cop at the window spoke the voice sounded a million miles away. He gripped the .44 Magnum. *I'll shoot the asshole in the face!*

"Sir, put your hands on the wheel!" The cop screamed.

He heard the cop loud and clear. He didn't notice the cop unsnapping his holster and sliding his 9mm semi-automatic pistol behind his right thigh.

"Let me see your fucking hands or I'll shoot!"

The cop sounded desperate. He looked and saw a gun pointed right at his head.

"Yes sir. I ... I'm sorry. Please officer, please don't shoot." He had lost the advantage; he'd waited too long. He placed his hands on the wheel, leaving the gun buried in the crease. He needed to calm this cop down, get him to put his gun away. Then he could go for his gun.

The cop held his flashlight and gun, both arms extended. He could almost feel the site aimed at his right ear. The cop was semi-crouched so he could see into the car.

"Put your hands on top of your head, nice and slow, now!"

He complied. *How do I get a drop on this asshole? Shit! I need a new plan!*

"When I tell you to, take the keys from the ignition with your right hand, and drop the keys out the driver side window."

The cop's voice was still serious, but he was calming down. Compliance was working.

"Do it now, very slowly."

He carefully removed his right hand from the top of his head, spread his fingers and slightly turned his palm toward the cop so he could see he had nothing in his hand.

"Yes sir. I'm real sorry; I'm doing it right now." He reached down and slowly removed the keychain holding the shaved ignition key. He'd filed it himself, so it would work in plenty of locks and ignitions. If the cop saw that key, the game was up. He cupped the shaved key in his hand so the cop wouldn't see it.

"Okay sir, I'm gonna' drop the key out the window." He slowly moved his right hand across his body and extended it out the open window. The keys jingled when they hit pavement. He placed his right hand back on top of his head and listened. Suddenly, he realized the cop wasn't talking to the other cop anymore. They had to be in sight of one another. He knew the closer together the two cops were to one another, the better for him once he started shooting.

The cop talked into the radio microphone clipped to his lapel. "Control Six-Nora Thirty-One," The cop said.

He heard a female voice on the other end. "Six-Nora Thirty-One, go ahead."

"Code Ninety-Nine control."

What the fuck is a Code Ninety-Nine? And why isn't the other cop doin' the talkin' on the radio? It wasn't making sense.

"Ten-four, Six-Nora Thirty-One, break ..."

He strained to hear the woman. "Unit to respond for Six-Nora Thirty-One?"

Suddenly, it clicked. *Yes! The fucker's alone! He's calling for a backup.*

He heard: "Six-Nora Thirty-Three, roger, I'll take the fill, ETA nine." The radio crackled then fell silent.

He thought he knew what this meant: *In nine minutes backup would arrive. But, what if he was wrong? What if there was another cop out there?*

"When I say so, slowly open the door, step out and keep your hands on top of your head." Now the cop was much calmer.

He turned and looked at him. "Yes sir. I'm sorry sir, anything you say." He tilted his head sideways. The spotlight from the police car was less blinding that way. The cop diverted the flashlight so it wasn't right in his eyes. He watched the shadowy figure outside the door. The cop hadn't moved an inch. *Good for me,* he thought, *bad for you. Just keep your big ass in the same spot. How much time had passed? Two minutes? Three? Either way, the cop had stopped talking to his partner. He was still unsure: one or two? Guessing wrong could get him killed.*

"Slowly get out. Do it now. So I can see you."

He carefully took his left hand from the top of his head, grabbed the door handle and pulled. The latch popped loose and the door was free to swing open. He paused a moment before moving. *Fuck! This is it!* His mind raced. *Do I grab the gun and go for it? Do I shoot this fucker from here or get out and start shooting? How much time has passed? Three minutes or four? Fuck it! I'm dead anyway.* He snapped the driver's door open with his left hand and pulled the gun from the crease with his right.

"Freeze! Don't do it!" The cop screamed.

He scrambled out and simultaneously fired. The gun exploded with an enormous kick. A yellow fireball lit up the car's interior.

He heard gun shots: not his own. Flames spit from the barrel of the cop's gun. He fired in rapid succession. The barrage of gunfire ripped through the still air and into the dark night. As he fired back at the cop, the muzzle flash temporarily blinded him. Gunpowder seared his nostrils. He tasted it too.

He scrambled toward the front of the car moving like a spider. *Everything works, fuck yes! I'm not hit!* Every time he put his hand down for balance, the big revolver scraped the pavement. As he moved around the front of the car, his own headlights blinded him. He felt their heat as his face passed the beams. He searched for the other cop. *Am I still being fired on?*

Then he heard the cop scream, "Code thirty! Code thirty! Shots fired! I'm fucking hit!" The cop's voice came from the ground, somewhere near the shoulder of the road and the rear of the car. He didn't know where he'd hit him, but the fucker wasn't dead.

He snaked away from the car into the darkness. He desperately searched for the wounded cop or his partner. He couldn't see shit. Nobody was standing. Then he spotted the cop on his butt on the ground, legs spread and sticking straight out. His body was wavering like a big fucking tree ready to fall. No one else was firing. Sure enough, the cop was alone. The cop struggled to stay upright. He hadn't spotted him in the bushes.

He scrambled to his feet and moved sideways across the front of the cop. The cop was shocked to see him moving. His eyes and mouth were wide open. The cop let out a gut-wrenching scream as he raised his right arm. He saw the gun in the cop's hand.

Fireballs exploded from his own gun barrel, blinding him as he moved. The cop fired a barrage of shots. He heard bullets whiz past his head as he dashed toward the darkness just off the highway. He dove into a clump of bushes and he waited. *Am I hit?* His heart felt like it was going to explode. His gut twisted, he coughed, gagged, and then puked in the dirt. He waited and heard nothing except the hysteria on the cop's radio.

I'm not hit, he realized. He wiped puke from his chin and scrambled up from the bushes. He ran back to his car, not even looking back toward the cop. He scraped the key from the pavement and dived into the front seat. While keeping his head low, he started the car, slammed the shift lever into gear and punched it.

Trooper Haynes' frantic scream from the radio shattered the night. Trooper Thomas recognized his friend's voice, but he'd never heard him sound this way: desperate and panicked. Thomas tried to form a mental picture but it was unimaginable. He gripped the steering wheel so hard his fingernails left indentations in the plastic. His back went rigid; he shook with adrenaline. His thigh tightened as he mashed down the accelerator pedal, but the pedal had nothing left to give. At 125 miles per hour time seemed to stand still.

Trooper Thomas screamed into his radio microphone, "Control, respond paramedics and fire, code three!"

"Copy, Six-Nora Thirty-Three. Fire and medics are code three!" Every second counted. Trooper Haynes' life was on the line.

Thomas turned his radio up to a blare so he could hear it over the wail of his siren. The dispatcher repeatedly beeped the high-pitched emergency alert tone. She controlled her scream as she called: "Six-Nora Thirty-One, confirm you're hit!" Her message drew only haunting silence.

Thomas and Haynes had graduated from the Academy together. They both worked graveyard watch and covered each other's ass. In 19 months they'd become close friends, hanging out together on their days off. Normal people don't call Tuesday and Wednesday their weekend. Only cops, firefighters and nurses do that. Haynes' little girls sometimes called him "Uncle." Thomas loved that. He didn't even have kids ... or a wife.

Thomas was first on the scene. As Haynes' cruiser came into sight Thomas fought the urge to drive in at warp speed. He was scared to death. He didn't want to get shot. His training taught him that he was no use if he didn't use his head. With his high beams on, he inched closer. He leaned toward the passenger side as far as possible in case someone fired into his cruiser. Nobody was in the lanes nearest the driver side. He stopped a short distance back and watched. Thomas was not going to cross in front of his own headlights and reveal his position. The suspect might be lying in wait. He shut off his rear amber lights so he wouldn't be illuminated when he circled around the back. He started for the 12-gauge pump shotgun in the locked rack, but decided his handgun was the smarter choice. It would leave his other hand free for a flashlight or to reload if need be. He was unsure of the best tactical response. No Academy drill prepared him for this nightmare.

He crept from his car, crouching, with his gun and flashlight in hand. His head spun and his heart raced. A cacophony of voices blared from the radio. He darted around the back of his car into the shadows on the road shoulder. He stayed low, searching for a target. Finally he approached the cruiser. It sat — a weirdly lit ghost in the night. The engine was running, top lights were spinning, and the headlights and high beams were on. Both the driver and passenger spotlights shone forward. It looked like an empty carnival ride set in an ocean of darkness.

The smell of burnt gunpowder hung in the air. It reminded him of the 4th of July. He recognized the angled position of the cruiser as the officer safety method they'd both learned at the Academy. Parked this way, an officer could use the engine block for cover in a gun battle.

Thomas knew his perceptions were off. He had trouble distinguishing time and space. Some things moved slowly in his mind, yet his thoughts seemed to be racing. It was the mind's adjustment to a combat situation. He'd learned about that, but this was his first experience of it.

He sensed an oddity: no vehicle in front of the cruiser. He crept another few feet, then, with a snap, he stood and shone his flashlight inside — no one there. He snapped his light off, crouched low and moved three feet to his right. If the suspect fired toward the flashlight beam, he would already have changed his position. Thomas squatted close to the ground, gun pointing into darkness, and waited for gunfire. None came. He became aware of a pumping sound: his own heart. Sweat poured down his face. *Where the hell is everyone? Is the suspect hiding or shot? Where the hell is Haynes?*

Thomas scanned the area, scared to death at what he might find. He moved several feet toward the front of the cruiser, still crouching and alert. The darkness made him feel safer. He saw nothing in front of the cruiser. Then he saw the figure. His eyes locked on the light-colored stripe running down the side of the pants. He saw the shininess of the thick leather duty belt and the combat-style boots. It was a uniform.

Thomas felt the sick realization that this was his friend. Part of his body lay in the dirt. His arms were spread wide. His eyes were fixed open. He seemed suspended in a puddle of bright red, frothy blood. His mouth hung open full of blood. His face was still.

Thomas stepped in next to his friend. He scanned the area: no other bodies. He knelt down on the asphalt, getting blood and dirt on his own uniform. Pebbles tore into his knees. He holstered his gun.

That was when he broke. His flashlight clanked onto the pavement. He grabbed his friend. Thomas screamed, "Please God no!" He leaned close and felt the carotid artery. His friend's skin was warm but there was no pulse. There was no rise and fall in his chest. Thomas ripped open the uniform shirt and immediately saw the remnants of a large bullet gnarled in the Kevlar fabric of the bulletproof vest. The vest had worked and caught the bullet.

He tore the Velcro straps of the vest free and pushed aside the front bulletproof panel exposing his friend's chest. His chest looked grotesquely deformed. The impact had torn the Pectoral muscle from Haynes' rib cage. The muscle had ripped loose and now rested under his right armpit. Blood poured from under his armpit, then stopped.

Thomas fought the urge to vomit. Tears and sweat burned his eyes. He thought about his friend's little girls and his wife. They were at home, safe and completely unaware of what had just happened.

Thomas turned his friend's head to the side to clear the blood from his mouth. He instinctively tilted back the head and gave two quick hard blows of air into his mouth. He felt the wetness on his lips and he tasted the sweetness of blood. His gut wrenched. Thomas centered his shoulders over his friend, clasped his hands together, and started pumping his chest with compressions. He automatically counted out loud. He heard cartilage and bones cracking and he felt it under his palm. After a few compressions, there was much less resistance. His hands slipped from the center point of the Sternum as he pumped. Blood made everything slick. The more he pumped his friend's chest, more blood gushed from under his right armpit. Thomas realized CPR was pumping his friend dry of every ounce of blood left in his body.

Tears streamed down his face. *When did I start to cry?* Snot ran from his nose. His throat burned. He felt his stomach coming out his mouth. He had thoughts of God and he could faintly hear counting. It didn't seem like his voice. Thomas didn't notice anyone else until the hands of a paramedic pulled him away.

"He's gone," said a voice. "There's nothing we can do."

Thomas sat up straight. He was soaked in sweat and blood. The paramedic crouched next to him and put his arm around his shoulder. Thomas felt an ache in his lower back and realized other parts of his body hurt too. He saw a 9mm pistol near his friend's hand. He hadn't noticed it earlier. The hammer was cocked. Haynes had returned fire. He'd fought to the end. He would remember that when he told Haynes' wife and little girls that their daddy would never again come home. Before the paramedic had him completely up, Thomas sunk back down on his knees. He wept.

*   *   *

The muzzle flash was blinding and the tasty bitch crumbled under his weight. She deserved to be taped up. After all, that was how he fantasized about her in the bar. Yeah, all ho-bitches look good taped up with the fear of God in their eyes, knowing what's comin'. He took the small roll of tape from his pocket and bound her hands and feet. He'll return her lookin' her best.

THIRTEEN

Jack and Casey sorted through endless notes, messages and information. It was critical to look at every detail. Jack knew that it was often impossible to recognize which piece would link things together. A key piece of evidence was there, probably right in front of them. It was always that way. Clues don't arrive in sequence. They blow in like a hurricane, spinning your head around. As the whirlwind blinds you, your gut whispers: "This one! Don't ignore this one!"

"That's the voice you have to listen for," Jack told Casey. "It's the same gut feeling that keeps a cop on the street from getting killed. The courts tell us instinct isn't real, and we can't use it to arrest somebody. Maybe not, but we can still use it when we're going down a blind alley — or when we step into a room and look at a scene. Those DAs and judges are the smartest people in the world. Just ask one. But they don't walk down those alleys or feel their stomachs go funny as they walk into a room where somebody died."

Casey nodded. This wasn't new to him. He'd heard a thousand cops say it.

A possible breakthrough came one afternoon when Richards called out for them to come into his office. Both detectives heard the urgency in his voice. They came in and took their usual seats.

"This might be the break we need." Richards handed Jack a piece of paper with four things written on it:

Escape Bar
2611 22nd Avenue
Cody Sines
(415) 677-9177

Jack handed the note to Casey. "Okay, boss. We're listening?"

"Apparently, a busboy was cleaning up the bar and found a small purse."

Jack leaned forward in his chair. *Is this it?* He thought.

Richards took note and went on: "Cody works at the Escape Bar and the busboy gave him the purse. He looked in the purse to see who it belonged to. It's Lisa's."

Jack recognized the sense of elation. The clue was like a shot of adrenaline. He felt lightheaded as his mind spun with scenarios. Just minutes earlier he'd felt the draining exhaustion of dead ends. Now it was full speed ahead.

"Let's go Casey." Jack jumped from the chair. "We're talking to Cody ourselves."

Casey matched pace with Jack. He'd already guessed the plan. *This is the big break,* he thought, *and it might be my break too.* The case was serving Casey's agenda just as much as it was Jack's.

*   *   *

After shooting the cop, he drove through the night. Darkness gave way to morning. His body was crashing fast as the crank wore off. He needed to get his thoughts straight. He needed to dump the car and get a cold one. That was the key to survival and staying free of the law.

Neighborhoods in Nevada were different than San Francisco. Nothing grew as fast. Trees were smaller. Streets were wider and curbs taller. It probably rained like hell, just like in Texas.

He pulled off the interstate into a shopping mall parking lot. He saw the Wal-Mart, the big bookstore and all the other stores and restaurants. The lot was a sea of cars. He parked in a crowded area near the multiplex. That part of the lot would be full until late. The cops wouldn't find the car for hours if not days. He wiped the car down for prints, just as he'd done with the last one.

The thought of that last car reminded him of that stupid bitch. *If she'd just acted a little like she liked him. Instead she'd teased, and then tried to deny him, treating him like white trash. Fuck me? No, fuck you dead bitch! I don't care who your Daddy is! He didn't know who she was until way after. That was his fucked-up luck.*

As he moved through the lot, the weight of the heavy .44 Magnum pistol pulled down the front of his pants. He had extra ammunition in his back pocket. He held the gun securely with his right hand. He'd kept his shaved key. It wouldn't fail him. He just needed to find the right car. It would be even better if it was good on gas. Things would cool down in a few months, but right now he needed to head toward safety. His sister in Texas would take care of him. She had plenty of room and always believed whatever story he told her. She loved him no matter what; but Texas was a hell of long way away.

*   *   *

Jack and Casey arrived at the Escape Bar within 30 minutes. The bar was closed, but the front door was unlocked. Jack walked in from the bright sun, paused and let his eyes adjust to the dim light. Casey was right behind him.

The bar had the familiar smell of all bars after closing: stale booze, dirty glasses and mustiness. When a bar is full of people eating and drinking, it smells like perfume, sweat and hot bodies. The patrons are used to the dim light, and they know what they're looking for. The music is loud, the crowd is louder, and there's not supposed to be much personal space. It's only when the evening ends that lights illuminate the seedy side of the bar. In the daytime those bright lights are low again, and the place is big, empty and almost asleep.

That's how the Escape Bar looked.

A shadow of a young man with a slender build appeared in a hallway next to the bar.

"We're closed. We open at 5:00."

"We're the police," said Jack.

"Oh finally, are you here about the bums living behind the bar? They're nothing but a bunch of fucking hippies."

"Actually, no. We're here to see Cody."

"Cody?"

"Yeah."

The figure stepped from the shadows and swished into the open. He was very thin and his "Peace Needs a Voice" T-shirt stuck to his rib cage. His jeans were European-looking, tight-fitting and hugged his hips. He had a wide white leather belt and his dark wavy hair was perfectly gelled. His face was an olive-skinned sculpture that never seemed to shave clean. He had big white, bleached teeth and green eyes.

"I'm Cody."

Jack was shocked. *This is Cody? Maybe it was all the talk about cowboys and whatever, but he half expected something more than this. For Christ's sake, every cowboy movie since Jesus had a tough guy named Cody. What was this?*

"Hi, I'm Jack and this is Casey," Jack reached out to shake. Cody shook his hand. It was soft and the hand was small for a man's. "We're here for the purse."

"Oh yeah ... that's some totally crazy shit about that girl. I mean, being here and all."

Jack noticed a very slight lisp.

"Do you have the purse?"

"The purse, yeah, it's in back ... but, like I'm not totally sure you're allowed back there. It's for employees only and ..."

Jack cut him off: "I'm sure the boss wouldn't mind. This is important." He could see this was a tough decision for Cody.

"Ahhh, I hate it when I'm the only one here and this kinda' shit happens. Gawd!"

Jack stood silent while Cody struggled with his dilemma.

Well okay ... I guess. I mean, you guys are real cops, right? I don't see any badges or anything."

Jack pulled his coat back revealing his badge and gun.

"Shit dude, okay. It looks real enough to me." He flipped his hands into the air. "This way."

His pace was fast and direct, even though his hips had a barely discernable swivel. They followed Cody through a narrow hallway lined with boxes of booze, wine cases and cleaning supplies. The office was cluttered with papers, receipts and many photos of other metro-sexual people in unknown places. "Here, this is it." Cody held it out like it reeked of dog shit.

Jack was sure that every employee there had already handled the purse, so there was no need to think about prints. It was the purse's contents that might tell them about Lisa's last night alive. The contents seemed intact: Credit cards, identification, make-up and cell phone; but, no car keys. Maybe she kept them separate from her purse in case her purse got stolen.

"This stuff never left the bar," said Jack.

"That explains why we didn't get shit on the tracks," said Casey.

Cody listened without saying a word.

"Dude, were you working the night Lisa Russell was here?" Casey asked.

As Jack looked through the purse he let Casey run with the interview.

"Uhh, yeah. I guess."

"You guess? Or you were?"

"I mean yeah, I was here. But ... I, like I don't really want to get involved cause' this job is totally cool ... and the tips are good and I'm signed up for Cosmetology school, and I need the dough right now. So, if I could be out of this whole thing it would be really cool."

"Look dude, we're not looking to jam you up here. I'm sure the boss would expect you to cooperate."

"Let me call him real quick to check." Cody reached for his cell phone.

"Cody, put the phone away. This is bullshit, okay? We could already be done if you'd quit fucking around."

"Okay, okay. I'm like super busy so can you do this fast?"

"Yeah, just a couple of questions."

"Do you remember Lisa Russell in the bar?"

Cody looked upward. "Yeah, I remember her sitting at the bar."

"Alone?"

"Mostly."

"Do you remember what she drank?"

"Wine, I think ... maybe a martini at first ... look, I really can't remember. I gotta'..."

Casey cut him off: "Dude! Hang on, man. We're talking about someone's life. Are you fucking kidding me right now?"

"Noooo ... I just don't like this kinda' energy in my life. I hate talking to the cops. I mean. No offense, but ..."

Casey pushed on: "Was she a regular?

"No way ... never seen her before." He shook his head.

Jack listened, noting that Casey knew the right questions.

"You said she was 'mostly' alone. Was someone with her?"

Jack paused, the answer distracting him from his search. Casey was onto something. Jack wished he had turned on his tape recorder, but it wouldn't do any good to stop this now. Casey was on a roll. They could always bring Cody in later for a taped interview.

"Do you ... think, like he's the killer?"

"I don't know. Tell us what happened."

"I served her a couple of drinks, I think. You know, I don't pay a lot of attention to women."

Casey let that one go.

"She wasn't here very long when this guy like, totally moved in on her."

"What do you mean, moved in?"

"You know, got in her space. They got all close and were hangin' on each other."

"You remember him?"

"Oh yeah, of course," Cody got a sassy look. "He was tall."

"What else?"

"He was wearing Wranglers."

"Wranglers? Like jeans?"

"Yeah, super tight."

Bingo! Jack thought. Cody had seen Lisa's murderer.

"What else?" Casey asked.

"He was real tall and thin. Like 6'3." He ordered Beam and Coke. We don't get a lot of those in here." He said it in a tone that expressed his disapproval of the drink.

"Had he been here before?"

"No way ... I mean, not with me here."

"How long were they here?"

"I don't know. Not long, I guess. She got totally fucked up. He helped her outta' here."

"Who paid?"

"I don't remember. I think he paid cash. Yeah, that's right." Cody nodded. "He left me 20 bucks for a tip. It was Hella-cool. I don't get tips like that a lot."

"Where'd you find the purse?"

"I didn't. The cleaning guy did. I mean, the busboy or whatever he's called."

"You know where?"

"Yeah. I think it was hanging on the hook under the bar in front of her stool."

"Do you think you would recognize him if you saw him again?"

"Do you think he was the killer? Shit, I hope I never see him again."

"Would you know him if you saw him again?" Casey pressed.

"I think so, maybe. I don't know."

"By the way, does your bar stamp people on the way in?"

Jack remembered the autopsy. Lisa didn't have any stamps on her hands.

"Fuck no! That's 80's disco shit."

"Cody, I'm gonna send a police artist here, okay? You need to describe this dude so we can get a sketch, okay?"

"I'm not good at this shit. I mean, like I said, I can't get involved."

"Dude, I'm just asking you to do the right thing, okay? Just do your best."

"Okay, okay. Shit, you cops are always so pushy."

"Cody, do you have any video surveillance of the bar?"

"Video? No, I mean you'll have to ask the owner. But I don't think so."

"Is there anyone else who may have seen this dude with Lisa?"

"No. I mean, we've been talking about it and no one said anything."

"What time were they here?"

"Early, I think. She got here around 9:30. The dude came in, like right behind her. They were here, maybe an hour, I guess."

Jack thought Cody would be great witness someday, if he ever got the chance.

"Okay, Cody, tell me as exactly as you can everything you can remember about this dude, okay?"

Cody looked upward again, his habit when he was thinking. "Like I said: tall and thin. He maybe weighed a 185 pounds. His face was like, sick-thin. All sucked in like he was a fucking speed-freak."

Casey nodded without interrupting.

"What else can you remember?"

"Really, that's all. Hey man, I was busy that night. I was tending bar alone. You know what I mean? I'm surprised, I mean, I'm even shocked that I can remember everything I told you. Are we done?"

"Hang on dude. What'd he look like? Hair, face, you know?"

"Yeah, yeah, okay. Light sandy hair. Like, kinda' long and wavy. I think it was past his collar. I think he had a mustache. I don't know, maybe not."

"How old?"

"Mid-thirties, it's hard to tell. I don't know. His face was fucked up."

"What do you mean, fucked up?"

"Like rough and ruddy — maybe too much sun or drugs. I don't know. Just fucked up."

"Thanks dude, we're about done. You got anything, Jack?"

"No, you got it all." Jack smiled at Cody.

Casey got Cody's personal information so they could easily contact him in the future.

*   *   *

He drove southbound in the newly stolen, medium-sized SUV. His shaved key worked perfectly. There were hundreds to choose from in the lot and thousands on the road. He was lucky enough to steal one with a child's car seat strapped in the back. The child's seat was a great cover. If a cop bothered to look at him, it would lower any suspicions.

He didn't know what year the stolen SUV was, but before he left the lot, he found a similar model. Using his pocketknife he took out the screws and swiped the front plate. Most people don't notice their front license plate missing so it can take forever before they report it stolen. In the business this is known as a "cold plate."

He drove to a Quick Stop, bought a RockStar and a tube of Super Glue. He drove to a secluded area a short distance from the highway and pulled over. His hands were shaky. He took the front plate from the stolen SUV, bent it in half, and ditched it in the bushes. He removed the rear plate from his SUV and sat back in the driver seat. He desperately needed to recharge.

He opened his soda and took a sip. The drink was cool and the can stung his chapped lips. The fizzle burned his raw throat. He felt it travel down his pipes into his empty stomach. He took a small paper packet from his pocket and opened it. He didn't want to spill a speck of his golden treasure. The yellowish-white powder had a combination dirty sock/chemical aroma. He loved the smell of crank. He snorted a heavy line, squeezing his eyes shut. The crank fried his nasal passages. The burn was a small price to pay. He loved the feel and taste as the crank dripped from his nasal passages into the back of his throat. The burning eased and a sweet euphoric high warmed his entire body.

He sat for a few moments, enjoying the high. The tingling subsided. He felt good, alert and back in his game. He used his pocketknife to carefully remove the month-and-year stickers from the rear license plate of the hot SUV. He opened the tube of Super Glue and put a few drops on the back of each sticker. Moving quickly, with no wasted motion, he glued them into position on the cold plate. He'd manufactured many cold plates in his life. He ditched the other plate in other bushes away from the first one, and then put the cold plate on the rear of the hot SUV.

He pulled onto a southbound lane of the highway. His hot SUV had a full tank and a very cold plate. His registration was current. If the cops ran the plate, it wouldn't be likely to come up stolen. The vehicle description matched too. It even had plenty of his favorite music. He popped in a CD and started to sing along with Waylon and Willie: "Mamas, don't let your babies grow up to be cowboys."

FOURTEEN

The metal cell door opened and Justin loomed in the doorway. His twisted smile didn't mask his anger or true desires. Kyle's eyes were still swollen nearly shut from the last beating but he could clearly see his enemy. Kyle didn't move from the bed. *Now what? This asshole gonna get on me again? He gonna rub me, beat me or what?* Kyle didn't say a word.

The shackling chains in Justin's right hand clanged together. Justin threw the chains on the floor near the cot. "Get up and strip off them clothes, one piece at a time." Justin smiled, loving it.

Kyle got up slowly. Every muscle in his body was bruised and beaten. His aches sharpened as he stood. He felt light-headed and had to concentrate to keep his balance.

"Take off that shirt and hand it to me real nice."

Strip searches were a part of Kyle's life like changes in weather are for a free man. Or they were more than that. After all, in the joint, the weather never really changed. Any difference between rain, sun, cold and hot had lost meaning long ago. But he still hated the strip searches; they never ceased.

Justin massaged and fingered Kyle's thin prison shirt, searching and feeling for anything concealed that might be used as a weapon.

Justin threw the shirt on the ground at Kyle's feet. "Now gimme' them pants."

Kyle stripped. With the aches in his legs it was hard to balance on one foot as he removed his pants. He wanted to sit down to undress, but that wasn't his call. He wasn't quite up for another beating ... not yet. He politely handed his pants to Justin. Justin searched and massaged the pants just as he had the shirt. He tossed them on the floor.

"Take off the skivvies and hold them up so I can see them real good."

Kyle removed his underwear and held them on display for Justin.

"Turn 'em inside out and show me the inside."

Kyle complied, just as he had a thousand times before.

"Good boy, now drop 'em on the floor."

Kyle dropped the underwear and stepped away from the pile of clothes. Standing naked in front of Justin, he felt more exposed than ever. Justin grinned and looked up and down his body, taking it in long enough to make the moment awkward.

The next steps were as choreographed as a ballet. Justin barked the orders and Kyle complied. The orders weren't really for direction because the dance steps were ingrained. The words merely set the tempo.

"Rub your fingers through your hair. Shake it out real good. Let me see behind your ears."

Kyle turned his head from side to side as he displayed the backside of each ear, pulling them away from his head.

"Open your mouth wide. Now lift your tongue. Pull your lips away from your gums."

Kyle manipulated his mouth with his hands like a chimp in a cage.

"Spread your fingers and let me see between them. Put your arms up and show me your armpits." Justin stood a few feet away during the visual inspection.

"Spread your legs a little and lift your dick. Now lift you balls. Turn around, bend over, grab your ass and spread your cheeks."

Bending over made Kyle even dizzier. He thought he might fall.

"Now lift your feet one at a time so I can see the bottoms."

Kyle lifted each foot and the dance recital was over. Just like the weather changing, natural, like a downpour, only different.

"Put your clothes on, then shackle up your ankles. You're going back to your cell." Justin applied the front wrist shackles that wrapped around Kyle's waist keeping the prisoner's hands bound tight against his lower abdomen.

When you can only shuffle 12 inches to a step, it takes time to walk the distance from the hole to the cellblock. Kyle didn't care. He had nothing but time. Back in his cell several letters had arrived. *That's what happens when you spend all your time on vacation,* Kyle thought. One letter in particular caught his attention. He noticed the guards had peeled it apart. The stamp had been removed and the thicker envelope paper was sliced and dissected. The letter and envelope had the distinctive odor of the chemicals they used to check for liquid drugs. The guards had been extra careful with this envelope. They had reason to be suspicious: There was no return address.

Kyle relaxed his aching body on his bunk and began to read the typed letter.

Do you remember the old days? We were so young. Playing, not a worry in the world. How did it ever get this way?

I remember that time you hurt the back of your head real bad. It only happened one time. You were pretending to be an Indian. Yeah, that was it. You were an Indian in search of a cowboy. I remember your bow and arrow. You used to run around with it saying you could take anyone with that thing. I used to laugh at you because cowboys always carried guns. Big ones like .44 Magnums. You know what kind of music cowboy's like? We used to pretend to dance to it. That's all there was in those days. Be safe.

Kyle read the letter several times and smiled. This was the best news he'd had in years. He picked up his prison notepad and pencil and began to write.

FIFTEEN

Several thousand people, all in uniforms or suits, packed the auditorium. The lights were dim. The folding chairs were beautifully arranged to flow toward the front of the stage. On stage left, slightly behind a wooden podium, was a line of 10 chairs. Perfect floral arrangements served as a backdrop. The front of the stage was dressed with dark-blue fabric. Two fire engines were positioned outside with extension ladders diagonally reaching 75 feet in the air and the ends touched. Huge American flags hung from each ladder. These swayed gently in the slight morning breeze.

Irate citizens were already phoning in to complain about the traffic disruptions. Dispatchers were bearing the brunt of the calls. Some people were delayed a few minutes on their way to work. "What in the hell do these cops think they're doing?" asked one caller. The dispatcher tried to calmly explain, but the caller hung up.

The police procession stretched for miles. Police cars and motor-cycles wormed their way from the funeral home to the auditorium. All the stoplights were flashing and cross streets were closed for the few minutes it took to pass.

Drivers kept honking and revving their engines in protest. One woman screamed into her cell phone: "What in hell is this? I'm late for my manicure!" She stared at the procession, and then noticed the motorcycle cop holding his hand up to keep her halted. She gave him the finger.

The motorcade carried its special cargo: a young widowed mother and two little girls in black dresses. The girls wore bows in their hair. Somehow that was the most heartbreaking sight of all. Along with the mother and daughters were the parents, brothers, sisters and others who'd been part of the lives of the dead. It was all headed up by a coach carrying the flag-draped casket of a young fallen hero, Nevada State Trooper Haynes.

*   *   *

Trooper Thomas had put incredible effort into preparing his fallen friend's service. The job distracted him from fresh memories of that night on the highway. Trooper Thomas hadn't slept since.

They'd seen pictures of officers killed in the line of duty when they'd been at the Academy, but neither of them had expected death. Certainly nothing could have prepared Thomas for what he found that night.

Now the job was to catch the killer. A multitude of agencies and hundreds of officers participated in the investigation. Every single cop wished he could be the one to find the killer. Any one of them would have taken pleasure in shooting him like a rabid dog.

*   *   *

He drove for two days straight. He still couldn't believe the cop hadn't shot him. *It was a fuckin' miracle*, he thought. He flashed back and forth between invulnerability and sheer paranoia. His body was powered by fear, caffeinated sodas and crank. He needed to sleep, but there was a lot of highway between him and his sister's.

Once he crossed into Texas he felt more secure. This was a big state, lots of room for him to lose himself, and shake off any leads the law might have. He'd been born here in Texas, and he vaguely thought that should mean something.

He was looking for a particular kind of place: a little fleabag motel not far from the highway and near a truck stop. Truckers like cheap motels. That way they save enough money to pay their favorite local whore — and they can shower before getting back on the road.

His search led him to the perfect spot, a crappy little single-story motel just off the highway. The busted pavement and worn-white lines in the parking lot signaled that this was the kind of place where there wouldn't be too many questions. If they asked anything at all, he could get by with excuses.

The sun had faded the tan stucco exterior. The last paint job was well over a decade old. Small rusted air conditioners hung from the windows with ratty curtains above.

He took his time driving in and stopped several parking spaces from the office. With sun glaring off dirty windows, it was difficult to see into the office. He could make out a clerk shuffling papers. As he got closer he figured the guy was about 50 years old. The clerk's hair was a gray mess, and he had a beer belly.

The door scraped across the tile floor as he went in. That caught the clerk's attention.

"Howdy, partner. I need a room for the night," he said, smiling.

The clerk eyed him. He knew he needed a shave and looked like he hadn't slept in a week. He noticed as the clerk looked past him to the SUV in the lot. The SUV had been a smart choice: new, but not brand new.

The clerk looked down at his hands. He suddenly remembered the cuts and scrapes on his knuckles. The guy was trying to figure him out. *How much time had gone by?* His head was swimming in the fading vapors of crank. "Hey, your sign says vacant. You got a room, right?" It worked. The clerk looked up, and seemed to recall that there was business to be done.

"Sure do, son. All I need is a driver's license and a credit card." The clerk put out his hand.

He knew there wasn't a truck driver in Texas who'd ever had to give this asshole ID. "My ID got stolen a couple of nights ago. I can't do anything about that till I get home. They got my cards too. All I got is cash. You folks still take cash, right?"

The clerk paused and thought about his response. He could see the guy was dying to figure him out. *If he pushes it, he just might end up dying.*

"I don't see nobody else in line wantin' to give you 29 dollars, so what is it? You got a room or not?"

"Take it easy, son. I don't move as fast as I used to. Sure we have a room. You're in Room eight, just around the other side of the building. Go left out the door and follow it around to the side. You can park there if you want." The clerk's fingers trembled as he handed him a room key attached to an oval plastic holder — "8" was printed on both sides.

He threw several wrinkled bills on the counter, grabbed the key and was out the door.

*   *   *

The family sat in the first row closest to the stage. Nevada's State Police Chief spoke first. Like every uniformed officer there, the Chief wore a black band across his badge. "There is nothing more difficult in my duties than burying one of our own family members," he started.

Behind the stage a 30-foot screen showed the smiling image of Trooper Haynes. The Chief spoke of the bravery of all officers and the essential support of family and friends. He described the calling one gets to become an officer, and the sense of honor and duty that spurs them to put themselves in harm's way so that others can live safely. His voice cracked more than once. Each time he paused until he'd regained his composure. Earlier he'd taken a few minutes to learn a little about Haynes' family, and now he used their first names. He wanted them to understand that even in as large an organization as this, they were members of a family.

Following the Chief came the Attorney General. He spoke for the people of Nevada, thanking the trooper's family and friends for all their support, and for all they had given to Haynes in his far-too-brief life. The AG promised to provide every resource, for whatever time necessary to bring Trooper Haynes's killer to justice.

Finally Trooper Thomas spoke through tears. He commended his friend as a comrade, father and husband. He voiced the things every officer there felt. He spoke of barbeques, vacations and his friend's quick sense of humor. He recalled the funny voices and imitations his friend often did. Those who'd known Haynes well chuckled behind their tears.

The bagpipes shrieked, filling the auditorium with their notes of sadness and death. Thousands stood at attention, saluting or holding their hands over their hearts, as the pallbearers wheeled the casket through the center of the auditorium. Trooper Haynes' body was loaded into the coach for the ride to his final resting place.

*   *   *

When Sam was in training to become a Texas Highway Patrolman, his officer taught him to run license plates of cars in motel lots. It was a habit he kept. Sometimes he turned up stolen cars. Other times he'd run a check on the registered owner to see if anything came up. It made for some good pinches. Making good pinches and building great cases was fun. Sam got bored writing tickets and accident reports, and arresting drunk drivers.

Sam had run a couple of dozen plates today, but so far he'd struck out. There was one vehicle left to check: an SUV with a Nevada plate. He ran it and it came back clear. Sam noticed a baby seat strapped in the back. *Odd,* he thought. *Folks with a car like this and a baby don't*

usually stay in cheap motels. I'm not rich, but the hell if I'd bring little
Sammy into a dump like this.

Sam radioed communications and asked for a registration check on
the SUV. After a minute or so, the dispatcher advised him the names
of the registered owners and the Nevada address. It sounded like a
married couple. The dispatcher followed up with vehicle information
including the model and year.

Bingo! The year of the vehicle didn't match. Sam and his wife had
been looking at SUVs lately. From that he knew that this one had a
plate from an SUV two years earlier.

Sam advised the dispatcher, requested another officer to assist,
and asked for the VIN. He asked the dispatcher to contact the plate's
registered owner to see if they were missing a license plate.

Sam parked his cruiser near the office door so that suspicious eyes
couldn't tie him to a specific room.

Sam walked into the office.

"Hey Earl, I'm lookin' at that SUV around back with a Nevada plate.
What's the story?"

"I don't know, Sam. All I seen is a white fellow, bout' thirty-five.
He's skinny, dirty and worn-out lookin'. He came in a few hours ago
and paid cash for a room."

"Did he have a kid with him?"

"Didn't see a kid. Why?"

Sam didn't answer the question. "What name did he give?"

"Didn't have ID. He said someone stole it." Earl winced, knowing
Sam wouldn't like it.

"Earl, how many times do I have to tell you? You have to get ID
from people!"

"I know, I know, Sam. What could I do? The guy creeped me out!"

"Okay Earl, what room is he in?"

"Room eight. I think he's alone." Earl handed Sam the passkey.

Sam walked around to the back of the motel and saw the second patrol car coming toward him. It was Chris, his regular beat partner.

"Hey, dude. Thanks for rolling over."

"No problem, pal. I love this shit. Fuckin'-A man, you're on fire! How many is that this week? Like three?

"Just fuckin' luck dude. I just got lucky."

"Which one is it?"

"The white SUV with the Nevada plate. Earl said he's a white dude, like thirty-five. And trashy lookin'."

"Just the one dude?"

"He thinks so. He's in eight. Bin' there, like a couple of hours."

"Cool, let's go get that fucker." Chris was pumped for some action.

"I gotta' check the VIN before we do it."

"Cool." Their training took over as they moved into position. Chris took cover behind another parked vehicle to cover the door. The curtains were drawn and the metal "8" hung crooked on the faded white door. There was no light from inside. Chris pointed his gun at the door. If the suspect came out, he'd take him off. The SUV was in the kill zone, and Sam felt vulnerable as he approached it to check for the number, but he knew Chris had his ass covered.

Sam got the VIN number, radioed it in, and quickly moved out of the kill zone. Moments later, the sultry voiced dispatcher confirmed the SUV was stolen out of Nevada. She also confirmed the cold plate was stolen, but had not been reported.

Sam and Chris pulled back around the corner.

"Okay dude, I got the passkey.'" He held it up to show Chris.

"Okay, then I got the hinge side," said Chris. He knew the routine. "And I'll go first."

"Cool."

"Dude, don't fuck around in the doorway. Just get your ass in fast."

"Bro, how many fuckin' times have we done this?" Chris said.

"I know, I know. I'm just remindin' you. You got your flashlight?"

"Yeah, let's go."

No matter how many times they'd done this in their careers, they got pumped up. There is very little out there that is less dangerous than entering a pad.

Sam called in again and asked the dispatcher to restrict their channel and send all other radio traffic to another channel. He didn't want to be at the door and have unrelated traffic making radio noise.

"All units, code 22 channel nine for an entry." She paused. "Repeat, code 22." The radio fell completely silent.

Sam and Chris positioned themselves on both sides of the door, and then moved slowly, so their leather police belts wouldn't squeak.

Sam noticed his right hand tremble when he gripped his 9mm pistol. Adrenaline pumped through his veins. He put his flashlight in his left-rear pocket and held the passkey in his left hand.

Sam gave Chris the nod. Chris nodded back with gun and light in hand, ready.

*   *   *

The cemetery wasn't far. Officers on horseback lined the curb. They wore dress uniforms and white gloves. The horses stood in perfect formation saddles and bridles shined and polished. The bridles had police badges on each side, showing that these were members of the Department. The manicured green lawn was interrupted with headstones and flowers. At a distance stood a large white marble mausoleum, 20-feet tall and as large as a house, and it was covered with flowers in tiny cups and the carved names of those entombed. Several feet above the ground, one tomb was empty. The doors stood wide open. An empty casket cart waited in front of the doors.

Seven officers stood at attention, rifles at their side. A Sergeant-at-Arms stood several paces away. Another officer stood to his side. His white-gloved hands held a polished silver trumpet that glistened in the sunlight. The Chaplain stood, bowing his head. He cradled a Bible in both hands at his waist. Folding chairs waited for the family. A semi-circle of beautiful floral wreaths sat on tri-pods, their ribbons and banners fluttering in the breeze.

*   *   *

The door suddenly swung open. Piercing light burned his eyes and blinded him. With a head heavy from sleep he wasn't sure what was happening. Suddenly he realized it was people moving with flash-lights, and guns — cops. He snapped up to move.

"Hands up fucker! Now! Or I'll blow your fuckin' head off!" He could barely make out an image. He blinked to clear his sight. It was a cop, with a fuckin' gun pointed at his head. Another cop moved into the bathroom and shouted, "Clear!"

His sense of time was shot to hell. The black-out shade was pulled shut and the rattle of the air conditioning unit blocked out noise — no wonder he hadn't heard them coming. Through the fear came one clear thought: no choices. He remembered that he'd left the gun hidden in the SUV. *Probably the best place for it,* he thought. *If I'd had it here I might be dead.*

He held both hands up, shielding his eyes from the blinding light. The cop with the gun to his head grabbed his wrist and yanked him off the bed. He quickly rolled him onto his stomach and drove his knee into his back.

He grunted in pain. *Every fuckin' cop has gotta' take a free shot. Fuckin' pussies, he thought. The cop nearly crushed his damn spine.* The cop was pumped up. He thought the cop was going to rip his arms out of their sockets when he pulled his hands behind his back.

The cop slammed the cold metal cuffs onto his wrists. He figured they knew about the murders; but then again, if they knew he killed a cop, why hadn't they just shot him? Here, they had him in this shitty little room with no witnesses. He would keep his mouth shut and find out what they knew.

He sat in his underwear as the cops searched the small room. They found dirty clothes and a shaved key. They stood him up and made him put on his pants while he was cuffed. They took him outside and threw him in the caged back seat of a police car.

Two more cops arrived. He watched as the younger cop searched the SUV. The older cops ordered the young one around. *He's in training,* he thought. *Maybe I've got a chance.* If they found the gun under the dash, he was finished. His knees trembled. His back and arms ached. All he could think about was going back to the fucking joint.

A tow truck arrived. The older cop filled out paperwork and handed it to the driver. He was the only one paying attention to the search. The young cop never got on his knees. *Probably doesn't want to get his uniform dirty,* He thought. *Come on, man.* Miss the gun.

He got the little bit of luck he was wishing for.

*   *   *

Uniformed pallbearers carried the casket from the coach across the lawn, and rested it atop the metal cart. The silence was eerie as the family settled into their chairs. Other guests sat behind or stood amongst the headstones.

The Chaplain spoke, "Please everyone, let's bow our heads and pray." He read a short Scripture and began the service.

People wept, remembering Trooper Haynes. They saw his widow and his two little girls, and remembered the families of others who'd fallen.

With the help of chirping birds and a slight breeze the warm sun gave the day peace. The scent of fresh cut grass, flowers and oak trees hung in the air. A low hum of traffic hung in the distance.

The Sergeant-at-Arms startled everyone as he barked the order. The officers in line snapped their rifles into position, vertically in front of their chests with elbows extended. At another barked order the rifles snapped into shoulder position; pointing toward the sky.

"Fire!" Seven rifles cracked the air. "Fire!" Another crack. "Fire!" The third shot echoed away while the officers snapped their rifles back into position at their sides.

*   *   *

The young cop nodded, said something, and waved the tow truck over. He motioned to hook up the SUV. He couldn't believe it. The young cop missed the gun and the ammo. The big cop who'd busted him climbed into the police car.

"Hey pal, what's your name?"

"I don't even know why ya'll fuckin' with me. I haven't done a damn thing."

"Cut the bullshit, dude. Where'd you get the car and the shaved key."

"Fuck off! I got rights? You ain't read me my fuckin' rights. Gimme' my lawyer."

"Dude, we got you nailed. Your fucking rights ain't gonna' help you. I know you drove that fuckin' thing here and your prints are gonna' be all over it."

"Then take me to jail you bitch."

"Fuck you! You're the bitch. The poor bastard you stole it from has to fly out and drive it all the way home. I was just trying to help your sorry ass out."

He thought for a moment and realized the assholes didn't know he did the killings. They actually pinched him for stealing a car. *This is fuckin' hilarious, they don't know,* he thought. He wanted to laugh out loud. He quickly realized he needed to get out before they figured out what he'd done. *Time to be honest, he decided.*

"Danny."

"What?" asked the cop.

"My name is Danny, Danny Fields," He smiled to himself with relief.

*   *   *

Two officers removed the American flag from the casket and folded it with sharp, crisp movements. Ten police helicopters hovered in formation overhead. The polished silver trumpet sounded Taps. Behind sunglasses the mourners' eyes blurred with tears. An officer presented the folded flag to Mrs. Haynes. She and her daughters held one another and wept. The pallbearers slipped the casket into its final resting place. Vault doors closed. A final darkness fell upon the casket of Trooper Haynes.

SIXTEEN

When the detectives met with Richards again, Jack could see the pressures mounting on his boss. Richards' eyes were more red and glassy, and the bags under them were getting darker. The hours he'd spent shielding the team from political interference weighed on him, but Richards didn't give an inch. He kept up with every detail. He was in the hot seat, and Jack wanted nothing more than to get him out of it.

Jack had known Richards his entire career and knew this guy's biggest concern was taking the heat off of the detectives. Richards always said, "When you take good care of the detectives, they put cases down."

"Cody had good information and Casey did a good job on him," Jack told Richards, starting off on a positive note.

"Finally, some good news."

"I think he'll stay cooperative too."

"What's next, Jack?" Richards asked.

"We need 18 patrol guys to canvas Golden Gate Park. We'll make six three-officer teams. They need to focus on the area closest to the bar." Jack wanted 12, but knew a request for 18 should get the dozen.

Richards took detailed notes, knowing the scrutiny they might have to withstand. That's what experience did to you.

"We also need 10 detectives to hit the Escape Bar tonight at 9:30 or so. It's pretty big joint to canvas." Asking for 10 was his way of trying to get six. "Maybe someone knows this guy." Cody Sines hadn't thought there were any other witnesses, but that meant nothing.

Richards never looked up from his notepad. "We've been tapping Patrol hard on this case. I'm going to ask for four teams. That's 12 total."

Jack and Casey nodded.

"Then I'll grab five detectives from the Assaults Unit. They'll cover the bar," Richards looked up, "That's what you really need, right?"

Jack went on without responding to the question. "We need the canvas guys to get rolling. We're losing daylight. I'll put together a quick Ops Plan for them."

Richards nodded in approval.

Jack and Casey were up and moving.

A moment later they were back at their desks, both shoving papers aside, creating space to work. Jack saw Andrew coming.

"Hey guys. I finished the purse." He handed his report to Jack. "Not much there."

"Thanks, Andrew. That was fast."

"Anytime." Andrew turned to leave.

"Hang on a sec ..."

"What's up, Jack?"

"We've got guys going into the park to try and find our shooting scene. Would you mind running it out there? If they find the scene, I don't want it screwed up."

Andrew nodded, "Sure."

"Thanks, I'm working on the Ops Plan. It'll be short."

"Okay. I'll grab another Crime Scene guy. Do you want me to run the plan over to Patrol and get things going?"

"No, I'll fax it."

"Okay, I'll get loaded up."

Jack finished and sent the plan. Richards had called ahead, so they were expecting it. As Andrew headed out the door Jack gave him a copy. "Call if you dig something up."

"Will do," Andrew disappeared.

Lieutenant Richards stood in his office doorway and yelled: "Casey, the Assaults guys are meeting you guys in the upstairs conference room." He turned and walked back into his office without waiting for an acknowledgement.

Casey had already worked up the sheet for the Assaults detectives, briefing them for their canvas of the bar. Up to then, they'd been in the dark. Homicide information was always need-to-know. It was the only way to stop leaks, even in a big city PD.

Casey hit "print" and copies spit from a printer across the room. Casey went over, took them, and handed one to Jack. They both silently reviewed it.

"Looks good," Jack said. "Let's go."

The detectives were already in the conference room. They sat at the oval-shaped table in the blue, ergonomically correct rolling chairs. They all knew one another's names. Casey handed sheets to a few detectives seated close and threw the rest on the table. Detectives divided their attention between the sheet and Casey.

"First of all, thanks for the help."

Many of the detectives nodded. They'd already been briefed that they would be doing a canvas, probably long into the night.

"Our victim was last seen at the Escape Bar. The address is in the plan."

Now all the detectives were reading the plan as Casey spoke.

"We're hoping you guys can find the dude she was drinking with. He's pretty distinct; his description is in the plan. Hopefully we'll have a sketch real soon." Casey paused for those taking notes. "The only guy we talked to so far is that Cody Sines dude. He's listed on the bottom of the sheet. He was the only one at the bar earlier when me and Jack went out there. Cody's cooperative. He served Lisa and the suspect. So if you can, hit up the other employees too."

One detective asked, "If we come up with something, you want a call or you want us to run with it?"

"Yeah, good point. Just give us a call and it'll depend. If it's something that's gonna' get real involved, we'll try to keep you guys out of it, okay?"

The detectives mumbled and nodded.

"Cool then, hey guys, thanks again. We appreciate it. Anymore questions?" There were none. "Thanks." The room emptied. Casey watched each one, and thought: *Five more cops involved ... five more possible leaks ... good or bad?*

Suddenly he realized Jack was looking at him. Casey nodded. "I think we got it covered, Jack."

"Nice work. We need to meet with the Mayor and his wife. Update them and ask if they might know anything about our cowboy." They headed back to Homicide.

Jack popped his head into Richards' office. The Lieutenant was on the phone, but wasn't talking. Jack said, "Just for info, boss, we're going out to update the Mayor. I'll let his security know we're coming."

Richards nodded his head up and down, and gave the thumbs up sign. He didn't bother taking the phone from his ear.

It wasn't long after that the two detectives stood at the entrance to the Russell home. The mood hadn't changed.

"I don't like coming here, man. This part sucks," said Casey.

"Yeah, it does," Jack said, ringing the doorbell.

The Mayor answered quickly. He looked none the better. Greetings were always awkward. Most greetings start with 'good' and there was nothing good about being there.

"Come in, detectives." He swung the door wide. "Let's go into the living room."

They followed the Mayor through a wide entryway into the elegantly decorated living room. They hadn't seen this room before. The furniture was tasteful and sat under a 12-foot ceiling. Jack noticed the coping around the edges. The center of the ceiling was recessed. The door-ways and windows were framed in multi-layered hardwood casings. The room held a rich wood odor: typical San Francisco. It reminded Jack of an old formal theatre. They sat on a long sofa covered with a fabric in a subtle green floral design. The low-slung high-polished coffee table held magazines in a perfect display. The Mayor sat in an overstuffed armchair at the end of the table. *The life that had been sucked out of the house was still gone. It probably would be forever,* thought Jack.

"Sir, we're sorry to bother you. We want to bring you up to speed." Jack said in a low tone.

"It's not a bother. We're anxious to hear any news." Jack could hear the fatigue in his voice.

"Would it be possible to speak to your wife as well?"

"No, she's not up to it. I'm sure you understand."

"Of course," Jack said, nodding. "Sir, Lisa was at a local bar called The Escape. It's over on 22nd Avenue near the Park. Are you familiar with it?"

"No, I'm not."

"She was there for about an hour, maybe less. She left the bar with a man. We're looking for him now."

"A man? Are you sure?"

"Yes. He's a white guy about 35 years old and tall. He's described as a cowboy-looking-type guy. Does he sound familiar to you?"

"No ... not at all. I can't believe Lisa would leave with a man. You said ... 35 years old?" The Mayor was searching desperately in his mind for an understandable reason. "Are you really sure?"

"That's where we're at sir. We're looking for answers." Jack didn't say anything else about the case. The Mayor was already beyond overwhelmed. They just needed to ask if the guy sounded familiar and just their luck, he didn't. "Oh, another thing sir ..."

"Yes."

Jack's words pulled the Mayor back from his thoughts. "Please don't discuss this with anyone except your wife."

"Okay, I understand." The Mayor nodded. "Please, just catch the one that did this to our girl." The voice held none of the tones of Russell's political orations. Here he was a grieving father, like any other.

"Sir, we're doing everything possible, I promise." Jack felt his cell phone vibrate. He glanced at the number: Andrew. "Excuse me; I have to take this call."

"Of course."

Jack whispered, "Hey, Andrew."

"We got it Jack! We found the crime scene!" Andrew couldn't control his excitement.

"Excellent. Where are you?" Jack kept his voice even. The Mayor and Casey both stared at him.

"Four blocks from the bar, off 26th Avenue. It's a dirt driveway in the park."

"We're on our way. It'll take us about 20 to get there." Jack hung up.

"Was that good news, detective?" The Mayor sounded desperate.

"I think they found where Lisa was taken after they left the bar."

"Where is it?"

"It's in Golden Gate Park, close to the bar, sir."

The Mayor nodded. "Thank you."

They were conflicting words. *How does a man thank someone for finding his own daughter's murder scene,* thought Jack.

Jack and Casey followed him to the door. As they stepped out Jack said again: "Please, sir, not a word to anyone but your wife. It's critical."

"I understand."

At the crime scene, Andrew had already locked down the entire area. Yellow tape stretched from tree to tree keeping the park urchins and their shopping carts out of the area. The displaced park urchins gathered on the edges, watching.

Andrew met Jack and Casey at the entrance of the driveway. "We found it Jack," Andrew said with a smile. "Lisa's shoe." He showed Jack a picture with his camera phone. It was the same silver high-heeled shoe with thin laces they'd seen at the coroner's office.

"Nice work, Andrew," Jack took out his notebook and looked around at the crowd. "I know it's a stupid question but, any witnesses?"

Andrew laughed. "Are you fucking kidding me? With these trolls?" He pointed toward the crowd. "The guys are asking but no one's talking."

"I don't' expect much from any of those folks. Hell, we can't get them to talk when one of their own gets killed." Jack grunted with disgust. He'd worked homicides involving homeless and learned the hard way that they were unsolvable.

"Got anything else in there?" Casey asked, nodding toward the scene.

"Yeah, a shitload of blood. I'll get samples. The plant material looks similar to the stuff Lisa had all over her. I'll take that too and go through it with a fine-tooth comb. I'm hoping we find her fingernail or a bullet casing.

"Me too," said Jack.

Casey turned toward Jack. "Now what?"

"Now we let these guys do what they do best and we wait."

Sooner or later, thought Casey. *Timing ... in the end, it's all about timing.*

SEVENTEEN

Processing the crime scene was going to take all night, so Andrew borrowed portable lights from the Fire Department and the Vehicular Crimes Unit. The lights, which were often used while investigating fatal car crashes, lit up the scene as if it were Monday Night Football. Not wanting that kind of audience, Andrew brought in pop-up canopies with side panels. Those blocked the view from the ground and sky.

Jack walked over to Andrew's unmarked car. Andrew had the engine running so the on-board police computer wouldn't kill the battery. The driver door was open. Andrew sat with one leg hanging out.

"The guys got nothing from the canvas on the north side," Jack said.

"I think Casey's still with the other guys checking the south side." Andrew was finger pecking the keyboard and didn't look up from the CAD (Computer-Aided Dispatcher). "I've been sending messages to dispatch so nothing goes out on the air."

"Good, we don't need the media crawling all over this place with choppers."

"Actually, I'm surprised they haven't picked up on anything."

"Whoever's listening to the scanner tonight must be sleeping on the job."

Jack hit the speed dial button on his cell phone, calling the Lieutenant.

"Richards, Homicide Unit." His voice rasped from fatigue.

"Hi boss. You sound like shit. You need some rest."

"As soon as you guys put this case down, I'll get some ... what's goin' on?" he barked.

Jack saw Casey approaching. He frowned and shook his head meaning they got nothing on the canvas.

"We got this thing locked down. Andrew and his guys will be on it all night."

"Good. Is the media out there yet?"

"No, were doing everything over the cell or CAD. Nothing on the air."

"Well, that won't last long. I'm already getting calls," Richards said. "They're sniffing around. Someone dropped a dime."

As both men knew, good reporters always find a source "close to the investigation," usually a cop or a personal friend. You hear it in every major story in every city.

"We let the Mayor know before we left the house. He's up to speed."

"Good, thanks."

Jack knew they'd have their asses reamed if the Mayor learned about the crime scene from the evening news.

"I'll let the chief know you spoke to the Mayor. Anything else?"

"No, we'll see you in the morning." Jack hung up and turned to Casey. "Let's call it a night."

"Yeah, I'm running low. I could use a recharge."

"I'll drop you off at your car."

*　　　*　　　*

Jack stepped in his front door and felt his body release tension. The smell of homemade food made him comfortable. The house was quiet. Sarah's car was in the garage, and he'd thought he would see her downstairs, but she'd already gone up to bed. Jack emptied his pockets on the hutch in the kitchen. He hung his keys on the decorative holder, unclipped his badge from his belt, and threw it in a drawer along with his gun. He walked upstairs and found Sarah sleeping. She woke up as he entered the bedroom.

"Hi, honey." Sarah smiled, rubbing sleep from her eyes.

"Sorry I woke you. You been asleep long?" Jack sat on the bed next to her.

"I was tired and had no idea when you'd be home."

"Did you eat?" asked Jack.

"Yeah, there's food in the fridge." Sarah sat up in bed and pulled the sheets up to cover her bare top. "How's it going?"

"Tough, but we're getting there." Jack told her about the cowboy, and Lisa being taped up. He mentioned the Escape Bar and details of the crime scene. "But it doesn't make sense. Why leave the car at a gas station?" he asked.

"Jack, don't you see it?"

Jack shook his head. He didn't see anything at the moment.

"He showed her off! She was his prize. He conquered that poor girl and wanted to show the world."

Jack saw sadness in Sarah's eyes. He realized it was the exact look she got whenever she was reminded of the violation she'd experienced as a college co-ed, long before they met.

"What do you mean?"

"He could have left her in that park and taken her car. She may not have been found for days. He wanted her found in a dramatic way, to show he controlled everything. So he put her in that trunk, in public, for everyone to see."

Jack was silent. He hadn't looked at the case from that perspective.

"She was raped."

"I don't think so, but he tried. We found cum on the back of her pants."

"Then she might as well have been raped," said Sarah.

They both sat for a moment, collecting their thoughts.

"So, how's Casey?"

"He's working out. I like him. He keeps up. He can interview too." She nodded.

"I mean, he's a little quiet and private. You know, like he was the other night."

"I'm glad," Sarah scooted back under the covers and smiled. "I'm glad you're home, for a few hours at least."

Jack kissed her on the cheek and went into the bathroom. He grabbed a towel, razor and shave gel. He went to the spare bathroom to shower. The hot water was heaven on his neck and back. He closed his eyes and rested his chin on his chest. The steam slowly filled the shower and his sinuses cleared as he slowly inhaled and exhaled through his nose. The shower warmed his entire body. He felt himself slowing down. But he couldn't clear what Sarah had said from his mind. She was on target. They weren't looking for a murderer; they were looking for a rapist who murdered — *a different animal.*

Jack toweled off, and then slipped into sweat pants and an old sweatshirt. Sarah was asleep. He walked downstairs into the kitchen. He read a few notes Sarah had left on the table regarding dinner appointments and other social engagements she'd committed them to attend. As usual, he would make the few he could. They always drove in separate cars, and he had to carry a suit and extra shirts, socks and underwear. It never failed, as soon as they arrived at dinner or a show, he would get called out. Either a new homicide happened or a lead on a case. He rushed to work leaving Sarah alone. Homicide detectives that still have a spouse, usually have a good one.

Jack found leftover pasta and salad in the fridge. He threw the pasta in the microwave then mixed himself a gin and tonic with two olives. He grabbed his drink, food and fork and settled into his favorite leather recliner. He loved the smell of the leather chair. He clicked on the TV with the remote and started watching sports highlights. The volume was low, but he didn't care to hear what they were saying. He was hungrier than he realized. He knocked down the food and a couple more gin and tonics. It was the perfect medicine.

A doctor had once told Jack, "You know what the problem is with alcohol?"

"No," Jack asked. "What?"

The doctor smiled. "It works."

Jack was disappointed when that doctor retired. He'd liked him a lot.

Jack woke up in the chair sometime during the night. He clicked off the TV, walked upstairs and climbed in bed with Sarah. Her body felt warm next to his. He liked the feeling of home.

It hardly seemed like a moment before the alarm woke him up from a dead sleep. He saw light coming through the edges around the closed bathroom door, and he was alone in bed. His vision wasn't yet clear. Sarah was in the shower. He felt good from rest but his head hurt a little from the gin. He lay in bed until he heard the shower shut off and Sarah moving around. He got up and went into the bathroom. Sarah had a towel wrapped around her body and her hair was wet. She was athletic and kept herself in good shape. She still looked great to him.

"Good morning, babe. How you feeling?" Sarah asked.

"I feel good. Your hunch last night was right on target. I haven't been able to get it out of my head."

"You would have seen it yourself soon enough," Sarah said with a smile.

*   *   *

Within an hour Jack was at his desk with a fresh cup of coffee. Casey arrived a few minutes later. Andrew walked in from the evidence room carrying 8x10 color photos and copies of evidence sheets. He needed a shave and hadn't changed clothes. His shirt was stretched and wrinkled. His eyes were bloodshot with dark bags underneath.

"You do get tired," said Jack.

Andrew ignored the comment. "We finished up about 6:30 this morning. I didn't want to go home until I briefed you guys."

"Thanks, Andrew."

Lieutenant Richards walked out of his office. He looked fairly decent and his suit was fresh. Obviously, he'd slept. "Let's meet in the conference room and get each other up to speed."

Jack, Casey and Andrew followed Richards down the hallway into the small conference room, and they all sat around the table.

"Andrew, why don't you start by briefing us on the crime scene from yesterday," said Richards.

"Sure boss. Here are the still shots. I've got video too." Andrew stood and spread copies of photos and evidence sheets across the table. They all grabbed copies and reviewed the list of items.

Jack and Casey nodded.

"The shoe's a definite match, and it had blood on it. The same type as Lisa's. We'll run DNA to confirm."

Jack looked at the photo showing a big puddle of blood. "She must have been lying here awhile," he said.

"Yeah, he was probably taping her up," said Andrew. "Those tire tracks match her Benz." He pointed them out in the photo.

"You didn't find a bullet casing or fingernail?" asked Jack.

"Nope. We could have missed the fingernail, but no way we missed a casing. It has to be a revolver. Or he picked it up."

"I don't think he could have found the casing in the dark, even if he wanted," said Casey.

It was extremely rare for murderers to clean up bullet casings. He'd seen it done once, maybe twice in the all the cases he could think of, Jack remembered.

"As far as the nail goes, it had to have fresh blood or meat on it. A rat or something probably picked it up and ate it," said Andrew.

Sick, thought Jack.

"The guy must have seen her drive up or park, right? How else would he know where her car was?" asked Jack.

Everyone nodded.

"We need to check all the public parking lots around the bar for video."

"I'll get that handled," said Richards.

"I think the guy is a rapist first, then a murderer," said Jack.

Everyone looked at him, puzzled. He told them about the conversation he had with Sarah. He left out the reason she was so familiar with how rapists think. "Has anyone checked with Sexual Assaults to see if they got any cases with a tall cowboy?"

"I'll take care of that," said Casey.

There was a rap at the door and a detective that had been sorting through new leads walked into the room. Richards looked up, annoyed.

"I'm sorry to interrupt, Sir, but I thought this was important." The detective handed Richards a letter. As Richards read, his demeanor changed dramatically.

"What's up, boss?" Jack asked.

Richards looked up at him. "It seems we have a convict doing a life sentence in Angola State Penitentiary in Louisiana." He turned over the envelope. "It's addressed to the investigators on the Mayor's daughter's case ... no names." He glanced at the letter again. "It says, 'The cowboy you're looking for used a .44 magnum.'"

"What?" Jack cried.

Richards continued, "'And, she was shot once in the back of the head.'"

All eyes were on the letter, and then they looked at each other.

"How the fuck can a convict in Angola possibly know that?" Jack demanded.

"The inmates name is: Kyle Sanders." Richards looked at Jack and Casey. "I want you two on a flight to meet this guy and figure out what the fuck is going on!"

"We're on it, boss," Jack said. "I'll call Angola and confirm that Sanders is an inmate."

"You guys better get to him before someone finds out he's a snitch. He's no good to us dead!"

Casey hadn't said a word. Jack noticed his partner was white as a ghost. It was the first time Casey had showed that much emotion.

"You okay?" Jack asked.

"Yeah, yeah, I'm cool," Casey said, his jaw setting. "I'm ready, too. Let's see if we can break this thing open."

EIGHTEEN

They took a flight to Dallas and then connected to a small plane to Baton Rouge. As they flew across Louisiana Jack saw green vegetation spreading everywhere. Wide swaths of land looked like plantations, each with a huge southern-style mansion surrounded by landscaping as well manicured as a properly tended golf course. He knew that Angola was north, near the Mississippi border.

"These are your old stomping grounds, right, Casey?"

"Yeah some of it. Man, it's been a long fuckin' time since I been here." Casey stared across the row, out the opposite window. "You ever hear what the inside of Angola is like?" Casey asked Jack.

"No, I haven't."

"There ain't no mansions up there. When I was kid, they'd say it was like hell on earth on the inside."

"Who said that?"

"Everyone. We didn't live too far away from it for a little while. Man, I remember, it scared the shit out of all us kids."

Jack chuckled. "Why?"

"It was a fucking scary place to us kids. They had a death row, and they had executions. The Warden actually gave the electric chair a fucking name: 'Gruesome Gertie.' Did you hear of that?"

"No."

"I remember they executed this one dude, and right after they threw the switch, his fucking head burst into flames."

Jack laughed. "No way."

"Yeah, dude. I'm not shitin' you. We heard about it the next morning. It scared the hell out of us." Casey laughed too.

Jack remembered reading something about Gruesome Gertie. He recalled that it was now the centerpiece of the Angola Prison Museum.

"There've been dudes who spent as much as 35 years in solitary at Angola. Even though I'm a cop, I think that's fucked up."

Jack couldn't imagine being locked in a cage alone, with no human interaction for a major portion of your life. He heard what Casey was saying, but he also got the message Angola was sending: it wasn't meant to be pleasant.

"Dude, you're a movie guy, I'm sure you've seen movies about the place."

"I don't remember any."

"And the songs. A lot of dudes wrote songs about it too."

Jack sat, listening in a way he hadn't before. Casey was opening up for the first time. Jack knew this guy was shaping up into a first-rate detective, but that was about all he knew. Here was a chance to get inside his new partner's thinking.

"It's the toughest maximum security prison in the entire fucking country," Casey said. "I knew that then, and I've read up on it since. It's still got that reputation. Way back in the Civil War days it was a huge plantation. It's on, like, 18,000 acres or something. I mean, it's fucking huge. They got like 5,000 inmates in there. I think it's the biggest prison in the world."

Jack nodded to keep Casey talking.

"The Mississippi River is on three sides of it. It's a shithole. I remember, man, it would rain like hell. And then flood the shit out of everything. The fucking mosquitoes are big enough to carry you away. And then they eat you alive. It's a fucking swamp. The mosquitoes thrive in that shit.

"Were there slaves on it when it was plantation?"

"Oh yeah, there were slaves. There's a lot of reminders of that shit down here. We don't see that kinda' shit in California." Casey paused. "It's weird, man."

"What is?"

"That's just a fucked-up piece of real estate. I mean, first slaves were there, and then it turns into a fucked-up prison."

Jack hadn't thought of it that way. He never looked at prisons as fucked up. Actually, he never gave it much thought.

"It's like, life is fucked up for everybody that steps foot on that piece of land." Casey shuddered.

Heavy humid clouds hung in the air making the approach bumpy, but things were smoother once they landed. Their rental car was ready to go, and Jack was glad the car's air conditioner worked. The humidity was even too much for the defroster. As the car chilled, condensation formed on the windows.

Outside the world was green. Lush crabgrass carpeted every spot of unpaved earth, including the divider on the two-lane highway. Most of the homes on the highway were trailers, and most of these had a dog or two on long ropes.

"Let's get the rap on this guy from the prison guards before we meet him," Jack said.

"I'm good with that. Actually I thought I would hang low, and back you up on this part. If you're cool with that?"

"Yeah, fine. They should be able to tell us anything we need to know about this guy."

"Either way, the dude knows something," said Casey.

"Regardless of how the case goes, we need to find out how he knows those details."

They parked in the visitor lot and stepped out of the cool confines of the car. The hot, sticky air bit into Jack's neck, raising an immediate sheen of sweat. Though the sun had already sunk low, Jack felt heat radiating from the asphalt. They followed the signs along a walkway to the Administration building. It sat outside the massive walls and razor wire. Jack pushed the metal door open and felt a blast of cool air hit his face and body. They stepped into the office.

"Good afternoon gentlemen, how can I help ya'll?" The guard sat at a desk behind the counter and smiled as he waited for a response.

"Hi, I'm Jack Paige and this is Casey Ford. We're homicide detectives from San Francisco." Jack held his badge for the guard to see. "Man, it's hot out there." Jack wiped sweat from his forehead.

"Uh huh, ya'll don't get hot like that in San Francisco." The guard got up from his desk. "Ya'll's a long ways from home. What brings ya'll here? I know it ain't the good weather." The guard laughed at his own joke.

"We're here to see an inmate: Kyle Sanders. I called yesterday and they confirmed he was here." Jack set his badge on the counter and took out a business card, as did Casey

"What's his name again?"

"Kyle Sanders."

The guard typed, while looking at a monitor on the counter. Jack couldn't see the screen.

"Uh huh, we got him, for life as a matter of fact." The guard kept reading. "Murder in the first. He bin' here 'bout 16 years."

"What kind of prisoner is he?" Jack asked.

"Well, ya'll wouldn't want him at yo' house for supper, that's fo' sure," The guard laughed at his own joke again. He touched the screen with his finger while scanning the page. "He's been in the hole some, but nothin' that's got him killed." The guard paused. "Hmm, looks here like he recently attacked one of our new guards."

"Does that happen a lot here?" asked Jack.

"Oh yeah, but not with him. First time. I'll print this out for ya'll to have."

"Thank you" said Jack.

A printer at the edge of the counter began to chatter. The guard looked toward a clock hanging on the wall. "I believe they all done with supper by now. When do ya'll wanna see him?"

"Now would be great."

"All right then, gimme' a minute." The guard tore a sheet from the printer and handed it to Jack. Jack took the paper and his badge. The guard got on the phone and examined their business cards as he spoke.

Jack didn't know what to expect with Kyle Sanders. It was tough to interpret the inmate's expression in his prison picture. Frozen images make people look more sinister than they actually are. That's why the media loves those black-and-white booking photos when they report a crime story.

"The Warden said ya'll could use his office for your interview," the guard said, looking up from the phone. "I'll escort ya'll over there myself."

"Thank him please. That's very generous," Jack said.

The Warden's office was like any other Jack had visited: large wooden desk, scattered paperwork, reading lamp on the corner and walls covered with framed pictures. These were images of Angola over the past hundred years. The prison had changed, grown. The only thing that didn't change was the marsh of the Mississippi always encroaching, always threatening.

The bookcase behind the desk contained lines of binders and books with titles like: "Prison Reform Act and Policy," and "Psychological Aspects of Incarceration and Rehabilitation." On top of the bookshelf were family photos, an autographed baseball and a bottle of *Gentleman Jack* with a bow. Directly above the bookcase was a large window. Jack looked out and saw inmates wandering around the main yard a few stories below and some distance away. It looked like a football field surrounded by a white gravel track. Several inmates had their shirts off and were running laps around the track. Jack couldn't even imagine running in that heat. Men watched each other do push-ups, some sitting on each other's backs to add weight and build more muscle. Jack had seen it in every prison he visited.

From that distance it might have been kids outside a high school, but then you saw the jungle of razor wire and the guards with automatic weapons up in the towers.

Jack turned back to the room and he and Casey started rearranging the chairs so they could sit next to Kyle. If they kept a guard in the room, he could sit on the black vinyl sofa against the back wall. Jack put his digital tape recorder on the desk. He heard an exterior door open and a guard giving directions: "Walk on to the end. They're in the Warden's office." Metal shackles clanked, accompanied with a shuffling sound of short footsteps. The footsteps echoed louder as Kyle approached. Casey looked nervous.

The inmate stepped into the office and stopped. His wrists were shackled in front, close to his waist. His ankles were shackled with 12 inches of length between them. The stare he gave Jack was expressionless. He turned and looked at Casey. Both held their stare on one another. Suddenly, Jack felt awkward, as if these two Southern boys might share something he could never really know — a culture, a background or just some kind of innate sensibility born from life in the endless heat. Casey looked away first and sat down.

Kyle had lived a long time taking orders and it showed. It was there in the pale skin and the gaunt look that came from a rotten diet. Nothing about him looked healthy. His face and arms were a blotchy gray with yellow patches from bruising. Jack thought about what Casey had said about this place. It was obvious Kyle had been beaten. Jack wondered who'd done the beating. Maybe it was the guard he attacked.

"Where you gentlemen want him to sit?" The guard asked.

The guard was huge and not so much muscular, just a big farm boy. Tobacco stained his mouth giving him a hard edge. Jack sensed no southern hospitality here.

"This chair is fine." Jack pointed toward where he wanted Kyle to sit. Jack was almost eye-to-eye with the guard; but the guard was slightly taller and had 50 pounds on him.

Kyle didn't move.

"Sit down!" The guard barked.

Kyle shuffled to the chair and sat without speaking.

"Hi Kyle, I'm Jack Paige and this is Casey Ford." Looking at the shackles, Jack didn't extend his hand. "We're detectives from the San Francisco Police Department. We're here to talk about the letter you wrote." With the mention of the letter, the room's mood changed. It was subtle, but apparent as a heart attack. Kyle tensed up. Oddly, so did the guard.

Jack looked to the guard. "You mind if we talk to him alone?"

"Alone?" The guard thought a moment. "Sure, no problem, sir. I'll wait outside. Ya'll just call me when ya'll are done." Guard Justin Pierce gave Kyle a warning stare and he closed the door and left. He would've liked to listen, but didn't dare. The Warden would be keeping a close eye on this one.

"We record everything, Kyle." Jack pointed to the tape recorder.

Kyle nodded.

"Tell us about your letter. How do you know about the case?"

Kyle leaned toward Jack and spoke low. "What I wrote is true, right? Otherwise ya'll wouldn't be here."

Jack kept a poker face. "Are you planning to tell us how you learned the information?"

Kyle nodded positively.

"Do you know who killed the Mayor's daughter?"

Kyle grinned and nodded again.

"I get the feeling, talking here is not a good idea." Jack let that hang in the air.

Kyle spoke in an obvious hushed, but strong tone. "I'll tell you everything I know. I just got one condition." Kyle's dark eyes pierced Jack's. "You get me out of this shithole. I'm doin' life. I wanna' do it somewhere nice, like California." His shackles rattled as he started to lean back.

"I don't know if that's possible Kyle."

He froze and gave Jack a hard stare. "Don't bullshit me. I seen it done before. You trade me for some other inmate. I bin' in here a long fuckin' time. I'm sure ya'll know that. I seen it done over and over."

"Okay Kyle, tell me what you know. That way I can see if it's worth the price." Jack knew Kyle had thought this out, but he hoped he could bargain.

"Listen ... I already told you something no one should know. Right?"

Jack didn't respond.

"That bitch got one shot in the back of the head, right?"

"Let's assume you're right ..."

"Fuck assume! I'm fuckin' right! And ... Ya'll know it! It was with a .44 Magnum! Right? He waited for an answer. He finally figured it out: He wasn't getting information. He had to give it. "Okay, I hate fuckin' games. Before he got out, he told me he was gonna kill the bitch!

How the fuck else would I know?"

Jack silently absorbed what Kyle just said.

"Who said that?"

Kyle lowered his voice again. "When ya'll ready to know who, ya'll jus' pack my sorry ass to California." Kyle stood up.

Jack was stunned. The conversation seemed to be over before it had really begun. Casey gazed at the prisoner with an odd look, almost as if he admired the sheer balls of it.

Kyle shuffled toward the door, yelling: "Guard Pierce, I'm done talking to these assholes. Please get me outta' here, sir."

Jack noticed the door opened immediately. Obviously, the guard had stayed as close as he could, probably listening. Kyle shuffled past him into the hallway. He seemed as confused as they did.

The drive back to the airport provided time to digest what had happened. Jack called Richards repeatedly but couldn't get through. Angola seemed like a huge abyss where no cell phone worked.

"What do you think?" Casey asked.

"We got to get him back to California ASAP. He knows he's holding a golden egg. It's his ticket." Jack stared forward as he drove.

"The dude said some interesting shit. He knows something, that's for sure," Casey said.

"It makes sense too, if it wasn't random, and it doesn't look like it was. I think he's got something for us. Someone Kyle knows had it out for Lisa."

"We can always ship him back if he doesn't pan out, right?"

"Probably not," Jack corrected. "We'd end up with him in California. But I don't care. He's locked up. It doesn't affect us, right?"

"Yeah, I guess so." Casey said staring ahead.

*　　　*　　　*

The walk back to the cell felt long, as if time were extending. Justin was keyed up. Kyle could feel it. Was it curiosity? Hostility? Or both? Justin followed him into the cell to remove his shackles, which was not normal thought Kyle.

As Kyle slipped out of the last ankle restraint Justin snapped. His heavy body forced Kyle against the wall, nearly crushing him. Justin grabbed Kyle's throat, squeezing his windpipe. At the same time, Justin reached down and twisted his balls. Pain streaked through his stomach and kidneys.

Justin's breath was against Kyle's cheek. The position had a horror that had become familiar. "You ain't gettin' outta here boy! Not unless it's in a fuckin' pine box!"

Kyle couldn't speak. Pain and lack of air left him on the verge of passing out. He thought his eyeballs might explode.

"Them assholes ain't takin' my bitch!" Justin's voice pitched high, like whining brakes. Kyle could feel the trembling strength in Justin's muscles.

Justin grabbed him by the hair. Kyle didn't feel himself getting slammed to the floor. He had already passed out.

NINETEEN

Danny had no transportation and just a few bucks left. Not that he was complaining. He still couldn't believe the cops had let him out so fast. All they had on him was car theft, and the county lockup was jammed up enough that a car thief didn't rate a cell. They gave him a trial date and let him go. Hell, they probably didn't even expect him to show up in court. They might have to convict him, and then pay for his upkeep for years.

When those assholes had burst into his room, he'd thought for sure he was done, but they hadn't found the gun in the SUV. That was all right. There were plenty of guns around.

Danny hopped on a bus headed east. He wanted to keep moving. He rode the bus as far as his ticket would take him. He didn't catch the name of the town he landed in.

He didn't much care.

Danny got off and started walking around. He found a likely neighborhood right near the bus stop. It was a nice day. Nobody paid attention to him. He searched for a house that looked empty but had cars, focusing on ones with their curtains drawn. People usually close curtains and windows when they leave. Most folks in this small working class neighborhood had jobs. It wouldn't take long to find the right house. Most people in Texas had guns too — that was on his list.

Danny looked at several homes, pausing to listen for the hum of an air conditioner or a dog barking. If he heard either, he moved on. There was a nice house on the corner of a cul-de-sac. From the three sides he could see it appeared nobody was home. He banged his knuckles on the side fence as he walked along. No barking dog.

He checked the windows for alarm stickers or contacts. There were none. He noticed the gate to the backyard was on the concealed side of the house. Perfect. Danny walked onto the front porch as if he were expected. He pushed the doorbell and heard it ring through the closed door.

If someone answered, he would ask for a random name then act confused, saying he must have the wrong address. Danny pushed the doorbell again. He listened for the telephone. *Sometimes nosey neighbors call to say there's a stranger on the porch.* The house was silent. He turned the front door knob and felt the resistance of the lock. If he had to kick in a door, it would be around back or in the garage. That would be safer.

Danny moved across the driveway to the side gate accessing the backyard. All the while, he scanned the neighboring houses to see if anyone was watching. He saw nobody. The gate wasn't locked. He slipped into the backyard. The house was locked up but the door leading from the side yard to the garage gave way as if it were cardboard. He noticed a Chevy in the garage. The door from the house into the garage was unlocked.

Danny felt the rush of walking through someone's house. He loved every minute of this: looking through photos, opening closets, rifling through drawers. He fondled the panties and bras in the bedroom dresser until he got hard. He discovered a sexy silk G-String, wrapped it around his dick and jacked off. He came fast, as usual. He wiped himself with toilet paper and flushed it down the toilet. In the bathroom he searched the medicine cabinet for good prescription drugs. He grabbed a toothbrush from the counter and brushed his teeth. He put the toothbrush back where he found it, laughing to himself.

He searched through every closet and under every mattress. Jackpot! There was a fully loaded, 9mm semi-auto pistol under the mattress in the master bedroom. Danny found over $400 in cash and gold jewelry. Taking whatever he pleased got him high. He helped himself to a beer and leftover chicken from the fridge. The keys to the car were hanging in the kitchen next to the phone. He put them in his pocket. Danny took a piss and tucked the gun in his waistband. He grabbed the rest of the chicken, a bag of chips and all the beer. He noticed a file on the workbench in the garage. He used it to quickly file another key on the ring— another shaved key. *The goddamn cops kept my last one.*

Danny backed the car out of the garage, while watching for nosey neighbors. *No one's around,* he thought. *This neighborhood's deserted.* Danny smiled as he saw the house disappear in his rear view mirror. *My lucky day!*

*   *   *

Jack and Casey touched down in San Francisco International Airport. They didn't check bags so they got moving. Both checked their cell phone messages as they walked.

"Hey, Casey."

"Yeah?"

"This is it!" Jack felt ecstatic. He hoped it wasn't just exhaustion, but he was pretty sure this was good — maybe great. The case was breaking open.

"What's up?"

"I got an urgent message from Auto Theft. Remember, we flagged all stolen vehicles taken the night Lisa was murdered?" Jack talked while listening to the message.

"Yeah."

"A Nevada Trooper called to confirm a stolen car they recovered in a movie theater parking lot."

"In Nevada?"

"Yeah, the car was stolen 10 blocks from the gas station the night Lisa was murdered. They say it looks like it's been there about a week."

"No fuckin' way?' Really!"

"Yeah, the Nevada cop called too, he left his number. I gotta' call him back." Jack quickly dialed the phone number.

The trooper answered: "Mike Simpson."

"Hi, Mike. This is Jack Paige from the Homicide Unit, San Francisco PD."

"Hey, detective, yeah, thanks for calling back. You're calling about the car, right?"

"Yeah, I just got off a flight and I'm walking through the airport, so if I lose you …"

"Got it. Yeah, we recovered a car from your city. When I called your Auto Theft Unit to confirm it, they said I needed to talk to you."

"Thanks for leaving me a message."

"Hey, no problem."

"This is what's up, Mike: I don't know if you heard about our Mayor's daughter getting killed?"

"Oh yeah, I heard about that case."

"That car you got, was taken 10 blocks from the place we found her body … the same night"

"What! Holy shit!"

"We're still on it," Jack said.

"She was shot, right? I heard that on the news." The trooper's voice suddenly became shaky.

"Yes, why …?"

"Was it a .44 Magnum?"

Something in Simpson's voice made Jack's ecstasy turn into nausea. "I'm afraid to ask why," he said.

"The same night your victim was murdered, my friend, Thomas Haynes was gunned down on a traffic stop. He was killed with a .44 Magnum."

Fuck! thought Jack. He felt sick. His stomach knotted and a choking sensation clogged his throat. He remembered when his first partner was killed in the line of duty. Jack always felt responsible. The pain never went away. The funeral was etched into his memory. He still saw the distraught faces of his partner's wife and son. He hadn't realized he stopped walking until he noticed Casey staring at him with a wondering look.

"Mike, I'm really sorry. Did he have a family?"

"Yeah, a wife and two little girls," his voice trailed off.

"That's fucked up."

"Yeah man, it's really bad."

Jack collected his emotions. "Mike, this is important. Are you listening?"

"Yes sir," his voice just above a whisper.

"I guarantee the killer took another vehicle from the lot. You need to check your stolen vehicles from that night, ASAP."

"Yes sir. I'm on it now. I'll call you back." His voice invigorated with the idea.

Jack hung up. "It looks like our guy fled to Nevada. He probably killed a Nevada Trooper along the way."

"Ahhhh fuck!" said Casey while shaking his head.

"I gotta' call Richards." Jack started punching the numbers into his phone.

"I'll be right back, I gotta' take a piss," said Casey.

Jack nodded.

Casey headed for the men's room. Once he was out of Jack's sight he took the business card from his wallet and punched in the hand-written number.

"Hello," the sexy voice answered.

"Hey Traci, it's me Casey."

"Hello detective," Traci sounded sleepy. "Umm ... I love when you call. I'm in bed you know, catnapping."

"Listen, I have important shit to tell you."

"Can't you come over and tell me in person? Come on baby?" She was still groggy.

"No-no-no ... I don't have much time. It's about the Russell case!"

"What is it?" Traci recognized his tone and was all business. When she baited the hook this was what she was fishing for. Now the fish had the worm.

"There's a dude in Angola State Penitentiary in Louisiana."

"Okay, go ahead."

"We just got back from talking to him. We just landed. I'm at the airport."

"Okay, okay ... I'm getting it!"

"His name is Kyle Sanders, got it? Kyle Sanders."

"Yeah"

"He's got very specific information about the murder, okay? He says he knows it was planned, and he knows who did it." People were passing by. Casey cupped the phone with his hand.

"You're kidding? What else does he know?" she asked.

"That's what we'd like to find out. I'm just worried that it might take the brass too long to see this guy's true value and we gotta' move fast on this dude. He's key. But, listen Traci."

"What?"

"You can't fucking tell anyone it came from me, okay?

"Of course I won't."

"No really, not a single fucking person, including your editor."

"I promise baby. You do like me, don't you? That's why you're telling me, right?"

"Yeah, I do, a lot. But remember, when they start asking about sources, just hint that you know somebody down there in Louisiana, okay?"

"What's next? Are you close to making an arrest?"

"I'll let you know, I gotta' go," he said, his hands sweating. "But promise me, not a word about me, okay?"

"Yes ... yes, of course. I've got it. Thanks sweetie."

"I'll talk to you later," Casey heard her squeal with excitement before he hung up the phone. He didn't wait for Traci Townsend to say goodbye. He had to trust her on this one. Hopefully, she wouldn't fuck him over and give him up. It would totally destroy his career. Casey knew Traci was a weak link and a promise from a woman like her was as shallow as a desert mirage was risky. This window of opportunity wasn't closing fast, unfortunately, it was slamming shut.

*　　*　　*

Jack recognized the anxiety in the Nevada trooper's voice when he called back.

"Detective Paige, you were right!"

"I'm sorry I was." For Jack, it was like watching a train wreck. Too many people had already died. He wondered how many were still in line.

"We had an SUV and a cold plate stolen the same night," said the trooper. "They were both recovered at a motel in Texas several days ago."

"Texas? Okay, what else?"

"The guy that owned the SUV had to fly to Texas to pick it up. He drove it all the way home. We got troopers heading over to search it right now."

"Excellent! Do you know what went down in Texas?"

"Yeah, apparently, some cop saw the vehicle at a motel and figured out it was hot and they arrested the driver."

Yes! Jack got an instant rush of adrenaline. *They got him!* Is he still in custody?"

"Uhh, no, they just fucking kicked him loose. They only had him on the stolen car, and they don't hold non-violent felons."

"Damn-it, please tell me they ID'd him before they kicked him loose." Jack held his breath.

"Yeah, they did. Danny Fields is his name."

Jack heard the crack of the bat and the roar of the crowd. The trooper had hit a grand slam: the name. Jack had never heard of Danny Fields. Why should he? But when a name is finally attached to a suspect who's consumed the time and energy of so many people it's like a spotlight suddenly lighting the sky. All the grueling days and sleepless nights gain meaning with a single name: *Danny Fields.* "Danny Fields," Jack said, tasting it. "Who's your contact in Texas?"

"A guy named Herman Porter. He's a detective. He sounds like he's got his shit together too."

"Good, what's his number?" Jack scribbled the number in to his notebook. Jack's mind was racing. "Okay Mike, listen real good, okay?"

"Yeah, yeah, sure. I'm listening."

"You tell your guys to rip that fucking vehicle to shreds. You hear me?"

"Yeah, I hear you."

"That .44 Magnum is definitely in that SUV!"

"Okay, sir. I'll tell them."

"Excellent! Do me a favor. Call me when you guys find that gun."

"Yes sir, will do!"

Jack punched in Porter's number. He answered on the first ring. "This is Detective Porter."

"Hello Detective Porter. I'm Jack Paige"

"I've been waiting for your call Detective Paige. And please, call me Herman." His voice sounded articulate and bright.

"Sure thing Herman."

"I guess you know why I'm calling?"

"I do. I'm sorry we couldn't hold him. If we only knew sooner."

"I understand, it happens. I'm just glad you guys got him ID'd."

"We got cops searching all over for him."

"Hopefully they'll pick him up."

"Or kill him. This is Texas, Jack."

"Right, sorry."

"I just need an email address from you. I got a six-pack of photos, including Danny Fields. I'll shoot them over to you."

"Excellent, you read my mind," said Jack.

"Is there anything else I can do for you?"

"Yeah, let me give you my partner's name and number too. In case you can't reach me."

"Sure."

Jack gave Casey's info to Herman.

"Anything else?"

"Yeah, what does Danny look like?"

"Well, he's a white boy. He's 34-years-old. He's 6'-3" and skinny. It says here, 165 pounds. His head is shaved. It looks new cause' there's some tan lines. He looks like a doper, all sunken' in."

"Are you always this dialed in, Herman?"

"I try."

"You're doing one helluva job! Can you fill me in on the details surrounding his arrest?"

Herman Porter filled in Jack on the rest of the details before they hung up. They headed for the police department. Jack's cell phone rang just as they arrived at the office. Jack recognized the number on the caller ID. It was Trooper Mike Simpson.

"Hey Mike, what's up?"

"They got it, detective. Just like you said."

"Outstanding." Jack gave Casey the thumbs up sign.

"It's a .44 magnum revolver. The serial number is ground down, but our lab will try to pull it up."

"I'll have our crime scene guys email you the ballistics on our case. You'll have it in 10 minutes."

"They also found a box of ammunition. Everything was tucked up under the dash. The fucker hid it in a wiring harness. It would've been a bitch to find."

"It's going to match the gun that killed your friend, no doubt," said Jack.

"I promise you one thing for sure, Detective Paige."

"What's that Mike?"

"It's gonna be a helluva race between you guys and us to see who's first to catch this son-of-a-bitch."

"Mike, we're on the same side. We all want the same thing. I promise."

"I'm not sure I agree with you on that one, sir. It's tragic he killed that girl. But that mother fucker killed one of my best friends."

"I understand, Mike. I really do."

TWENTY

Traffic was heavy and being that the San Francisco Airport is actually in San Bruno, not San Francisco makes it a helluva drive back to downtown SF. It took them forever to get to the PD. Jack and Casey sat in Lieutenant Richards' office with the door closed. Now that the case was breaking Jack didn't want any possibility of a leak.

Jack sat on the edge of his chair and leaned forward. He looked like a sprinter in the starting blocks.

"Get out your notebook and pen." Jack waited a moment while Richards fished for writing materials.

"Now, write this down: Danny Fields." Jack exhaled, slid back in his chair and smiled for the first time in a week.

"Excellent, Jack!" Richards slammed his hand on the desk. "How the hell did you guys break it?"

"I just got off the phone with a detective from Nevada. They lost a state trooper. They think this scum, Danny, killed him during a car stop." Jack didn't hide his anger.

"That son-of-a-bitch," Richards muttered.

"Afterwards Danny drove to Texas and got pinched for having a stolen vehicle."

Richards looked up. "So?"

"Don't get too excited. They already kicked him loose. But at least they got him ID'd."

"Texas? Why's he in Texas?" Richards thought aloud. "Sorry Jack. What happened to the trooper? How'd that go down?"

"I didn't get all the details. But he was shot with a .44 Magnum."

"Richards nodded, making the connection in his mind.

"It was a real shitty scene for those poor bastards."

Richards swallowed hard, feeling the same chill Jack did.

The three men sat silent for a few seconds. Richards spoke first. "Did he have a family?"

"Yeah, a wife and two little girls." Jack's voice thickened.

Richards didn't say a word. He nodded his head from side to side and pursed his lips tight. His eyes took on a look cold and hardened.

Jack continued with the details, finishing up with the recovery of the gun.

"What's next Jack? What do you need?" Richards stopped writing and rubbed a cramp in his palm.

"On my way in here, I asked Andrew to fax the ballistic information to Nevada."

"Good."

"I also talked to a detective in Texas. He's emailing a six-pack of Danny so we can do a photo line up with Cody at the bar."

"Excellent. So I know what you told me about Kyle Sanders, but how does he fit into this case? I don't get it. And why did Danny go to Texas? Is he related to Kyle or Angola?"

"Hell if I know. We're working on that now. But either way, Kyle has some very specific information."

"What's he want?"

"He wants out of Angola. He's doing life and wants us to do a prisoner exchange so he can do his time in California."

"What the hell for?"

"I don't know. But it's his bargaining chip, and we don't have much choice at this point."

"Do you wanna' get him out? Is it worth it now?"

"Yeah, I think it is. I mean, we gotta' find out who he talked to. It's important."

"Okay, I'll back you on it then."

"Thanks ... I'll write a quick affidavit and get a spring order for him. I think I can get Judge Ambrose to sign it. I figure we get him out and over here first, and then we can work out the exchange later."

"Where you gonna' house him?"

"I'll call my buddy in Sacramento at the Board of Prisons and make arrangements to house him at San Quentin. If that don't work, fuck it, we'll throw him in the county jail."

"Sounds good."

"Casey can use the same affidavit and get a Ramey Warrant on Danny. That way, we don't need to file the entire case with the DA's Office. It's far from ready anyway. We don't have time to wait for an Arrest Warrant."

"Casey, do you have a judge for the Ramey?"

"Absolutely, boss."

There was a knock at the door. "Come in," Richards yelled.

The door opened slightly and Andrew peeked in. "Sorry to interrupt Lieutenant. We just got the call. The media discovered the place Lisa was murdered. That reporter, Traci Townsend is doing a live report. It's on Channel Four."

"Thanks Andrew." Richards used the remote to turn on the television hanging in the corner of his office.

The station flashed the San Francisco Police badge on the screen. It was the same background they used on all crime stories. The letters

'Special Report' flashed across the screen.

The anchor said, "We're going live to Reporter Traci Townsend. She has learned of an incredible break in the Lisa Russell murder. Traci?"

"Don't tell me either of you have done a press release," said Richards.

"Press release? We just got back for Christ's sakes," said Jack.

Traci looked spectacular, gleaming with the inner glow of her secret. She stood with the park scene as backdrop.

"Thanks, Bill." Her TV voice wasn't so sweet, though sex still permeated her delivery. "Earlier, we discovered Lisa Russell was murdered 50 yards from where I'm standing." She pointed. "Just beyond those bushes in the park." The camera panned to the area.

"Even more incredible, we've learned from sources close to the investigation, that there is an inmate, named Kyle Sanders in Angola State Penitentiary in Louisiana, who knew Lisa Russell was going to be murdered."

"What the fuck?" Jack jumped from his chair.

"Our Channel Four Action Team contacted officials at Angola. They have confirmed they have an inmate in their custody named Kyle Sanders. The officials would not confirm nor deny whether or not investigators from the San Francisco have spoken with Sanders."

All three watched, completely stunned. *What more could this bitch possibly say to fuck up this case*, thought Jack.

"We've just learned that the inmate is serving life in prison for a murder he committed 16 years ago." Traci smiled in triumph.

Jack stared, not even noticing the phone ringing on Richards' desk. Richards picked it up.

Onscreen Traci said: "This incredible case is certainly twisting and turning as we speak. Our investigators here will certainly need to ask Sanders to reveal how he came to his knowledge of the murder."

"I can't believe this is happening," Jack yelled.

Richards' face was beat red as a voice screamed through the phone. "I'll handle it, damn it!" Richards shouted. "I hate leaks!" Richards slammed down the phone. "That was the Chief. He's already getting calls. Get that asshole, Sanders, here ASAP!"

Casey was silent.

*   *   *

Judge Ambrose was great for law enforcement. He had started out as a cop decades earlier. He was smart enough to recognize the streets were mean and he wanted to work in a different part of the judicial system. He went to law school at night, graduated, passed the bar exam, and got a job at the District Attorney's office. He was a prosecutor for seven years, and then got elected to the bench. That was 15 years ago.

Jack had known Judge Ambrose since he was a young prosecutor. They had many trials together over the years. Judge Ambrose had presided in a good number of homicide trials where Jack was the lead investigator. Judge Ambrose had recognized that Jack was special, that he cared about people and was fair. It made no difference whether Jack was answering questions under direct or cross examination. He was open and honest to both sides. Jack had a unique appeal to jurors ... almost fatherly. They liked him. They saw that he was a professional who did it right. Prosecutors loved it. Defense attorneys hated it.

Jack liked Judge Ambrose's courtroom. American flags were framed on every wall. Some were tattered, others pristine. They represented a collection Judge Ambrose had assembled over decades. The bench was built with solid oak, hand-crafted and finished in high-gloss. All Superior Court judges rule their courtrooms from high in the bench. This courtroom actually felt like American justice.

From the corridor Jack peeked through the crack between the two tall doors. He didn't see attorney's backs or hear voices, so he assumed the court was quiet. He walked in to find Judge Ambrose relaxing in the Jury Box, talking with his deputy bailiff and clerk. Judge Ambrose wore a white shirt and tie, sans jacket or robe.

"Hi Jack," Judge Ambrose said, grinning across his courtroom. He put his hand to his forehead as if to concentrate. "Let me guess … the Russell murder."

"As usual, Judge, you're absolutely right." Jack hadn't calmed down from the news report.

"Then we better go into my office." Judge Ambrose pushed open the jury box gate and stepped out. He shook Jack's hand. "How are Sarah and the kids?"

"Good, Judge. Everyone's good."

"Excellent. Tell her I said hello." The Judge walked around the front of the bench to a door leading into a corridor. This corridor connected to every courtroom on the floor and had a private elevator for the judges. The Judge's chamber was directly behind his courtroom.

Jack took a seat in front of the red cherry desk with Judge Ambrose behind. The Judge eyed him. "You've got quite a case, Jack."

"It's breaking open, Judge, but there are twists."

"I thought as much. What do you need?"

Jack told Judge Ambrose the details and before he finished, Judge Ambrose nodded, already knowing what Jack needed. Then Jack paused, Judge Ambrose said, "I'll write the order to get Kyle to California."

"Thanks Judge," Jack said.

Within a few minutes the Judge had drafted and signed the order. "Good luck, my friend. Be careful. Your family needs you around."

Jack ran the order down to the Superior Court Clerk and had it imprinted, then he hurried it back to the office. Here was the key to Angola State Penitentiary and the secrets of Kyle Sanders.

TWENTY ONE

Danny smiled when he saw the freeway sign for the airport. He desperately needed two things — and both would be there.

He pulled into a seedy neighborhood full of rundown government housing: two-story red-brick apartments landscaped with cement and half-dead crabgrass. Near every third building a broken-down swing set sat in a bedding of dried-up tan bark. Cyclone fencing lined the perimeter. Curtains wafted outside screen-less open windows. The front doors on some the apartments hung open. Children in diapers played in the dirt, their hands and faces filthy. No one watched them.

They're lucky I'm no child molester, Danny thought. *I could take any one of them.*

The ground shook as jets thundered overhead. The children seemed unaware that they were growing up on the end of a runway.

Danny quickly spotted what he came for. The guy was standing on the corner with no intention to cross. His head was swiveling, searching for customers, cops or some other dealer wanting to gun him down. The slightest hint of a cop would send him running on a pre-determined route, usually over fences.

Danny rolled up in his car and waved the dealer to his window. The guy looked around, and then approached with his hand tucked deep under his shirt and into his waistband. Danny knew he was a new customer, and this dude wasn't going to take chances. Danny played it cool, He wasn't here to do a dope rip; he just wanted to buy his shit and go. It took Danny exactly 20 seconds to score his beloved crank. *Why can't supermarkets work that fast?*

From the ghetto Danny headed straight for the airport, and then followed the signs to the long-term parking lot. He grabbed a ticket from the machine. The arm lifted and folded away so he could drive in. He covered his face as he passed under the camera aimed at the entrance. He parked in an area crowded with cars and close to the pick-up area for the shuttle bus.

His luck with the cold plate at the last motel sucked. He wasn't going to make the same mistake twice. He needed to dump this car for one that would stay cold for at least a couple of days. Danny tried his shaved key in two cars without luck. The third was a charm.

When Danny drove back out the parking attendant looked at him and his ticket. "You've only been here eight minutes."

"Yeah, I'm real sorry man; I got screwed up and took a wrong turn. It took me awhile to find my way out."

The attendant gave Danny a look of disgust. The gate lifted. The attendant waved Danny through without taking any money.

Danny headed straight for his sister's house with his crank and his very cold car.

*   *   *

When Jack returned from court he was thankful he could slip through the side door. The media had taken over the front lobby. Extended booms with satellite dishes reached into the sky. Both street and parking lot were lined with coaches from every major station. Jack was surprised no one was selling silk-screened T-Shirts adorned with Lisa's face. The crime scene and the leak had put the story back in the lead. They were starved for details, but Jack wasn't about to give them any. They were close to putting this one down.

When Jack got back in the office things were moving. Casey had the Ramey Warrant for Danny, and Andrew was looking for Jack.

"Jack, Herman Porter emailed me the six-pack," Andrew said. "I printed it and gave it to Richards."

"Excellent, things will tighten up when Cody picks him out."

Jack and Casey met with Richards and saw the image of Danny. This one's eyes looked steely cold.

"He cut his hair. It's way shorter than what the bartender said," said Casey.

"Good ... sign of guilt. He's trying to change his appearance. I love when they do stupid shit like that," said Jack.

"Do you want to show this or you want someone else to go?" Richards asked.

"Someone else. We got to get moving." Jack nodded toward Casey.

"Got it," Richards left to find another detective and returned quickly. "It's on its way."

"Thanks, boss. We need to brief the Mayor and his wife. We'll let them know we have a suspect now."

"I'm surprised it hasn't been leaked yet," said Richards.

"Maybe it has. Everything else has been leaked ..." Jack said with disgust.

"After we brief the Mayor, we'll head straight to Texas. Hopefully, we can get Danny in pocket and then work on getting him extradited. Then we can hop over to Angola and grab Kyle."

Richards nodded. "I'll handle the media. I haven't figured out yet what the hell to say about Kyle."

"Just try to keep them about two steps behind us." *Such a crazy relationship, Jack thought. We chase the bad guys and the media chase us. And we always have to keep that gap between us and them until the end.*

*   *   *

This time Jack was glad to meet with the Mayor. Now they were on the road to doing something good, the first step in healing the loss. Without answers closure never occurs.

They sat in the same living room, this time with Mrs. Russell there. Jack was glad to see she was able to get out of bed. The four of them collectively looked like they had been to hell and back. Mrs. Russell's eyes moved but never focused — a symptom of heavy sedation.

"Sir, we've identified a suspect," Jack let the news sink in.

"Is he in custody? Has he confessed?" The Mayor's hands started to shake. Jack didn't know if it was from shock or anger.

"No, we don't have him yet. He's on the run. We think he's in Texas."

"What's his name?" It was the first words Mrs. Russell spoke. Her voice was deep and raspy.

Jack looked at her and saw her staring with foggy eyes.

"Danny Fields."

"I never heard of him. Did Lisa know him?" Mrs. Russell asked.

"We don't think so, but we're not sure yet."

Jack did not disclose that the case did not appear random. He didn't have answers for the questions they would ask. Instead he gave an abridged version.

He saw the pain and disgust in their faces as he reached the part about the Trooper Haynes. They saw that others were losing so much to Danny Fields. As he finished all four of them stared at one another, each caught up in thoughts, processing information and wondering.

"We … my wife and I saw the news report. Who is this man in prison that knew about Lisa?"

"He sent us details about the case. We met him. He wants to be moved in exchange for information." Jack realized his answer sounded confusing without the background information.

"You mean there was a witness?" The Mayor looked shocked.

"Not an eye witness, no. This guy has been locked up in Angola for 16 years. He committed a murder when he was young, and he's doing life."

"I'm confused," The Mayor shook his head as if to clear his thoughts. "You already know who killed Lisa, right?"

"Yes, sir. But, this guy knows details about the murder. He told us details before we even identified the suspect."

The Mayor nodded, obviously still confused.

Jack went slowly. "We have to find out how he knew. We can't leave it open. What we did was negotiated a deal. We're bringing him back to California to do his time, and then he'll talk."

"How come all of this has to do with the South? I mean... Angola, and ... Texas, I don't get it?"

"That's what we're trying to figure out."

"Lisa has never even been to the South," He said.

"I think Danny is from the South, I think that's the key," said Jack.

"Sir, the media is all over the case and as usual, we wanted you to hear the facts from us rather than from a leak," Casey said.

"I see," said the Mayor.

"We have to go now. We're heading to Texas. Do you have any other questions?" Jack asked.

"We have a million, but I don't think you can answer them," said the Mayor.

Jack and Casey left the Mayor and his wife standing in the doorway with their arms around one another.

*　　　*　　　*

When Jack and Casey returned Andrew was waiting.

"Big news guys! The lab called, Lisa came back positive with Rohypnol. You were right Jack, she was drugged."

"It's coming together," Jack said. "There's something else, right?"

"Yeah, the gun matches too; it's the same in both cases."

"Andrew paused a second then dropped the bomb. "Cody picked out Danny in the six-pack. He's positive on the ID. You guys got him!"

I knew it would all match up, Jack thought. It felt good to finally hear the words.

Jack looked at Casey. "You ready to go get Danny?"

"Hell ya', let's go get that fucker!"

"Then let's go."

TWENTY TWO

Jack and Casey landed in Texas and rented a non-descript SUV. Jack drove and Casey navigated.

"Let's go see Herman Porter," said Jack.

"Cool." Casey snapped his fingers. "Ahh man, we forgot to call him. You think he'll be there?"

"From the sound of Herman, he'll be there. And besides, we didn't call ahead on purpose."

"Why's that?"

"I'm not real trusting of cops I don't know. I feel better if they don't know when we're coming."

Casey changed the subject. "Good job on the rental, this is a nice ride," He rubbed the sill under the window.

"Yeah, I like it too. And we can shut off the automatic headlights. We need that."

"Oh yeah, it's fuckin' tough to do surveillance in these new cars, man. You can never turn off the lights. It sucks."

"Plus, we don't have a hotel, this is it."

Casey nodded.

"Did the Nevada Troopers say when they were gettin' here?"

"Late tonight. I plan on us being on Danny before they touch down."

Casey gave Jack directions to the Texas State Trooper Headquarters. On this, his second trip south within 48 hours, Jack felt hot and tired. He was relieved when the building's air conditioning hit him full blast. The officer behind the counter reminded Jack of the prison officer at Angola.

"Hello, gentlemen. How can I help you?" He was as polite as a concierge in a five-star hotel.

Is everyone down here this polite? Jack wondered. *Where are the pissed-off front desk cops I'm used to?*

"Hi, we're from the San Francisco Police Department-Homicide." Jack held out his credentials. "We're looking for Herman Porter. He's been helping us out."

"Yes, sir, Detective Porter is here, but he didn't say he was expecting ya'll." The officer inspected Jack's badge and identification card.

"Yeah, sorry about that. We were rushed to catch the flight. I didn't have a chance to call ahead."

"Yes, I see."

"We've been working on this case and weren't really sure when we'd get here, too." Jack said.

"He did tell me there were some fellas coming from Nevada. I believe they'll be here later tonight."

Jack smiled. *I guess Nevada cops are a lot more trusting than I am.*

"Let me call Detective Porter for ya'll," The officer picked up the phone and had a short conversation. Jack couldn't hear what he whispered into the phone. Within seconds, a handsome gentleman came in from a secured door.

Detective Porter was a slight man with a perfectly cropped short afro. His hair reminded Jack of Colin Powell's. He wore a perfectly-tailored, lightweight navy blue suit. His yellow tie had touches of violet that accented the subtle stripe in his suit. His white shirt had medium starch with a French cuff. His cufflinks matched the violet, and his Italian shoes had stylish buckles on the side. Herman wore a small pin in his left lapel indicating he was a detective. He was exactly what Jack imagined from the phone call: he looked like a Southern Baptist television preacher. *Perfect.*

Detective Porter extended his soft hand. "Hello gentlemen, I'm Herman." No titles or rank.

"Hi Herman, I'm Jack. This is Casey."

"I didn't expect ya'll so soon. I thought you might call first." Porter raised an eyebrow.

"Yeah Herman, I apologize for not calling ahead." Jack said while running his fingers through his hair. He could tell Herman clearly knew they'd never intended to call ahead.

"I understand," he smiled.

"By the way, thank you for the Six-Pack. We got a positive ID on Danny with it."

"Excellent! I have some other stuff for ya'll as well. Follow me, please." Herman unlocked the secured door and held it open for Jack and Casey. They walked down a short hallway into a small detective office. There was nobody else there.

"I understand ya'll working together with the Nevada State Police."

"Right, yeah, we are." Jack stumbled on his answer. "You see, we're working together to some degree ..."

"Of course, I understand."

"Frankly, it's tragic about the trooper. We've all lost friends, but the priority is to just catch this asshole."

"I agree," said Herman. He turned toward a table and a stack of papers.

"I did a workup on Danny. Here's his info." He handed the papers to Jack. Jack noticed yellow highlighting on several sheets.

"Here are four addresses Danny used while in Texas. He did time here for sexual battery. He also did about eight years in Louisiana for a rape. He's been out about five months now. He skipped parole. They've been looking for him, kind of ..."

"Was he in Angola?" Jack asked.

"Angola? I don't believe so, but he could have been, I guess. Why?"

"We have a snitch in Angola that said the killer told him he was planning to murder our victim."

"Interesting, what's his name?"

"Kyle Sanders. He's been in 16 years for murder."

"Have you checked him in the Family Court files?"

"No, I don't think we can do that from California." Jack had never heard of a Family Court File. "You mean like, divorce files?"

"Well, not exactly. I mean, we have a link analysis system that mines all public files: Welfare, Section 8, the usual. We have good reciprocal files with Louisiana too. That's how I got the address for Danny's sister's house." Herman pointed to a highlighted paper in Jack's hands.

"Nice work."

"I ran a credit check on him and he once listed her on a credit card application as a referral. I ran a check on her and she still owns the same house as she did back then. She's never been arrested. Here's a printout of her car with the address." He pointed to the highlight.

"Outstanding work, Herman." Jack said, genuinely impressed.

"Give me the details on Kyle Sanders; I'll see what I can do."

Jack gave Herman Kyle's vitals.

"I gave you the other addresses, but I think they're crash pads at best. They're all pretty close to his sister's house."

"How far is this?" Jack asked.

"It's about three-hours drivin'. Ya'll gonna' eat before you go?"

"No, we're anxious to get going. Well grab something on the road."

"All right, I listed the numbers for the local Sheriff, the Parrish Police and the State Police on back of one of those papers. You may need them."

"Herman, you've been a great help. Thank you."

"My pleasure gentlemen, I wish I could join ya'll. There's nothing more I would rather do than nail Danny."

They exchanged business cards. Herman gave them written directions to the county where Danny's sister lived. They were back on the highway. The cool air from the air conditioner felt good on Jack's face.

"I like the way he works," said Jack.

"That dude's got his shit together," Casey said as he wiped the sweat off his brow.

*   *   *

Danny had relaxed for a couple of days. His sister's house hadn't changed since his last visit. He hadn't seen her since he arrived so he figured she was out of town for a while. No big deal. She always loved when he popped in for a visit. She was a creature of habit. She always left a spare key in a small wooden shoe in the outside laundry room. Danny found the key and helped himself to her food, full bar, clean shower and linens.

Her ranch-style house was modest, in a neighborhood surrounded by similar homes. They were small, but comfortable, and cleverly situated on small lots with lots of privacy. It was a perfect place to hide out for a couple of months.

Even if the neighbors noticed him, it didn't matter; he belonged. This was his sister's house. She welcomed him, even though she wasn't home.

As he parked his newly-acquired vehicle in the driveway, Danny felt safe.

TWENTY THREE

By the time Jack and Casey found Danny's sister's house it was the middle of the night. There was no light but that from the street.

"There's a car in the driveway. Can you catch the plate?" Jack asked as they came up on the address. Jack shut off their headlights.

"Yeah, got it! It's different from the one Porter gave us. Different car too."

"I don't see the sister's car anywhere," said Jack.

"Me neither." Casey dialed his cell phone.

Jack heard him give the plate to the dispatcher and then hang up.

Jack eased the SUV along the curb, three houses away on the opposite side of the street. They had a good view of the front of the house and the car.

Casey's cell phone buzzed. He answered it, and Jack listened, keeping his eyes on the house.

"Okay ... it isn't hot? Do us a favor, call the registered owner and see if they know where their car is. Yeah, man, I'll hang on." Casey glanced at Jack. Jack nodded in agreement. "Yeah, I'm still here," Casey said. He listened for a moment. "No, that's all for now. Yeah, just leave a message on their answering machine. Hopefully they'll call back. Cool thanks, later." Casey hung up.

"The R/O lives three hours from here. You heard right?"

"Yeah, except it's hot and he's in there," said Jack.

They sat in silence for several minutes. Jack felt edgy. "This is one extremely dangerous dude — and we're on our own. We need to keep our cool, okay?"

"I hear you, Jack."

"Let's hop in the backseat. The windows are tinted darker and we won't get spotted." The two men climbed over the consol between the front seats, nearly kicking each other in the process. Once back there they settled in. Casey munched on sunflower seeds. They had several bottles of water. It was just enough for a long night.

A few hours later dawn light shone in the east. "Stakeouts were easier when I was younger," Jack yawned. He stretched and twisted at the waist. In the cramped space it was the best he could do.

"Dude, I'd kill for a fuckin' Starbucks right now." Casey's voice grated from lack of sleep and too many sunflower seeds.

"Yeah, me too. Hey, Casey, hand me that empty bottle."

Casey passed the plastic water bottle to Jack.

"One time I was on this stakeout all night," said Jack while cutting the top off the bottle.

"Yeah?"

"I had to piss so bad I couldn't think straight. I split to a gas station for two minutes. When I got back, the fucking guy was gone."

"Ahhh man, that sucks! Did you tell them how you lost the dude?"

"I had to. What else could I say?"

"That's some embarrassing shit, dude," Casey chuckled.

"From then on ... I pissed in a bottle," said Jack as he filled the bottle.

"Fuck! Jack! There he is!" Casey jumped up and pointed.

Jack didn't dare look up.

"He just came out of the house." Casey watched. "Yeah, that's the fucker, I can tell from here, dude."

"Okay, okay," said Jack, he wasn't finished.

Casey gave a play-by-play. "He's putting a jacket or something in the car. Yep, that's definitely him. This dude is fuckin' squirrelly. He's checking everything out. Fuck! He's looking our way! Duck!" Casey slid lower into the rear seat. Jack tried to do the same, but his situation was a bit more complicated.

"What's he doing now?" Jack finished his business without spilling.

"He's going back inside. Maybe he's gonna' split?" Casey sat up straight.

Jack got an adrenaline rush that made him forget his sore body. "Did he spot us?"

"He eyeballed the shit out of us, but there's no way he could see us back here. It's way too dark."

*   *   *

Danny went out to throw a light jacket in the car. He figured he'd gotten his use out of the car, and planned to drive it a few miles away and dump it. Then he spotted the SUV a few houses away. *Was that there last night?* He wondered. He couldn't remember. The bummer was he couldn't see the fucking thing from a window. That sucked. Unexplained SUVs and vans made him nervous. Some might call it paranoia, but he knew it was just being safe. He decided to stay put. He could dump the car later, after the SUV was gone. Y*ou die if you fly,* he thought. *This bird would avoid the hunter.*

Danny tucked his 9mm pistol in the front of his pants, then went out the back door and walked around the house toward the front fence. He grabbed a wooden crate and placed it next to the fence so he could peek over. He watched the SUV.

*   *   *

Jack quickly ran through their limited choices. "Option one: We let him split and try tailing him while we call in for help from the locals. Problem is it's getting daylight and we only got one car. We'd get burned in a heartbeat."

"I agree," said Casey.

"Option two: Let him get in the car, then jam him. But I don't think this SUV will block the entire driveway. It's too wide."

"Plus, we don't have a fuckin' light or siren. If he runs we're fucked," said Casey.

"Yeah, you're right. Okay, option three: call and wait for back-up. If he splits, we explain to Richards and the Mayor why we let him drive away." Jack winced at the thought.

"That's a shitty option."

"Option four: I hit the front and you go to the rear."

"I like it! Fuck him, Let's go get that dude," said Casey.

Jack grabbed the door handle and held that position. His breath was heavy from excitement. Casey held the same position at the other door.

"Nice and slow, buddy. Are you ready?"

"Yeah, ready."

"Then let's go get that asshole!"

They opened their doors and got out.

*   *   *

Danny saw the rear passenger doors of the SUV open. Two guys in suits got out. *Fuck!* This ain't good, he thought. They moved quickly toward the house. Danny felt the bottom fall out of his stomach. A wind gust blew one guy's jacket open. Danny saw the glint of a badge, a glimpse of a gun. *Shit! How did they find me here?*

He considered shooting them, and then realized they may not be alone. He should have looked around for other vehicles or cops. He'd had tunnel-vision for the SUV. Now he scanned the street. No other cops in view, and he hadn't seen any climbing over the back fence.

If he fired now, everyone would hear the gunshots, and the place would be crawling with cops within minutes. *They must've spotted me when I went to the car. Why hide? They know I'm here.*

Danny had his own options, but all of them sucked. He saw the bigger cop head toward the front door. He lost sight of the second cop but he figured that one was coming around back. *Shit!* He needed to find cover, fast. That cop would be in the back yard in seconds. Danny quietly ran toward the outside laundry room and dove into the heavy cover of the bushes. He pushed himself as deep as possible into the shrubbery. Within seconds, the smaller cop appeared near the corner of the house. He was crouched low and moved slowly. His gun was drawn, pointing forward.

Did he see me hide? Danny's heart pounded so hard he thought the cop could hear it. He sat as still as possible. Even the slightest movement would rustle the shrubs. The cop paused and scanned the yard. He looked back and forth between the back of the house and the laundry room. Danny ever so slowly raised his gun so he could better aim. The cop didn't seem to look in his direction or focus toward the shrubs. *That was good.* The cop was in a tactical dilemma and Danny knew it. He didn't feel safe with his back to the laundry room without first checking to see if it was clear.

Danny made his decision. If the second the cop fixed on him, he'd fucking waste him. The cop moved slowly across the lawn. He stared directly at Danny while he advanced. Danny couldn't believe the cop couldn't see him. Danny's hands shook so badly it was hard to steady his gun. Sweat poured down his face, stinging his eyes. He aimed through the bushes, squeezed one eye shut and put the bead of his gun sight directly on the cop's forehead. He put pressure on the trigger and felt the hammer draw back. *As soon as he sees me, he's dead,* thought Danny. He intensely watched the cop's face as he moved closer: looking for a hint of recognition or a sudden look of shock.

The cop was 10 feet away and closing the distance quickly. He had to decide now. *Shoot this fucker or don't.* He squeezed the trigger harder, keeping it fixed on the cop's forehead. Squeezing, waiting for the gun to explode. Suddenly, the cop's eyes shifted. Danny was a split second from blowing his head off. The cop's focus was the doorway of the laundry room, not him. It was right next to him. The cop moved toward the laundry room doorway. The cop hadn't spotted him. Danny eased the pressure on the trigger. The cop passed within three feet of him, then disappeared into the laundry room. *Perfect!*

Danny heard the faint sound of wood breaking from the house. A voice — the other cop — yelled: "Police!" Danny knew the other cop would be busy searching the house for a few minutes. He had a fraction of time. He couldn't waste a single second. Danny pushed himself from the confines of the bushes and rushed into the laundry room, following the cop. He saw the washer and dryer to his left and a small folding table to his right. The cop was opening a vented closet door at the rear with one hand while pointing his gun with the other.

Danny put his gun to the back of the cop's head and said with eerie calmness: "Freeze mutha' fucker or I'll blow your fuckin' brains out."

The cop did it, tensing up like a tiger.

Danny felt a sense of calm amidst the chaos. "You ever wonder if you hear the gunshot when you get shot in the head at point-blank range?"

"Ahh, no," the cop answered.

Danny wondered if you heard it or not: He was amused by his clever discussion. "You don't wanna' find out."

"No, no I don't Danny."

The mention of his name enraged him. How could this fucking cop know his name?

"What the fuck did you call me?"

"Danny. I called you Danny, Isn't that your name?"

These fuckers know who I am. They came lookin' just for me, he thought. What the fuck do I have to lose now?

"What you fuckers want? Why you here?"

"Don't make shit worse for yourself, Danny … there's a shitload of cops on their way, dude."

"Shut the fuck up!"

"Just run, Danny … I'm tellin' you man, don't make shit worse for yourself. Just split."

"So you can shoot me in the back? Fuck you!" I ain't stupid."

"Okay, okay. Then … just take it easy, dude."

"I said shut your fuckin' mouth. Now, slide your gun across the floor, nice and slow, fucker."

The cop hesitated.

"Hey, asshole, you're taking too long! In case you haven't noticed, I got you. You wanna' die today?"

"No, no man. I don't wanna' die. Just take it easy dude."

"You're not as fuckin' stupid as you look."

The cop put his gun on the floor and slid it away.

"Get on your knees and put your arms straight out."

The cop complied. Danny searched around the cop's waistband while holding the gun to his head. He took the handcuffs that hung from the rear of the waistband.

"Do you carry a backup? Don't lie mother fucker, or I'll kill you."

"I don't carry a backup. You got my only gun."

"Get your fuckin' hands behind your back."

The cop complied.

Danny squeezed the handcuffs on him as tight as he could. Ass-hole cops had done it to him enough times. It felt good to give it back. Danny liked controlling this cop. It felt almost as good as raping a bitch that deserved it.

Danny rolled the cop on his side and searched the rest of his body for a gun. Luckily for the cop, he didn't find a backup. He grabbed the cop's gun off the floor; made sure the hammer wasn't cocked, and then slipped the gun in his back waistband. Danny reached over, grabbed the cop's sleeve and said, "Get up!"

Danny tucked himself in as tight as he could behind the cop. He grabbed the back of the cop's hair with one hand, stuck his gun to the side of his head and asked, "What's your partner's name?"

"Jack."

"Let's go talk to Jack. Nice and slow, asshole. Keep your mouth shut or I'll kill you. Got it?"

The cop nodded.

They walked slowly across the backyard toward the rear door. Danny opened it, and they stepped into the all-white kitchen. Danny heard the other cop searching another part of the house.

"Shhhhh ... don't say a word fucker," he whispered. They stood motionless in the middle of the kitchen. Danny kept the muzzle of his gun pressed into the side of the cop's head. Minutes felt like hours. Danny heard the other cop moving closer toward the kitchen. Danny decided not to call out. He wanted the cop to be surprised. The cop turned the corner into the kitchen and froze. "Hi Jack," said Danny.

After a split second, Jack raised his gun, and then began backing out of the kitchen.

"Yo, yo yo, mutha' fucker, wait! Stop!"

"The cop kept backing up and pointing his gun."

"Stop now fucker! If you back out of here, I'm gonna waste this fucker."

Jack stopped, but kept his gun pointed at them.

"Listen Jack, put your gun on the floor and slide it toward me, nice and easy."

"Go fuck yourself!" said Jack.

Danny was well concealed. He knew the cop didn't have a shot.

"Casey, you okay?"

"Hey mutha' fucker, I'm running this show, not you! Shut yo' fuckin' mouth!" screamed Danny.

"He's got me handcuffed, Jack. Don't let this asshole go!"

"I said shut up." Danny twisted the cop's hair tighter in his fist.

"Jack, listen to me," yelled Casey. "Kill this fucker!"

"Put your gun down, man. You don't want me killin' your buddy. Put your fuckin' gun down."

"Don't do it Jack! Fuck him. Shoot us both!"

"Why'd you do it Danny? Why Lisa?" Jack knew he had to distract Danny if he were to have a shot at winning.

"Fuck you! Shut up man, shut up, and put your fuckin' gun down!" His voice rapidly became desperate.

"You had it all planned out since Angola. Kyle Sanders told us."

"Who? What?"

"Kyle Sanders ... Angola ... you know?"

"I don't know what the fuck you're talking about! Shut your mouth, now!"

"Jack, fuck it dude, take the shot. Fuck him, take the shot ... I understand, man."

"Did you do it alone, Danny? Or did you have a friend help you?"

"Fuck you!" He screamed. "You don't know what the fuck you're talking about."

"Lisa Russell ... the girl from the bar."

"Fuck her. She's lucky I didn't fuck her hard too. He's gonna' die, man, if you don't put your gun down."

Jack kept his aim. He could only see a small portion of Danny's head.

Casey struggled but his attempts were futile.

"Jack, I'm telling you!" Danny screamed. "Don't be stupid. Listen … you gotta' listen to me, man, I'm gonna cuff you up like your friend here, okay? And I'll be on my way."

Casey screamed, "Jack, don't do it. He's lying. Shoot this fucker, Jack! Please, I forgive you, man. I really do. Please, please, please … kill this mother fucker, Jack. Shoot us both now!

Jack's head spun like a top. This was something he'd never experienced in his life.

"Jack, listen!" Casey screamed. "Shoot us both! Don't let this fucker walk out of here!"

"Shut up! Shut your fuckin' mouth!" Danny rattled Casey's head.

"Jack, don't listen to him. I could have already wasted him and you. I got no reason to kill you fuckers. Don't make me do it! Put your gun down."

"Kyle Sanders, you remember him, right? Angola?" Jack tried to keep Danny talking.

"What ? Who?"

Casey screamed hysterically, "Jesus Christ, Jack! Shoot him now!"

"Shut up asshole!" Danny screamed.

The situation was surreal. Things moved in slow motion. The screams muffled in Jack's ears, and his whole focus was his front sight and Casey's face. He could see the machined marks on the front sight of his gun. He saw red veins in Casey's eyes. Their cops' eyes locked onto one another. Jack felt like Casey was trying to tell him something.

"Jack, put down your gun. Don't be stupid, man!" yelled Danny.

"My heart, I … I have a bad..." Casey coughed and spit flew out his mouth.

Jack kept his gun pointed at Casey's head. They were eight feet apart from one another. *Bad heart? What? Is he setting up something?*

Jack took deep breaths, calming himself. His arms and shoulders burned as he steadied his gun. It felt like a 20-pound weight in his hands.

Casey coughed harder then suddenly jerked and twisted his head sideways.

Jack saw three quarters of Danny's face. He instinctively squeezed the trigger. His gun exploded. The muzzle flash blinded him. He felt the fear of God. Casey and Danny crashed to the floor. Jack didn't know which one he shot.

The kitchen filled with the sweet aroma of blood and burnt gunpowder. Both men were heaped together on the floor. It was a bloody mess. Someone moaned — and then moaned again, the same man. Casey rolled over onto his side. His eyes were open. The side of his head and face were covered in blood. Jack saw Danny on his back on the white kitchen tile. His right eye and the top-right portion of his head were blown off. His left eye was fixed open and glazed like a dead fish. His mouth was stuck open in a silent scream. Casey was covered with Danny's blood.

"Dude, get these fucking cuffs off me."

It was over. The chase ended with Danny dead on his back, in his sister's beautiful kitchen. *She'll love the police for this,* Jack thought.

*   *   *

Jack and Casey sat at the kitchen table with Danny dead on the floor. Casey's gun was still in Danny's waistband. They would wait for the local police to remove it. Jack watched Casey fumble with the cell phone. His hands shook, and he had trouble dialing the local police. His wrists looked branded from the tight handcuffs and then the fall.

Jack called Richards. "Hey, boss."

"You guys got him?" Richards asked.

"Yeah ... kind of, I guess."

"Ahh shit, don't tell me?"

"Yeah, he's dead."

"Are you guys okay?"

"Yeah, we're good," Jack gave him details of the shooting.

"He didn't know Kyle?" Richards asked.

"He acted like he didn't. Maybe he was bullshitting."

"This case is crazy. And this place is a media circus. The Warden at Angola called me. He said reporters are showing up at the prison requesting an interview with Kyle for Christ's sakes! Kyle Sanders has become a household name!"

"What? That's insane," said Jack. *Everything had become insane to him. How the hell did Kyle know about the case? How did that bitch Traci Townsend know about Kyle? It didn't click together. One thing for sure, he was going to find out soon.*

"Are you guys okay to pick up Kyle? I can send someone else."

"No, we got it. I'll keep you posted." Jack hung up.

Casey was off the phone too. "Fuck! I'm sorry, man. That was so fucked up. I put you in a fucked up situation, dude."

"It wasn't your fault Casey. If I went around back, it would've been me, not you." Jack paused a moment. "I wouldn't have been smart enough to pretend I was having a heart attack."

"Pretend? Dude, who the hell was pretending? I thought I was going to die!"

Jack pondered a moment then said, "I don't get it, Casey. Do you think Danny was lying about Kyle?"

"I don't know, Jack. He had to be, right?"

Jack heard sirens approaching. Within seconds he heard a voice at the front door, "Police! Are you detectives in there?"

"Yeah, we're in the kitchen," Jack yelled.

TWENTY FOUR

Kyle couldn't help but smirk as he packed his letters and hand-drawn porn into a box. He didn't expect the detectives to move so quickly. *It wasn't like he was complaining about it either.* The Warden himself called Kyle to his office to tell him he was being moved right away. He hoped to see that fucker Pierce before he left. Just to see the look on his face. Pierce could go fuck himself, tonight and every night from now on.

Kyle finished packing, picked up his box of worldly possessions and called to the guard. "I'm done in here, sir!" With a loud crack the steel door electronically disengaged and fell ajar. Kyle pushed it open with his foot and stepped out onto the elevated steel walkway. He'd spent 16 years in that tiny cell, just about every day of his adult life. All those days had been supervised and planned by other people. It never changed. He felt a chill in his spine and a sense of fear of the change.

"Hey Sanders! Where you goin'?" An inmate yelled.

"Hey movie star! Don't tell us you're moving to Hollywood!" Another screamed. Others laughed and whistled.

Kyle ignored them. He couldn't believe it was really happening, but finally the promise had been kept.

The guard marched him into the receiving area, usually reserved for new inmates.

"Sanders ... get in the shower," he barked.

Kyle undressed and complied.

"Wash your hair and brush your teeth. I don't want you stinkin' on the flight to California."

Kyle followed directions without saying a word.

After the shower, they strip-searched him and gave him deodorant. They sat at a table on the opposite side of the metal detector and X-rayed everything. Another guard packed his stuff into a small brown suitcase, and then waved Kyle through the metal detector. Kyle noticed Pierce coming through a door across the room. His face was beet red. Kyle had never seen him so pissed off. Kyle looked away and walked through the metal detector. Once he got to the other side, he was given underwear, socks, a pair of blue jeans, a white cotton button-up shirt and a pair of black shoes with laces removed. Laces could be used to strangle someone or to hang himself.

Not in 16 years had Kyle done anything like this. Breaking his daily routine seemed foreign. He would soon exit the front gate of Angola State Penitentiary long before he was dead — that wasn't supposed to happen.

Jack and Casey sat in the receiving area, their rental car was parked next to them. As the prisoner walked up carrying his suitcase Jack thought he almost looked human. Three guards escorted Kyle. Jack immediately noticed the prison shuffle, slow, with steps never more than 12 inches. That was years of muscle memory at work. Those feet would always feel shackled. Kyle stopped a few feet from Jack and Casey. He didn't speak.

"Hi Kyle, you remember us?" asked Jack.

Kyle stared.

"We're taking you to California. We got a lot to talk about, pal."

Kyle looked at both men and nodded his head. His face was expressionless.

"Put your hands out in front of you." Jack reached into his rear waistband and grabbed a pair of handcuffs from under his suit jacket.

Kyle set his suitcase at his side and complied.

"I'm going to handcuff you in the front. It's a long way back and you'll be more comfortable that way," Jack placed the cuffs on Kyle's wrists. "I'm double locking them so they won't get overly tight on you, okay?"

Kyle nodded without speaking.

Casey grabbed the small suitcase and threw it in the trunk of the rental car.

Jack opened the right front passenger door. He stepped back and told Kyle, "Get in and buckle the seat belt."

Kyle sat in the seat. He noticed his window was rolled down. He reached up with his cuffed hands to grab the seat belt. It was the first time he ever used one. They'd never had a car when he was a kid and back then if you did get in a car no buzzers went off, making you comply. As an adult he'd only seen seatbelts on television. Casey and Jack shook hands with the guards and got in the car. Casey in the driver's seat and Jack directly behind Kyle.

There was a loud buzzer and a bell rang out. It sounded like a fire alarm, startling Kyle. Yellow warning lights on poles came to life, spinning and throwing light like a summer lightning storm. The large steel door rolled up slowly. Kyle stared out at the world. It revealed itself little by little as the door rolled toward the ceiling. Once the door was completely opened, the alarms and flashing lights stopped. Silence fell.

Kyle looked out the window at Pierce and caught him glaring. "Hey Pierce!" Kyle yelled.

Pierce looked shocked, like he expected Kyle didn't have the balls to say anything. It stunned the guards as well. Everyone stopped and stared, especially Pierce.

"I'll see you again … maybe on the outside, probably in hell."

Pierce froze for fear of what Kyle might say in front of the other guards.

"Either way, you best look over your shoulder. Cause' I'll be comin'."

"Fuck you Sanders! Fuck you!" exploded Pierce.

The other guards looked at Kyle and then back at Pierce with wonder on their faces.

Casey hit the gas and the window button at the same time.

"I take it you had some issues …," said Casey.

"Yes, sir. It's all good now, sir."

They drove through a section Kyle had never seen. Here inmates walked around unescorted, none shackled, some even holding rakes and brooms. They were working. Out here they had landscaping, bushes, trees and sidewalks. These were the low risk minimum security inmates. Kyle had known they existed, he just didn't know where. They passed through one additional security gate — the gate to the real outside world. The trees and bushes around the prison were bigger, more mature. Kyle had seen them once, 16 years before on his way in, a lifetime ago. He remembered them like it was yesterday.

Kyle seemed mesmerized by sights and scents. As soon as they left the receiving area, he was overcome with the clean sweet odor of fresh air. He could actually smell the fresh cut lawn and flowers. For years, the only scent he experienced was the pungent odor of the cleaning disinfectant used on the floors and walls. He quickly became accustomed to the smell of men who exercised but didn't shower. He actually had forgotten how sweet the outside world smelled. This was the outside.

A voice brought him back. "Kyle, I'm going to make something very clear to you right up front." Jack leaned over the seat onto Kyle's left shoulder.

"Yes, sir," Kyle whispered softly.

"I like you, but if you so much as think to reach for that door handle, I will blow your fucking head off."

Kyle didn't take the comment as threat. He knew Jack was simply explaining the absolute truth.

"I understand, sir."

"You are a convicted murderer. I haven't a single qualm in me. Handcuffed or not, I guarantee you, I'll shoot you before I allow you to escape."

Kyle nodded and watched Casey from the corner of his eye. Casey stared straight ahead, driving.

Jack continued. "I will not be on the national news because I let you escape. Quite frankly, nobody would give a damn if I killed you."

"Yes, sir, you're right."

"When we get to the airport, you're in custody for check fraud. We're extraditing you to California, got it?"

"Yes, sir."

"If we told them you were a murderer, the captain would never let us on the plane. We'd be driving back to California. And frankly, I'm not in the mood."

"Yes, sir."

Jack moved away from Kyle and sat back in his seat. "Oh Kyle, one more thing."

"Yes, sir?"

"Stop calling me 'sir.' I'm a detective."

"Yes ... detective."

They drove about 20 minutes without speaking. The swampland was endless and populated mostly with God-awful insects, poisonous snakes and man-eating reptiles. Those were the only things that survived the heat and unbearable humidity.

"Kyle, why don't you start telling us about the murder and how you know the details you had in the letter?" Jack asked.

Kyle felt a sense of panic. He hesitated a moment and looked toward Casey to see if he was going to say something too. Casey said nothing. He stared out the front windshield. He looked lost in thought and oblivious to Jack's question.

"I … uhhh, I will detective, just like I said. I'd feel a whole lot better if I started talkin' once we're on that jet. It'd be a lot harder for ya'll to turn around and take me back." He hoped Jack accepted the excuse.

Jack paused a long moment. It was dead quiet in the car. "Alright Kyle, I understand how you feel. Plus, it's a long flight."

He didn't have a shred of information except what was in that letter, and Jack would quickly figure it out. *Now would be a good time,* he thought.

"Hey, Jack, I gotta' piss like a fuckin' race horse. You mind if we pull over?" Casey looked at Jack in the rear-view mirror.

"Fine with me," Jack said, looking around at the empty landscape.

"Stop anywhere, there's nothing out here."

"How about you?" Casey asked Kyle.

"I gotta' piss too, if ya'll let me."

"Alright, I'll pull over and get you out."

Kyle wasn't sure how this worked, so he just followed along.

*   *   *

Richards made all the necessary notifications; first, about the shooting and then that Jack and Casey were picking up Kyle. He had to get the Mayor up to speed so that there would be no embarrassing surprises. He needed to brief the Press Information Officers. He did this personally so they would understand exactly what information they could release to the media. Reporters would be all over this thing within hours.

Richards' pager kept going off but he didn't even look to see who was calling. If they had to page him to reach him, they weren't important enough to talk to at his point. He had enough on his plate.

When he finally checked it, he realized Andrew was trying to get through. The damn thing was an emergency page. *What now? Andrew never pages me,* he thought. This happened just as Richards entered his office. Andrew was right there, with another phone message in hand.

"What's this?" Richards growled.

"Herman Porter called, said it's urgent, sir."

"Who the hell is Herman Porter?"

"The Detective in Texas who helped Jack and Casey. He sent that six-pack too."

"That's right. Jesus Christ! Does everybody have an emergency?"

Richards closed the door, sat down and dialed the number. Porter answered mid-ring on the first ring.

"This is Porter!" The Texan's voice was hurried.

"Porter, this is Lieutenant Richards. You called?"

"Yes, I left a message on your direct line, did you hear it?"

"No, I just got back."

"I think Jack's in trouble, Lieutenant!"

"What? Have you talked to him? Is he okay?"

"I tried him, I've been trying … but his cell phone, it doesn't work or something. It's urgent!"

"I'm not following, Porter … you haven't talked to him, how do you …?"

"Lieutenant, please! Listen carefully … Casey Ford and Kyle Sanders are half-brothers!"

"Who?" Richards wasn't sure what he just heard. It was so obscure, it didn't click.

"What? They're … what?"

"It's a long story, sir. But when Jack mentioned Sanders I said I would check some reciprocal systems between Texas and Louisiana, beyond criminal history stuff, okay? I looked at family-and-welfare. Kyle has a half-brother, and his name is Casey Ford! Could they be the same? Your Casey Ford?"

"What the fuck!"

"That's what I thought too. It couldn't be, right? I mean, no way, but it is — same mother. They have the same mother but different fathers."

Richards could barely concentrate on Porter's words. His mind blown beyond comprehension.

"When they were kids she got welfare on both!"

"Oh my God! And they're out there …"

"That's what I'm saying! I tried to call Jack but the area around the prison has no cell service," Porter rasped.

"It's a setup," Richards cried.

"Exactly!" Yelled Porter.

"Lemme' call Angola and see if they're there yet." Richards felt like he was going to vomit.

"Okay … I'll …"

Richards hung up, just as he noticed a number scrawled on a note-pad. Jack had written it. It was for Angola. Richards frantically punched the keys. He tried to tell the prison operator it was life-and-death, but he was suddenly on hold, then a mechanical voice transferred him around. A minute passed like an hour, and then finally an officer identi-fied himself — a real human being.

"This is Lieutenant Richards, San Francisco PD. Are the detectives still there?" Richards couldn't spit the words out fast enough.

"No sir, they left with the inmate about 30 minutes ago. What's the problem sir? Are you okay?"

"No, I'm not okay! Lives are at stake. You guys have to act fast," screamed Richards.

"Yes sir, okay."

"Casey Ford, our new homicide man who's with Jack Paige, is Sanders's half-brother."

"What was that sir? He's what?"

"They're fucking half brothers. It's a setup — a breakout, and Jack's gonna be the fucking victim. You got to get help to Jack!"

"Holy Shit!" said the guard. "We'll dispatch a team of guards immediately. There's only one road in and out, sir!"

Richards hung up without taking the phone from his ear. He called the operator and got the Baton Rouge Airport Police. Next, he sprinted to the Chief's office. The whole way he wondered if Jack was still alive. He pushed thoughts of Sarah and the kids aside. He couldn't go there.

*   *   *

Casey pulled the car to a stop onto the soft dirt shoulder. There was little room to park because the road was elevated about four feet from the surrounding flat terrain. Jack had noticed roadways built the same way in places where rainfall was high. It kept the road from flooding.

Once they stopped and the hum of the engine and the howl of the wind disappeared, Jack felt a real sense of desolation. For miles there was nothing but bushes, sparse trees and mosquitoes. Jack didn't have to pee, so he wouldn't venture far from the car.

Casey shut off the engine, left the keys in the ignition, and he and Jack got out. Jack stretched, gulping hot humid air. His head was still foggy from the shooting. This marsh felt peaceful, like it hadn't changed in a million years. Cricket chirps mixed into a continuous insect buzz, like a natural mantra.

"I'm going to take a leak, then I'll take care of Kyle," Casey edged down the embankment, balancing himself with outspread arms. Jack watched Casey disappear behind some bushes 50 yards away. Jack glanced up and down the desolate road. It was incredibly peaceful. Footsteps made him jump. It was Casey climbing the embankment toward the car. Jack marveled at how the lush landscape soaked up sounds of movement.

"Get out," Casey said to Kyle as he opened the door.

Kyle unbuckled his seat belt and turned his body so his feet were out the door and on the ground. He had to rock his body forward a bit so he could get out without the use of his handcuffed hands.

"We'll be right back, Jack," Casey grabbed Kyle's arm to help him down the embankment.

The two walked side by side.

Once they'd gone a few yards Kyle whispered, "What's next?"

"Shhh, not now," Casey hissed without so much as a glance at Kyle.

Jack watched Casey and Kyle head toward the same bushes Casey had used a moment before. They disappeared behind the cover. *Something seemed off, but he didn't know what. Maybe just being out here with this guy, and after all that shit in Texas, all this peace,* Jack thought. But somehow it was more than that. He could sense it.

He kept worrying about Casey behind the bushes with Kyle. Jack stared after them. *Am I paranoid? Did the shooting screw me up that badly?*

Once they were out of Jack's sight, Casey took out his key and removed Kyle's cuffs. "Take a piss, Kyle," he said.

Kyle undid his button and zipper and started to pee. "I can't fuckin' believe you did it, you got me out," Kyle whispered and shivered with giddiness. "What we gonna' do about him?" He motioned toward the car with his head.

"I'll take care of that. When it's time, you run like hell, Kyle … and don't fuckin' stop for nothin', hear me?'

"Yeah, yeah, okay, then what?" Kyle's hands quivered as he zipped himself up.

"Jack's too far away. If he shoots, he'll never be able to hit you. Just keep runnin' like I said. And don't look back!"

"Okay brother, okay."

"Here's three thousand in cash. That should hold you for a couple of months. Call me in a couple of weeks so I know you're safe." Casey took a sealed envelope from his inside jacket pocket and handed it to Kyle.

"I love you, Casey. Thanks for not forgettin' me." As Kyle took the envelope his eyes welled with tears. He hugged his brother.

There was a sudden rustling, and the two men looked up to see Jack. He stared at them.

He'd begun figuring what was wrong with the picture even before he started across the marsh. They'd walked this way with Casey out ahead — it was backwards. As Jack had gotten down in the brush he'd realized Casey wasn't even paying any attention to Kyle's movements ... not even a hand on Kyle to control him.

Christ, he thought, *they might as well be a couple of guys out for a walk in the woods. The cop walks behind. The cop controls. It's natural. But as Jack came within sight of them, he saw. Were they hugging? They couldn't be. He thought Casey might be in trouble.*

"J-Jack," Casey stammered. "You don't understand. It wasn't supposed to go this way." He looked visibly shaken. Kyle looked like he'd seen a ghost.

"What's going on?" There was no aggression but, everything felt wrong. Jack wished he'd drawn his gun.

Kyle stepped sideways and then stopped. He eyed them both.

"Kyle needs to escape, Jack. It's all going to be on me, my fault. You have nothing to do with it."

"What? What the fuck are you talking about?"

"Please ... please Jack, just let him go," Casey began to cry.

"Casey, I don't know what the fuck you're involved in, but nothing has happened that can't be fixed." Jack started moving his hand toward his gun.

"No ... this shit can't be fixed." Casey struggled for words.

"Yeah, it can," Jack said, astonished at the calmness in his voice. He didn't feel calm at all. His mind raced for a reason for this insanity. It also raced for options.

"No Jack, you're wrong, man! Kyle's my half-brother. They locked him up for a fucking accident! He was just a kid! You don't understand! He raised me! He fucking took care of me, man!"

Jack's jaw dropped. He knew one thing: He was in deep shit!

"I promised him, Jack. I wouldn't forget him in there. I wouldn't let him rot like fucking garbage." Casey was crying. "I promised. It wasn't fair! He didn't deserve it!"

Jack spoke more for time than anything else. "So, you fed him the details ... made him the important witness ... right?"

"Appeals are bullshit here! Not like California. It's not fair, Jack! You don't fucking understand. You've never had to live in this shit!"

"And you leaked to Traci ..." The pieces suddenly fit for Jack. "Telling her guaranteed the heat. We *had* to get Kyle out. You knew that would force it, whether we solved the case or not."

"Jack, please. Fuck it! Let him run. It's on me, man. I've thought about this my entire life! I know what I'm doing ... please."

"I can't Casey. You'll have to kill me."

"No man, no ... Don't go there, please ..." Casey turned slightly, then grabbed for his gun.

Jack's world went into slow motion. *Crazy! Casey's my partner.* Jack reached for his gun, moved right and hunched, putting Kyle between them. Casey was a half-second ahead. *Damn him!* Jack pictured his gun out, and his finger squeezing the trigger. *If my body can just catch up.*

Casey rotated right, around Kyle. Kyle hunched and ducked his head. He saw they were using him as cover.

Jack felt like he was watching a movie. Oddly, as all three bodies moved simultaneously, like a slow-motion dance, Jack saw the bulging eyes and open mouths of the brothers. *They looked similar. Jack felt the chill of centuries of Southern corruption.*

Jack heard rapid pops, saw fire spit from Casey's gun, and then someone hit him in the chest with a sledgehammer. It knocked the air from his lungs. Pain burned through his chest, like being impaled on a red-hot poker. He didn't even know if he fired or not. Jack landed on his back still gripping his gun. *Two guys,* he thought. *Which one's Casey?* One man dropped to his knees. The other still stood. Jack mustered all his strength, raised his gun and fired. He could hardly hold his arm up. The weight of the gun was unbearable. His chest burned with hell's fiery intensity. He squeezed the trigger again and again. He faintly heard gunfire and wondered if it was his own. His stomach convulsed and racked his body with pain. Something warm spewed from his mouth, like vomit, but it tasted sweet, like blood. Jack saw Sarah and the kids, playing on a beautiful green lawn: then all went dark.

TWENTY FIVE

Lieutenant Richards personally escorted Sarah and the kids on the longest flight of their lives. He shielded them from the media gauntlet in Louisiana. A sensational story had just gone nuclear: the murder of a Mayor's daughter, two brothers in a prison break, a good cop gone bad — or was he bad all along? A gunfight between cops, with a vicious murderer chained in the middle — it was all wrapped in one huge story.

Not long after his family arrived they moved Jack from the Intensive Care Unit into a private room. He remembered intense pain, falling and shooting. The time between the shooting and waking up was blank. Whole days were gone. He didn't care. Jack was lucky to be alive.

The 9mm bullet had struck his chest right of center, and then shattered when it hit a rib. A fragment tore through his right lung, causing it to collapse. A surgeon repaired the lung during an eight-hour operation.

It just wasn't my time to go, he thought. Had Porter not called Richards and had Richards not called Angola, they would not have sent a rescue team. In another few minutes he would have bled to death. The guards found him, treated his sucking chest wound, and minimized his massive bleeding. A medical chopper airlifted him to the trauma center. They saved his life.

Sarah sat on the bed feeding him ice chips.

"I love you," Jack said in a hoarse voice. It was painful to speak.

"I know. Shhhh," she smiled, and gave him another ice chip.

When Richards had run through the entire sequence of events, Jack tried to follow, but the story seemed as hazy as the morphine fog. In the end it sickened him.

His feelings about Casey were mixed. How could a cop do that? This guy had already shown himself as a good detective; but this guy was his brother, and that's a bond that's made for extreme behavior, both good and bad, since biblical times. And now both brothers were dead, Kyle from a badly aimed shot of Casey's.

Jack wished he hadn't killed Casey. He would carry that the rest of his life. He was glad it was Casey's bullet that had killed Kyle and not his. At least that had a strange justice.

Jack felt a nagging guilt for not sensing something about Casey. He didn't say it, but those closest to him knew he thought it; but no one had seen it, not in all the years Casey had been in law enforcement. No one had sensed the plan. *Plain and simple, he was dirty*, Jack thought. *Sad, but true.*

Jack was thankful he was alive.

"Jack, you did one helluva' job. The Mayor is going to give you a commendation. Every talk show and news station wants an interview," Richards told him.

Sarah rubbed Jack's leg over the covers. "I think this would be a good time to hang it up. Don't you, honey?"

He didn't try to answer any of them. He couldn't if he wanted. Commendations and retirement were the furthest things from his mind. He just wanted to get strong enough to go home. He missed his home. And then maybe spend a couple of weeks in some warm Miami sun with Sarah. After that he could answer all their questions, After all, he had a million unanswered questions of his own.

ABOUT THE AUTHOR

Wayne Farquhar is a 28-year veteran working with the San Jose Police Department in California. He has worked through the ranks from officer to lieutenant with detective assignments in Sexual Assaults, Homicide and Internal Affairs. He has also worked undercover assignments in Child Exploitation, Child Pornography and Vice. He spent 10 years as a street cop and hostage negotiator. Wayne has worked on Federal Task Forces with the Bureau of Alcohol, Tobacco, Firearms and Explosives (ATF) and the Federal Bureau of Investigations (FBI). He has appeared on national television, *America's Most Wanted* on a murder investigation. *Blood over Badge* is his first effort in crime-thriller fiction, and he hopes to write more books and speak to larger audiences about his experiences in law enforcement. Wayne lives with his family in the San Francisco Bay Area. To purchase a copy of *Blood over Badge*, please visit the 3L Publishing website (www.3LPublishing.com).